'Very happy to
McAllister.'

'I believe that I saw you this afternoon on the green before the Capitol.'

Mary found herself answering him, aware that Jared was turning the full force of his powerful personality on her. 'Yes, I sat there for some time. I needed to think a little. Spring in Washington is perhaps a good time for thinking.'

That amused him, it was plain, and she returned his smile, with interest. Why, she thought, horror stricken, I am flirting with him. How long has it been since I flirted with a man?

Dear Reader

A DARLING AMAZON is Sylvia Andrew's second book, a fascinating Regency story where the heroine accidentally causes real difficulty for the hero—Julia's efforts at reparation only seem to make things worse . . . After fifteenth-century Tuscany, Paula Marshall has moved to America of the 1890s in the first of a mother-and-daughter duo. WILD JUSTICE charts the unmasking of outwardly respectable Mrs Mary McAllister and her small daughter Sally-Anne in Washington's closed political society! Watch next month for Sally-Anne's own story.

The Editor

Paula Marshall, married with three children, has had a varied life. She began her career in a large library and ended it as a senior academic in charge of history in a polytechnic. She has travelled widely, has been a swimming coach, and has appeared on *University Challenge* and *Mastermind*. She has always wanted to write, and likes her novels to be full of adventure and humour.

Recent titles by the same author:

THE FALCON AND THE DOVE
AN IMPROPER DUENNA
COUSIN HARRY

WILD JUSTICE

Paula Marshall

The author wishes to thank Mercedes-Benz UK Ltd.
Evans of Leicester, Ltd.,—in particular Mr Ron
Andrews—for their help in providing information about
the early history of the horseless carriage. Any errors are
the author's responsibility, not theirs.

*First published in Great Britain 1992
by Mills & Boon Limited*

© Paula Marshall 1992

*Australian copyright 1992
Philippine copyright 1993
This edition 1993*

ISBN 0 263 78047 3

*Masquerade is a trademark published by
Mills & Boon Limited, Eton House,
18–24 Paradise Road, Richmond, Surrey, TW9 1SR.*

*Set in 10 on 10½ pt Linotron Plantin
04-9302-87694*

*Typeset in Great Britain by Centracet, Cambridge
Made and printed in Great Britain*

CHAPTER ONE

'Revenge is a kind of wild justice'—Francis Bacon

MARY MCALLISTER, putting on her wide-brimmed straw hat liberally decorated with mauve pansies, each with its mischievous face smiling at her, stared at her reflection in the gilt-edged mirror over Senator Wayne Hamilton's fireplace in his ornate office-cum-library. There were times when the gravely serene image it presented, blonde curls tamed, smoothed down and polished, blue eyes steady, serious mouth held just so, seemed to belong to a stranger, to have nothing to do with the slim, quicksilver girl she had once been.

It was almost as though that girl had never existed, as if she had been, all her adult life, the Widow McAllister, hard-working, dependable, calm and sober. Someone to whom the senator's equally sober son, Boyce, would propose, one day soon, a fit partner for herself, and a fit father for her daughter, Sally-Anne, who had never known her true father.

The elaborate French clock in front of the mirror weakly pinged out five in the afternoon, and the senator's typewriter, Miss Agnes Merry, looked up, and said, 'You're late today, Mrs McAllister. And Mr Boyce, too. Thought he would be here by now to drive you home.'

Mary, who had been checking her own little fob-watch, to find that it was running slow, as usual—almost a commentary on her life, she thought—said in the cool and measured voice which all official Washington knew, 'I expect that he's been detained at the Hill. Congress is debating the Western Territories Bill today, and I know that the senator particularly wanted him there.'

Boyce was a congressman who would almost certainly

inherit the senator's seat when he at last decided to
retire. 'Tell him that I had to leave before he returned,
and that I haven't forgotten that he's escorting me to the
ball at the White House this evening.'

'Oh, the Hill,' shrugged Miss Agnes. 'Always the Hill.
It dominates our lives in every way, doesn't it? Not only
because the Capitol stands on it, but its demands ruin all
our plans. Mr Boyce will be sorry to miss you, I know.'

'Well, I can't stay,' said Mary reluctantly. 'I promised
Sally-Anne that I wouldn't be late tonight, and working
for the senator means that I'm not often there when she
arrives home from school.'

She had been Senator Hamilton's aide-cum-secretary
for the last three years. It was not so much that she
needed the money—she was modestly wealthy these
days—but she needed occupation, needed to take her
mind off her own lonely condition, needed to do something useful to lessen boredom.

The senator was by way of being a reformer. She had
met him one evening at a White House reception, taken
there by a distant cousin who was part of the permanent
presidential staff, not a political appointee. Conversing
with him, she had impressed him with her knowledge of
current affairs, so much so, indeed, that impulsively he
had said, half in joke, 'Why, Mrs McAllister, I have just
lost my secretary and aide, John Haines, to a law firm. I
do believe that you would be more than capable of taking
on his work.'

'If you are advanced enough to employ a female as an
aide,' she had replied, half in jest herself, 'then I will
offer myself as a candidate for the post.'

He had looked at her carefully, rugged old face
amused. 'I might accept you at that, Mrs McAllister. I
might at that—like to try?'

Something of the unregenerate girl inside her, hidden
under layers of civilisation, polish and self-control, made
her answer him, in a parody of the Western drawl which
was all around them, 'Shorely would, Senator, shorely
would,' her face animated for once, so that the senator

thought suddenly, Why, she's beautiful, a desirable woman, not a nun at all!

'Bully for you, Miz Mary. Bully for you!' He had been a lady's man in his youth, and thought that were he thirty years younger he would have given this Mary McAllister a run for her money, tried to find the woman whose eager, amused eyes had shone at him so briefly. He had made his drawl match her own—he had been a country boy once, and had never forgotten the speech rhythms of his youth. 'Tomorrow morning, then, Miz Mary. Nine o'clock sharp?' And, speaking so, his voice had reverted to the statesmanlike manner which all Washington knew.

He saw by her expression that she thought that he might be joshing her, in the way in which many older men teased pretty women, not taking her seriously, and added, still in his fine old Republican mode, as though he were one of the Founding Fathers come back to earth, 'I mean it, Mrs McAllister. I need someone desperately, and I'm willing to bet that you would fill the bill, and you might as well start betimes, I guess.'

And that had been that. So, here she was, working for a busy US senator three days a week, a *habitué* of Washington's corridors of power, a citizen of the Imperial state, almost a figure of consequence herself, for lesser men had to approach her in order to gain access to the busy man Senator Hamilton was.

He had never regretted her appointment. She was so unobtrusively efficient despite her youth, and, yes, despite her sex, for the senator did have a few after-thoughts about employing a woman; but they soon disappeared. Besides, his support of female suffrage, the granting of the vote to women, was given a fillip by his appointment of a woman who was as clever as she was beautiful.

And yes, he thought, given that her father had been Professor Robert Nelson, and her mother no fool, that should not be a surprise. The blood lines ran true—the senator bred horses as well as helped to govern the

United States, and was liable to translate his earthy knowledge of life from one to the other.

He counted it a benefit that Mary was not a traditional female emancipist who felt it necessary to insult the men with whom she wished to share political power. An open espousal of such a controversial cause would have been contrary to the person she had become, would have clashed with the woman whose decorum was equalled only by her command of every social art practised in the nation's capital.

For Mary McAllister was nothing if not proper: a very model of well-behaved womanhood, so much so that the men who had tried to be easy with her joked about her behind her back, called her the Ice Princess. More than one had offered to end her widowhood for her by marriage, others had offered less official liaisons, but to all of them she had returned a regretfully smiling no, offering them nothing at all.

Only, now, at twenty-seven, she had begun to wonder if she was being fair to her daughter, seven-year-old Sally-Anne, to deny her a proper family life, and had started to encourage a little—just a little—the senator's staid son, Boyce, who had pursued her, mildly, ever since she had arrived in his father's office.

Pinning her hat firmly on her head, buttoning her light coat and listening for Boyce's step—he might yet arrive to save her a troublesome journey home—Mary thought again of the proposal which she knew was sure to come, and wondered what she would say when it did, and why her thoughts about marriage to Boyce were so unenthusiastic.

After all, to marry Boyce would be such a *wise* thing to do. He was a little older than she was—thirty-two—had once been engaged to a girl who had been foolish enough to be tempted away by one of the capital's notorious philanderers—and then deserted, leaving Boyce a wary man where women were concerned. He was such a safe person, not at all like his father who had been quite a buccaneer in his youth.

And that was the drawback: he *was* such a reasonable, safe person. Reasonably good-looking, reasonably clever, unlike his cunning, brilliant father, reasonably rich—and he would be richer when the senator died. In fact, he was reasonably everything, and that was the trouble.

The girl inside her, who would not die, however much she tried to kill her, said Yes, the senator wants it, because you will give Boyce steel, provide him with ambition, push him when he enters Congress—and, yes, make a man of him—but face it, Mary, do you want him? He's dull, dull, dull. What will he be like in bed? Dull there, too, no doubt. And once I wanted more than that, had more than that, wanted love and passion, not merely to end up marrying someone like Boyce, whom I don't love, because the marriage will be so suitable, and everyone will approve of it.

No, I do not love him. I like him, but is that a suitable reason for marrying him? And then again, but, after all, love let me down once, horribly; perhaps liking might answer better?

But if Mary McAllister could talk herself into accepting Boyce Hamilton the girl inside cringed away from the very idea—even to give Sally-Anne stability. And now not only the hidden girl, but Mary herself was beginning to have doubts. She shook her head—to clear it, perhaps—and said to Miss Agnes, 'I dare not wait any longer, and Boyce would not expect me to. Tell the senator that the memorandum I have written for him is on his desk.'

'I won't forget,' said Miss Agnes briskly. She knew very well that the 'memorandum' was, in fact, a speech which Mrs McAllister had written for the senator to make at the next meeting of a small committee discussing an Anti-Trust Bill, which the senator would give as it stood—barring the alteration of a few commas, that was.

She watched Mrs McAllister pick up her umbrella, and thought, not for the first time, that if women had their dues it was the Widow McAllister who would be

standing in Congress, among the nation's legislators, not
confined to being so much the senator's strong right arm
that she could have done his work for him.

Unaware of this tribute, Mary walked out into Washington's spring, the many trees here, in the capital's
heart, already showing a pale green in the light sun of
late April.

She moved briskly along M street, past the red-brick
town houses of fashionable Washington, wondering why
suddenly, today, the placid and orderly life which she
had made for herself, and which had contented her for
the last six years, and which would receive its crown
when she married Boyce Hamilton, should seem so
dreary and stale.

On an impulse, instead of taking the left-hand turn
which would lead her to the suburb where she lived, she
veered right, made her way to Pennsylvania Avenue, the
great ceremonial road which ran through the heart of the
city, walked along it, then past the museums, and the
galleries, their Greek columns lemon in the sun, to come
out on one of the giant greens in the Mall before the
Capitol, standing like an enormous wedding-cake, high
on the Hill, under the mild blue sky.

Mary stood and stared at it. One day, perhaps, she
thought, as Miss Agnes had done, a woman might sit in
Congress; not simply work there, as she sometimes did
to help a senator, but be a senator herself. She thought
that that would be a great thing, but it would not happen
now, in 1889, nor for long after she stood here. Mary
had no false illusions that any campaign for female
emancipation would gain victory easily, nor did she wish
to lead one. She would serve her sex by her personal
example.

She sighed, sat down on one of the many benches
under the trees, watched the squirrels leaping and
bounding around and up them, darting erratically in
sudden sharp movements. The girl she had once been
had resembled the squirrels——And what do I resemble
now? She thought. She did not try to give herself an

answer, but bent down suddenly, and with the ferrule of her umbrella traced a name in the earth.

A short name: a man's name. Rubbing it fiercely away, her eyes filled, for the first time for years, with tears at the thought of him, and of his betrayal. Why should such a ghost return from the past to haunt her now, when respectability and salvation were about to claim her finally—if she accepted Boyce, that was?

Would accepting Boyce mean that she finally destroyed everything which had happened to that girl of nineteen, with all her hopes and ambitions for a life of love and passion?

She sat back to let her mind wander, not towards nearly eight years ago, for those memories were forbidden ones, and normally she denied that they had ever existed, but in the direction of the life which would be hers as part of the senator's family. There were times when she thought that if Boyce was the man his father had obviously been she would have accepted him without a thought. But that was foolish.

Soon, now, she must make up her mind, and, depressingly, she knew what the verdict would be. She would accept Boyce and settle for second best—because there was nothing else left.

Mary was so engrossed with her own problems that she did not notice that a tall man, broad-shouldered, darkly and ruggedly handsome, well dressed himself, was staring at her with more than common interest. He, too, had been looking at the Capitol, walking towards it, when he had seen the elegant and well-groomed woman in her violet gown, with silk pansies pinned to her coat lapel and fashionable hat, seated alone on a bench.

Intrigued, for the public benches in Washington were rarely occupied by such figures of fashion, he had given her a second glance, to find that she reminded him strongly of a girl he had known long ago, except that this was no wild slim girl, but a woman, and a sophisticated one, her figure mature, its graceful curves celebrated by the beautiful cut of her dress, her hair, not short, rioting in curls around her head, but long, dressed high beneath her fashionable hat. Everything about her spelled money and position—and the girl he remembered had neither; had worn not a couturier's creation, but a plaid shirt and a man's Levi's tucked into her little Western boots!

He watched from a distance, interested, saw her pick up a violet and black tapestry bag, and walk purposefully away, calm and controlled, deliberation in everything she did. He thought of the impulsive girl he had known, of her vivacity, every movement lively and unconsidered, and, despite the hurt which the thought brought him, smiled a little at the memory, shrugged his shoulders.

I am growing maudlin, he thought, and fancy a likeness in every pretty blonde woman I see. I have not even thought of Charlie lately, and sure God, after all this time memory is like to deceive me. Whatever else, my Charlie could not be that composed and elegant creature.

'Most ladylike,' said Boyce approvingly to Mary that evening, when he called to take her to the ball. 'As always your taste is impeccable.'

Mary dipped him a curtsy, and flirted her eyes at him over her huge fan, a gesture of which, by his expression, Boyce did not entirely approve. She was wearing grey silk, a colour which might have extinguished most blonde women, but which, in some mysterious fashion, enhanced her beauty remarkably.

She picked up her shawl, a cobweb of a thing, and took Boyce's offered arm. 'I am sorry,' he pursued, in his somewhat stolid manner, 'not to return in time to take you home, but you know what it's like on the Hill these days. . .'

'Oh, indeed,' said Mary. 'And most important that you remained. Of course, I understand.'

'I knew you would,' he said; they were now outside her home, and he was handing her into his buggy. 'That is the thing I admire most about you—your understanding—after your discretion, that is.'

Mary bent her head at this, smiled her thanks for this praise, but thought, Oh, dear, how dull he makes me sound. Understanding and discretion. Such worthy virtues.

'I would like,' continued Boyce, 'to speak to you later this evening, over supper perhaps, to talk to you about the proposed Anti-Trust Bill. I am most concerned that not only should the measure go through, but that it prevents such pirates as Jared Tunstall from enriching themselves by their manipulations. You have heard of Tunstall, I suppose?'

Mary bent her head again, murmured, 'Yes.' Was it wrong that she should feel somewhat dismal at the prospect of an earnest political discussion over supper? For the hundredth time she wished that Boyce were the sort of cavalier who would forget such matters, worthy though they were, for at least the length of time required to say something exciting, amusing, and, yes, frivolous.

'The senator said that he is in Washington, staying with his brother Orrin, and I suppose that he has come here to lobby support against such proposals as mine. . .' And for the time it took them to drive to the White House he treated Mary to a disquisition on the Trusts— a matter about which she knew rather more than Boyce did, and could have expressed better—except of course, Boyce thought that as a woman she was in constant need of simple-minded instruction!

She wondered briefly, driving past interested spectators outside the White House gates, who had come to goggle at their political masters and their women enjoying themselves, of what they would think if they knew what an evening of paralysing dullness awaited her.

'He is the worst kind of adventurer, for all that he comes from such an old family. . .' Boyce was saying, and she really must pay attention to him. It was Jared Tunstall he was speaking of again. 'I saw him in New York once, surrounded by. . .' Boyce stopped, aware that no gentleman such as himself should speak to a pure woman like Mary McAllister of Tunstall's rowdy life, and the dubious women he consorted with. . . 'The wrong kind of persons,' he finished lamely.

Oh, shoot, thought Mary, wondering where such dreadful thoughts were coming from today, if he means that Tunstall is a philanderer, why can't he say so? Does he think I live in a dream?

But she said nothing, merely resigned herself to another virtuous, but boring evening.

Dressing to go to the ball at the White House with his much older half-brother, Orrin Tunstall, the senator for Nevada, Jared Tunstall thought again of the woman he had seen in front of the Capitol. He laughed at himself a little—a man whose reputation with women was notorious, to be caught by a passing stranger because of some half-seen likeness to a girl he had once loved as dearly as life.

He thought how Orrin would josh him: 'Jes' like you, Jared, not in Washington above a half-hour and chasin' the gals already.' Orrin was a man of good education but he found it politically expedient to speak and behave as though he were not, deceiving the many who thought that, because his speech and manner were rough and simple, so was the man. They were often to be speedily and unfortunately disabused.

Well, Jared already knew a few girls—and a few who were very much not girls—from his last visit to Washington some four years ago, and he would certainly not lack for entertainment, even if he could not track down the woman who had intrigued him so. He was staying in the house his brother rented whenever Congress was sitting, refusing to use the big old mansion which Jared had inherited from his mother. 'Like open spaces,' he was wont to say, whenever Jared offered it to him, 'Dam' place more like a mausoleum than a home. Like my little retreat here. Don' want to live in no tomb.' And liked the extra comforts his landlady also provided for him, was Jared's amused reaction to that.

He wondered briefly whether he ought to open up the

place himself: it depended on how long he was likely to stay in Washington, and at the moment he had no real idea of how long that might be. He thought again of his brother and the deceptions he cultivated to confuse people. And I, he mused, what do I cultivate? And knew without being told: a ruthless manner rendered the more cutting by his air of extreme civilisation, his beautiful Eastern voice, and careful, educated speech, all of which had amused Orrin ever since the two brothers had met for the first time as men, after many years apart, when Jared had reached eighteen.

It amused Orrin even more now that Jared was nearly thirty, because he knew that beneath all this civilised polish Jared was even more unregenerate than he had been then, that the air of civilisation was a mask which his half-brother could drop at will—although he seldom cared to.

He walked into Jared's room as his brother was arranging his cravat, and gently applauded his appearance. Jared thought that Orrin's at fifty was remarkable, too.

'Yuh shorely do look purty,' Orrin offered.

Jared gave a thin smile, straightened his cravat. Evening dress, the black and white of it, suited him. It went with his glossy blue-black hair, slightly waving, cut a little longer, perhaps, than fashion demanded, emphasised the strength of his somewhat harsh face, the power of his body, the length of his legs.

'Pretty is hardly a word I would use of myself,' he said.

'Nope,' said Orrin. 'But I look an ass in a monkey jacket, while you, you look as though you were born in it. Comes of goin' to Harvard, I s'ppose, while I got taught only in the great Academy of Life.'

Jared laughed. 'It's an academy I attended, too,' he said drily.

'Yo, but Harvard came first,' said Orrin, 'And you know the old sayin'?'

'"You can take the boy out of Harvard, but not

Harvard out of the boy."' Jared's laugh was mirthless. 'I
think I made a good first of trying to prove that saying
wrong.'

'Shorely did,' said Orrin, clapping Jared on the back.
'Mus' admit that, little brother. Yuh might have had an
Eastern grandpappy on yore Ma's side, but you shore
lived that down successful-like when yuh went West.'

He pulled out a big silver turnip of a watch which had
belonged to his father, and whose chain stretched across
a broad, but flat stomach. 'Want to walk—seein' as how
we can't take the hosses?'

'No,' said Jared. 'Important for us to arrive cool—and
sweet-smelling.'

'Fer yuh, perhaps, but not fer me,' grinned Orrin,
and then grimaced. 'Right, tell the butler to git the
carriage 'round,' he said, and later when they were being
driven up the road to the White House, 'Shall purely be
glad to be home agin, out of fancy dress. Why am I a
senator, I often ask myself?'

'Because Pa was,' said Jared, his own grin wide.
'Carrying on the name and the tradition. The least you
can do for his memory.'

'Yuh could take over,' suggested Orrin, 'seeing as how
yuh is the civilised one.'

'Not I,' said Jared emphatically. 'I don't want my
freedom of action spoiled.'

Orrin was amused by his brother's strong rejection of
the dubious honour offered to him. 'Prefer to be a bandit
prince on Wall Street, do yuh? What game have yuh
come here to Washington to play? No, don' tell me.
Then I ain't lyin' when I allows as how I don' know!'

'No game,' said Jared. 'I simply want a holiday. I'm
tired of wheeling and dealing.' And he refused to enlarge
further as their carriage reached its destination, and drew
up on the broad sweep in front of the main doors of the
White House.

Link-boys ran up to escort it away, and flunkeys
bowed them into the house itself. 'Too much dam'
ceremony these days for a good Republican state,' grum-

bled Orrin. 'Shall be back to kings an' princes yet.' A
statement of which Jared took no note, having heard it
many times before.

The White House was really too small for the functions
held in it. The crush was, as usual, enormous, and the
line waiting to shake President Benjamin Harrison's
hand moved along with paralysing slowness.

Later the ballroom was so crowded that the heat was
overpowering. Jared found himself alone. Orrin had
been taken off into a side room by a presidential aide to
speak to Harrison in private, but Jared was not solitary
for long. A large, handsome woman, fashionably dressed
in a gown which looked as though it had been
upholstered on to her, greeted him.

'Jared Tunstall, I do declah. When did you-all arrive
in town?'

Jared turned, bowed. 'Today, Sarah Lee. I trust I see
you well?'

Sarah Lee Chase ignored his question. 'Arrived here,
and never let me know.' She smiled warmly at him, a
moth-eaten tigress, he thought unkindly, who had
unashamedly and unsuccessfully pursued him on his last
visit, and was now apparently determined that he would
not elude her again.

She talked animatedly at him, rather than to him, of
her husband, a senator sold long ago to the railroad
interests, bought by them to block any attempt by
Congress to check their piratical operations. Jared's eyes
roved over the ballroom, he made mechanical answers to
her provocative small talk, stopped listening altogether
when he found the woman for whom he was looking, the
woman who had sat on the green before the Capitol.

She was now wearing a dress of dove-grey silk, cut
low to show magnificent shoulders, and a hint of shadow
at the front suggesting an equally beautiful bosom. The
glossy blonde hair was lifted high into a simple knot,
and there was an orchid in it. The dress itself was also
simple, the colour suggesting chastity, he thought, a

little wryly—a hard target for him, perhaps. But above all else it was the face which intrigued him again.

It was so like, and so was she, his memories of his lost Charlie. . .except. . .except. . .the face was almost Grecian in its purity, enhanced by an expression of lovely calm. . .whereas Charlie. . . Charlie had been quick-silver, nothing classical about her, and he remembered, too, the youthful hollows of her face, her joyful spontaneity, so different from what he could see of this woman's almost holy placidity.

He shook his head. He must be growing maudlin. . . Perhaps when he spoke to her? He watched her again.

She was talking to a tall man, her fan, a small delicate one with pale grey feathers running along its top, held high, as though she were protecting herself—from him, and from all men? For the man bending towards her so attentively had something of the proprietorial in his air, as though the woman were his possession. Except that Jared was quite convinced, why he did not know, that they were not husband and wife. The man's manner was too tentative, and hers, for all the apparent submission of the lifted fan, and the slightly averted head, was too independent.

'Sarah Lee,' he said suddenly, interrupting the ani-mated flow of her empty chatter, designed to impress rather than inform, 'the woman over there, the one in grey with Boyce Hamilton; do you know her?'

Sarah Lee looked at him, annoyed that his attention was so palpably not on her. She followed his eyes. What use to say no? Of course she knew the woman. All Washington knew Senator Hamilton's female aide. It piqued her that he could be attracted to another woman while she was speaking to him. Everyone knew that Jared Tunstall was so much his own man that he always did exactly what he pleased, but really!

'Yes,' she said, and then, a trifle demeaningly, 'That's the Widow McAllister, Senator Hamilton's assistant. All Washington knows *her*.' She made it sound an insult.

'Then, Sarah Lee, I must ask a favour of you. Introduce me to her, if you would be so kind.'

Anger ran through her, 'Oh, really. Why? She's not at all your sort of woman, Jared. If I tell you the men all call her the Ice Princess. . .'

Jared tired of this. 'Now, Sarah Lee. I asked you to introduce me to her, not instruct me in what kind of woman I prefer—I already know that, and do not need you to tell me. She intrigues me, that's all. Reminds me of someone I used to know. If you won't oblige me, then forgive me, I must find someone who will.'

Sarah Lee's expression grew even uglier. So, Jared Tunstall's visit was to be as unproductive this time as his last one had been. There was no help for it; she would lose any hope with him permanently if she let him leave now.

'Oh, very well,' she said ungraciously. 'But, I warn you, the Widow McAllister is not for such pirates as you are. In any case, Boyce Hamilton, the senator's son, with whom she came tonight, is sure to propose to her soon, and she's hardly likely to turn him down. Another bore. Like calling to like.'

But she led him across the room to the alcove where Mrs McAllister was standing, alone now, for Boyce Hamilton was talking to a group of legislators—one of the problems of being a woman at White House functions was that they were used as political forums where wheeling and dealing could be carried on behind the rites of social enjoyment.

Mary McAllister looked a little surprised on becoming aware that it was indeed herself whom Sarah Lee Chase was making for. She was no part of Sarah Lee's rather raffish set, and had already noted that Sarah Lee had apparently picked up yet another handsome stranger, although, near to, the face of the man she was towing along was strong and harsh rather than handsome.

His eyes, so deeply blue that they were almost black, were assessing her before he and Sarah Lee had even arrived, and she stiffened a little. She had long since

learned to recognise the signs which told her when men
were approaching her with sexual demands in mind, and
this man reeked of danger, and, yes, of sex.

'Mary, my dear.' The friendly words were belied by
the frosty voice. 'May I introduce to you an old friend of
mine, Jared Tunstall, who has expressed an overwhelming desire to meet you? I am sure that you must already
have heard of him, so little escapes you in your—er—
responsible post.'

This was all said so poisonously that the unspoken
comment—that what was heard of Jared was discreditable, and that Mary McAllister was little more than a
kind of superior servant—hung in the air between the
three of them. 'Jared,' she concluded, 'this is Mrs Mary
McAllister, Senator Wayne Hamilton's. . .aide, I suppose you would call it. A credit to the whole women's
movement.'

The curiosity which Jared felt about the woman before
him was heightened by the amused twitch of her lips at
Sarah Lee's dismissal of herself as a mad feminist.

'Delighted to meet you, Mr Tunstall. I fear Sarah Lee
flatters me. I may, by chance, have inherited a man's
post, but I am far from being a shrieking harpy pursuing
female emancipation. Believe me, I have no extraordinary ambitions, other than to further the senator's.'

While she spoke Jared had taken the hand she held
out to him, not to shake it, but to lift it to his lips, and
kiss the back of it. The moment he did so, the White
House, the ballroom and Sarah Lee disappeared for both
of them. For Mary the brief contact was stunning,
electric, giving her a sensation which she had not felt for
eight long years.

But for Jared time itself turned back. Looking into
the calm face before him—for Mary gave no sign of the
great wave of passion which had swept over her at his
touch—hearing her voice, almost overthrew him, calm
though it was, the likeness of it to his lost Charlie's was
so strong.

The likeness he thought that he had seen was suddenly

so profound, her voice carried such plangent overtones, that he was nearly overcome. No, she was not his Charlie, but, seeing Mary McAllister, the grief which had consumed him when he knew that he had lost Charlie was thick in his throat again. He was aware of her eyes sharp on him.

Shocked by the effect which his touch had had on her, Mary looked fully at him for the first time when he straightened up from kissing her hand.

Of course, she had heard of him, as who had not? Everyone in politics knew of the top Wall Street operators whose actions affected government, the robber barons who between them controlled the financial life and economy of the United States, whose decisions built and destroyed railroads, coal mines, oil wells, the lodes of copper, silver and gold, developed the great undeveloped areas in and around the frontiers, and who connived between themselves to corrupt and control Congress itself.

For these men bought and sold senators and congressmen, determined what Acts were, and were not, passed, and lived like Renaissance princes in palaces which contained the loot of Europe. The older ones married their daughters to the bankrupt scions of European aristocracy, and the younger ones, like Jared Tunstall, having first conquered American society, then went to Europe and enjoyed themselves in the courts of princes there.

It was said of him, she knew, that he was a friend of the Prince of Wales himself when he visited England, and that his own wealth was uncountable, and, for all his youth, mostly won since he first advanced on Wall Street some few years ago. To give him his due, his success had been his own, neither the reputation of his dead father nor his older brother Orrin having helped him in his piratical career.

And women. His mistresses were the famous beauties who lorded it over New York, and when he went to Europe. . .well, gossip had run over at that point, and

to give Mary her due she had always avoided listening to
tales of such creatures as Jared Tunstall.

But, looking at him, she could see his attraction, and
could understand his success with both love and money.
The harsh, hawklike face, clean-shaven, with its strong
mouth, the perfect evening clothes which could not
disguise the muscular body, enhanced it rather. His
height and his breadth were impressive, too. He towered
over most of the men in the room. When he spoke his
voice was pleasant and deep, with the accents of the East
Coast strong in it, not at all like his brother Orrin's
Western drawl, familiar to her from his frequent consul-
tations with Senator Hamilton. His effect on her was so
strong that she could hardly take in what he was saying.

'Very happy to meet you, Mrs McAllister. I believe
that I saw you this afternoon on the green before the
Capitol.'

Oddly, something about him struck her as familiar. A
bell rang, evoking echoes at the back of her mind, but
surely she had never met him before? She would have
remembered, would she not, such a distinctive face and
body, not handsome, but better, a man of such overpowering physicality, of such size, and above all the aura
of confident sexuality which surrounded him.

But yes, she had known such a man once who had
carried that same aura with him—only 'boy' might have
been a better description of him. For once, she allowed
the memory of him to return, a memory she had vowed
never to revive.

And that boy had possessed the blue-black hair of the
man before her, but he had been bearded, slim, and
light-hearted after a fashion that this man certainly did
not share. Sardonic cynicism was written all over him.
No, this man could not be her lost Link—nor did she
ever want to see him again. After all, she had spent the
last eight years denying to herself and the world that he
had ever existed.

It was his voice, perhaps, which had deceived her.
And how could that be? For Link's voice had been

lighter, rapid, and he had spoken in a thick Texas drawl, not in the polished, almost British accents of a man who consorted with kings and princes.

She found herself answering him, aware that he was turning the full force of his powerful personality on her, quite deliberately.

'How strange,' she said slowly. 'Yes, I sat there for a time. The afternoon was so pleasant, and I needed to think a little. Spring in Washington is perhaps a good time for thinking.'

That amused him, it was plain. He answered her gravely, 'Spring anywhere is perhaps a good time for thinking, Mrs McAllister. A time when all things are renewed, when winter and decay are behind us. A happy thought, that, to have at a White House junketing.' And he gave her such a dazzling smile that she was nearly undone, a smile which in its odd fashion reminded her again of Link. Spring madness must be assaulting her, that she should think of him so often today, and that a fancied resemblance could start her wits astraying.

After Boyce Hamilton and the other men she usually met, this man was a revelation. She could well understand Sarah Lee's baffled anger that he had escaped her, her annoyance that his attraction was all for the Widow McAllister, as she had spitefully named Mary. The sheer physical pull of him, the almost careless assumption of strength and power, again unlike Boyce, who usually seemed almost apologetic that he was the senator's son, was almost overwhelming.

He was speaking to her again, and she must attend. It was not like her to be so overthrown by anyone.

'Have you been Senator Hamilton's aide long, Mrs McAllister?'

She made a sudden unusual decision, a decision which was quite unlike her. It must have been the call of that forgotten past working on her, she thought afterwards.

'Mary, Mr Tunstall. I know your brother well. Strange for him to call me Miz Mary, while you remain so formal. Yes, Mary it shall be, seeing that you do not claim his Western manners. As to your question, I have been the senator's political secretary and aide for the last three years.' And she returned his smile, with interest.

Why, she thought, horror-stricken, I am flirting with him! How long has it been since I flirted with a man? Not even with Boyce. Particularly not with Boyce. He would hardly know what to do with a flirting woman.

Jared Tunstall did. His faint smile grew broader. 'Mary, then. Forgive me, but you hardly look old enough to be referred to as the Widow McAllister. A child bride, Mary? And do call me Jared. I refuse to run second to Orrin. His seniority in years is bad enough without him claiming it over me in the matter of pretty women.'

Mary felt like saying, I am sure that you are second to none when it comes to pretty women, Jared, but something, some remnant of sanity, saved her.

'Oh, but,' she said, and her smile was a delight, Jared thought, 'Senator Orrin Tunstall is so chivalrous, in the Western manner, you understand, that he would do nothing to disturb a lady—if you tell him I gave you permission. . .' And that, she thought, ruefully, is nearly as provocative as my unspoken comment.

Jared gazed at her with pleasure. How in the world could Sarah Lee hint that this woman was frigid? What on earth was wrong with all the men in Washington that none of them had got to first base with her? Except, of course, that stick, Boyce Hamilton, whom Jared had met once, in New York, a man who thought women were to be put on pedestals and worshipped from afar, not to be thrown on beds and pleasured.

He had a fleeting memory of the redheaded trollop he had had on his arm when he had seen and spoken to Boyce Hamilton once in New York, and Hamilton's condemning look at a man who engaged in such frivolities as escorting professional beauties. He would enjoy taking this far from professional beauty from such a stick as Hamilton.

His Charlie she might not be, but a woman to be pursued, and to be won. What a trophy! The Ice

Princess! And his internal grin grew greater still. What a set-down for poor Sarah Lee—to be passed over for the Widow McAllister!

'Oh,' he said, 'I promise not to duel with Orrin over the correct way to address you. And now, Mary, the music is starting again, you are on your own, no one has come to claim you, and to seal a new-found friendship will you do me the honour of waltzing with me?'

Mary looked at the eager, lively face of the man before her. Boyce had talked vaguely of returning to claim her for the waltz. But he was nowhere to be seen. And a kind of joy which she had not felt for as long as she could remember swept over her.

'No,' she said, 'no, I am not formally claimed. I will certainly dance with you, Jared, if that is your pleasure.'

She closed her fan and hung it from her wrist by its silken ribbon. He bowed, held out a hand, and swept her on to the floor. She knew at once that he was a good dancer, light on his feet for such a big man—but then, so had Orrin been when she had danced with him; but she had never felt like this with Orrin.

The touch of his hands, the nearness of his superb body, the faint scent of clean linen, and some hint of lemon, which must come from the oil he had rubbed in his hair, the whole powerful aura of dominant male animal, so different from the usual men she met in Washington, overpowered her. And again the sensation of familiarity was strong. She had felt nothing like this, nothing, since the days when she had renounced her past and come to Washington, not as wild Charlie, but as careful, composed Widow McAllister.

Half unconsciously she closed her eyes, leaned back a little against his confining arm, and the expression on her face had subtly changed from its usual calm impassivity to one of almost sensual acceptance—and she was quite unaware of this, although the man holding her was not.

Poor Widow McAllister, he thought, half in triumph, half in amusement, what has she been missing in life?

No, not my Charlie at all. And he thought of Charlie and her sweet abandon with him, with a bitter regret. For so long he had suppressed his memories of her, and now this fancied likeness had brought her back to haunt him.

He was not the only man in the room to notice the transformation of the Widow McAllister. Boyce Hamilton, arriving late from his conference, found that his Mary, for so he thought of her, had disappeared. He looked around for her, and heard Sarah Lee's mischievous voice half whispering in his ear, 'Beware, Boyce, beware; you are losing your white lily to a master at the game of opportunity.'

Unspoken was her further comment—a pity to lose yet another woman you thought of as yours to an adventurer.

Mary, unaware that an angry and jealous Boyce was watching her patent enjoyment at dancing with Jared, sighed with disappointment when the music ended. Her dream of pleasure over—for that was what the waltz had surprisingly been—she opened her eyes at last to see Boyce leaning against the wall, arms folded, an expression of acute displeasure on his face, scowling at her.

Jared saw him too, and, laughing to himself, did not stop, but waltzed Mary round the room once more, swinging her with him, until they arrived back where they had started from, before a Boyce whose scowl was now so ferocious that even his teeth were bared—a sight which Mary saw with dismay, and Jared with amusement. The poor devil would be grinding them next!

'I thought that that was our dance, Mary,' he greeted her, after he had flung an, 'Evening, Tunstall,' at Jared.

The dance seemed to have revived the unregenerate girl inside her, for she replied—oh, so sweetly, 'So did I, Boyce. But you were nowhere to be seen. Jared took pity on my forlorn state, and asked me on to the floor. He was alone, too, so what could I do but accept?'

'You knew I was returning. I told you so,' he said stiffly. Quite without meaning to, the three of them had begun to provide entertainment for those around them. 'Tunstall at his tricks again,' was the most common internal comment, and Boyce Hamilton was no match for such a thruster.

'You really must not be annoyed with Mary,' Jared said smoothly. 'I am afraid that it was I who lured her on to the floor. I am the one to whom you should direct you reprimands. If any are needed, that is.'

Mary looked from one to the other. For a moment she half thought to placate Boyce. And then the devil which had left her eight years ago returned and prompted her again.

'In any case, Boyce,' she said, 'you really have no call to be cross. You did not return, I believe, until the dance was almost over. Was not that so, Jared?'

Jared! Mary! It was plain from Boyce's face how much he resented the intimacy which they had so quickly reached. Mary remembered, with some compunction, how long it had taken for her and Boyce to reach Christian-name terms, whereas five minutes had been sufficient for her to beg Jared Tunstall to call her Mary! It must be the unwanted memory of Link which had led her to such an access of indiscretion.

She was full of conflicting emotions. One part of her was wishing that she had never danced with Jared Tunstall, that he would go away quickly, take away the unwanted memories which he had provoked, and stop Boyce being so cross. The other part was perversely glad that she had provoked the usually mild Boyce to such annoyance by dancing with Jared, and at the same time her heart sank into her light evening pumps at the thought that she was about to commit herself to a jealous and possessive man who had proved himself to be easily provoked. It was obvious that, although he had not yet proposed, Boyce thought she was already his.

And that thought was intolerable to her—to be so taken for granted that even before marriage he questioned to whom she might speak, and with whom she might dance. She reined her anger in.

It was now quite apparent that they were the subject
of some considerable interest. More than one person had
seen Jared Tunstall with Mary McAllister in his arms,
and some few so-called gentlemen were already quietly
laying bets as to whether Tunstall would not only freeze
the senator's son out, but would prove to be the man
who breached the widow's closely guarded fortress.

Mary might not know all of this, but she knew
Washington: a small-minded town with a nose for scandal. So far, she had walked a circumspect line, and had
no mind to give gossip-mongers something to get their
teeth into. Yes, it had been very pleasant to dance with
Jared Tunstall, having flirted lightly with him, but, after
all, she had come with Boyce, and he was right to think
that she should have put his interests first.

She smiled at Jared and held out her hand for him to
take and to kiss again—doubtless causing further comment. 'My thanks, Jared. And now I expect that Boyce
will want us to go in for supper. You are staying in
Washington? Perhaps we might meet and talk again?'

She was graciousness itself, but it was his *congé*, he
knew. Skilfully done, and one more proof that she was
not the woman he sought. He bowed again after the kiss,
said goodnight to that fortunate ass Hamilton, who
would now probably start to bully her all over again.
Dammit, the man did not deserve her.

The rest of his evening was ruined. He had not the
faintest desire to speak to, or dance with, any woman
now that the Widow McAllister was forbidden to him,
and his temper was not improved by his brother Orrin,
who said severely to him in the carriage on the way
home, 'Now, Jared, I know yore a great man for the
ladies, an' all that. But I trust yuh to remember that yore
a gentleman born, and ought not to go chasin' after good
women like Mary McAllister. She's not used to dealin'
with sharks like yuh. Pity to spoil her chance to marry
Hamilton's son. Yes, I know the man is a poor stick, but
he cares for her. While yuh, yuh rogue, I know yuh.

Another scalp for yore belt. Ought to have enough already, without makin' a good woman unhappy.'

'Hell, Orrin,' he said angrily. 'Don't you give me credit for possessing any sense of decency? I haven't the slightest intention of making love to, or seducing, the pretty widow. And as for ruining her! But it does seem a pitiful waste that she's going to be hitched to such a half-man as Boyce Hamilton. If he didn't look so much like the senator, I'd have wondered if he fathered him!'

Orrin was unrepentant. 'Yuh mind what I say, little brother. I'll come after yuh with a shotgun if yuh ruin her life, seein' as how she ain't got a daddy to do it for her. I mean it, Jared. Jes' behave for once, eh?'

Well, never mind all that, thought Jared. Whether I wish to seduce her, or court her, is my business. And, if I am truthful, it is not only her likeness to Charlie which excites me, but the woman she is. Ice Princess, indeed. How in the world could anyone think her that?

For Jared had seen immediately through the façade behind which Mary McAllister sheltered from the world, and not only did he wish to discover whether she was his lost love, but he also wanted to find out what sort of a woman she truly was.

CHAPTER TWO

'Ah, Miz Mary. I'm expecting the Tunstall brothers to call at four o'clock this afternoon.'

Mary looked up at the senator, who filled the office doorway, his presence still a dominant one, despite his seventy-odd years and his slightly stooped shoulders. His noble face, like an old Roman bust, and his mane of white hair, still worn long in disregard of the fashions of 1889, made him an instantly recognisable figure wherever he went. She could not help thinking, again, how sad it was that Boyce should have so little of his father's grand and imperious personality. She had been told that he was more like his mother, a retiring woman, a pale figure beside her dominant husband.

'I'll make a note of it right away,' she said, interrupting her task of sorting papers to pick up the heavy gilt-edged diary, to write in it in her neat hand, '4.00, the Tunstalls.'

'I expect,' said the senator, 'that they're coming here to lobby me over the Western States' plan to try to convince the United States Government to make silver a joint currency with gold, seeing that brother Orrin is the senior senator for Nevada.'

Both he and Mary knew that Nevada was the United States' prime silver-producing state. 'And,' he went on, 'I'm sure that brother Jared will be trying to convince him that supporting the Tariff Bill might be a useful carrot to offer me in exchange for my vote. After all, Wall Street wants us to protect American goods and services from competition from abroad, and Jared is nothing if not a good Wall Street man. I believe that there's a report on silver and the Nevada proposals somewhere there——' And he pointed at a pile of papers

30

neatly flagged and docketed on a shelf above Mary's desk.

'You could read through it if you would, make some notes and remind me of the relevant paragraphs. Deep fellow, Orrin, for all he comes on as a roughneck. Have to be ready for him.'

Mary finished briefing Miss Agnes for the day, then pulled out the report and began to leaf through it, making notes on a yellow legal pad as she did so.

She sometimes thought that, after all, she could take the senator's place in government, and then she thought of the sheer ruthlessness of Washington's politics, the smoke-filled rooms filled with good old boys, and the brutality with which they pursued both their careers and the almighty dollar, and thought again. Government would have to change if women were to participate in it. However decorous the behaviour of the country's legislators in public, she knew that their language and habits in private were very different.

The Tunstalls were coming to lobby the senator, she knew, to collect his vote if they could for the Silver Bill which Orrin was trying to push through Congress before it adjourned in the early summer. He was probably bringing Jared along to act as further weight in the balance, and almost certainly the senator would want her in the room with them. Not to speak, but to be there to provide information, and occasionally advice—but mainly to make notes, to be aware of what was said and done by all parties present. Perhaps to look up a reference.

Sometimes he told her to appear to make notes, even when there were none worth recording, to persuade his visitors that even their lightest word was receiving great attention. At other times he told her to put her pad away—'We're speaking off the record now,' he would say—although the moment such a visitor left he and she would reconstruct between them what had been said with as much speed and accuracy as they could muster.

His memory was remarkable, and hers no less so, trained by her dead father.

After one such particular piece of dealing when her memory had been invaluable to him in getting a clause on welfare admitted into a disputed bill to do with the working hours of women, he had bought her a small pearl necklace as a thank-you, and when she had smilingly tried to refuse it he had insisted that she accept it.

'I'm not buying you, Miz Mary,' he said. 'I've no designs on you, merely thanking you. I thought that Jack Haines was good. You're better. I'd have given him a slap-up dinner at Willards with the best French wines thrown in, if he'd done for me what you did, but etiquette says that I can't do that—so the necklace. Wouldn't like you to think me ungrateful.'

That had been early in their relationship, and Mary knew all about old men and their secretaries, but he had never said, or done, anything improper to her, and she had come to understand that he did have affection for her, but saw her as the daughter he had never had. She knew that he had a strong wish for her to marry Boyce, but he had never put any pressure on her to marry him, and she respected him for that.

The Tunstalls arrived a little beforetimes and she went out to greet them; they had been ushered into the senator's drawing room. Orrin was wearing Western boots with high heels, and carrying a large white Stetson hat, an elaborate buckle on its band. Jared was in Eastern clothing, sombrely magnificent as befitted a young lion from Wall Street, New York. Orrin was broader, Jared taller. It was the first time she had seen them together, and despite the difference in their age she could plainly see how alike they were—but in manner and expression rather than in direct physical resemblance.

'The senator was kept at the Hill longer than he had expected. He only arrived back a few moments ago. He asks if you would both do him the honour of waiting a little until he is ready to see you. He suggests that I

order tea for you while we do so. I hope this is agreeable
to you both?'

Orrin spoke for the pair of them. 'Surely is, Mary.
Honour to take tea with you. Jared agrees with me, I am
sure. Dam' right, he better had!'

Of course, Jared agreed, it went without saying.
'Delighted to take tea with you, Mary, I can think of few
things I would enjoy more.' And the dark eyes on her
were telling her another story. But she was determined
that this afternoon she would not be seduced by the Wall
Street pirate's all-conquering manner.

She smiled at him, instructed the black servant girl to
hand him tea and pound cake, which he ate and drank
with a polite gusto, sitting beside Orrin on the long sofa.

Well, he was at least more decorously dressed than his
brother; Orrin, as usual, looked like a refugee from one
of the Wild West shows which were currently touring
America. Except that his improbable clothes, his outlan-
dish boots—he must have had a struggle not to put on a
pair of ornate Mexican spurs, she thought with amusement—and his hat, which he had placed carefully and
reverently on a chair, were all elegant and superfine,
luxurious, not at all like the rough-and-ready working
clothes which Mary McAllister knew the real Westerners
wore. Leave that, she thought, I won't think of that, and
she concentrated on entertaining her visitors, putting the
past firmly behind her.

She could not, however, prevent herself from making
some light comment on Orrin's boots. He had once told
her that he disliked walking, preferred to ride—in a
carriage if not on a horse.

'Forgive a personal remark,' she said. 'But while I
admire your Western footwear—such splendour, such
richness is hardly fit for the plains or the desert, one
might think, and certainly not of a shape to render
walking rather than riding your choice.'

Orrin grinned agreement, 'Oh, bravely said, Miz
Mary. You should favour the House with your wit. But
then you would have had to be a man. What a waste!'

Jared put down his teacup, refused more, and asked, 'Since you seem to know which are the most useful boots for riding, I take it that you ride, Mary?'

Did she ride? Of course she did. As a girl it had been her passion, but here in Washington she only rode occasionally, had a good horse which she seldom exercised enough.

'Yes, Jared,' she replied, face a little animated, 'although I hardly indulge in Washington in the kind of exercise which I am sure Orrin is used to. And you, of course, must also ride. You could hardly be his brother if you didn't.'

Jared nodded. Her slight smile when she answered him had changed her face again. 'Oh, I am a Westerner by adoption, learned to ride with a European saddle, but Orrin cured me of that when I went West, taught me the Western mode. I slump over the saddle-horn as though I had been born to it. Will you ride with me one afternoon? A shared pleasure is a greater pleasure.' And this last came out almost provocatively, as though it were not riding of which he spoke. Oh, yes, he thought, brother Orrin will be after me with that shotgun yet!

Mary ignored the last phrase, gave him the answer he wanted.

'It would be a pleasure, Jared. I know you have visited Washington previously, but I am sure that I can find something to show you which you have not seen before.'

Dear lord, she thought, now I am doing it, too. What could make me say something with such a double meaning? It is not like me. I am not Sarah Lee, nor Rhoda Rennie, the madam who runs the Liberty Belle, for although good women never spoke of such persons they knew that they existed.

If Jared picked up her unintended innuendo he showed no sign of it. He merely said, 'I will take up your offer as soon as I have found a horse worthy enough to sit on. Orrin will help me, I'm sure. What he does not know of horses is not worth knowing.'

'True,' drawled Orrin, looking a little reprovingly at

both of them. 'But, Jared, you know as well as I do, if this horseless carriage which you are promoting catches on, horses will be like dinosaurs. Nasty, stinkin' things, allus breakin' down, but one day, like the locomotive, they'll change everythin'.'

Mary was not surprised by Orrin's perception, nor that Jared was into horseless carriages. Like most people she agreed with Orrin's preference for the horse, but like him had enough wit to see their possibilities.

Once they had driven into the conversation, horseless carriages did not leave it. Jared began to talk animatedly about them. 'They may break down frequently now,' he said, 'but think of early locomotives and railroads—how primitive they were, and what they have become. The possibilities are infinite. Why, we might even use their engines to power flight!'

'Now, there yuh do leave me,' Orrin said. 'But what I do know is, I shall never like them. Give me a good hoss any day.'

The door opened and the senator appeared, eyes approving the friendly scene before him. 'You have entertained my visitors so well, I see, Miz Mary, that they will hardly wish to abandon the tea-tray and come down to the mundane earth of everyday life.'

'Tea is like oil,' remarked Jared. 'It fuels everyday living.' He was amused at himself. Orrin *will* be pleased. I am being as proper as a dowager.

'You will take a cup, Senator?' Mary offered, the teapot in her hand, regretful that the pleasant half-hour was over. Jared Tunstall was not merely a lady's man in the ballroom. Her knowledge of his New York career told her that there were great depths to him, and, like Orrin, he had a fund of knowledge.

'With regret, no,' said the senator, declining tea. 'I have detained Senator Tunstall long enough and must not keep him further. If you are all finished I propose that we adjourn to my inner sanctum and begin our discussions.'

The senator's own room was not large and was strictly

functional. It was reached through the office-cum-library where Agnes and Mary worked. Once in it, and everyone disposed—the senator at his desk, Mary seated, pad on knee, pencil poised, the Tunstalls on a high sofa—the true meat of the visit began.

The bargaining, the haggling—the exchange of concessions for voting intentions—the harsh and cynical nature of government, so different from the arid philosophies in academic textbooks, never ceased to fascinate Mary.

'Now,' said the senator briskly, courtesies being over, 'there is no need for us to blink at the issues involved, Orrin. We have been friends, and occasional adversaries, too long for that. You are not going to pretend that you have not come here to do other than to offer me your support for the Tariff Bill, which I and my fellows are proposing, in exchange for us voting for the clauses in the Silver Bill which would demand that the US Treasury guarantees to buy silver each month at a fixed price.'

'Oh, I likes a feller that knows where he stands,' grinned Orrin. 'No shilly-shallying, no mugwumping. Jus' a plain statement of fack.' He seemed to grow more Western by the minute, thought Mary, fascinated. She had half expected them to go through the usual ritual of advancing sideways at one another like a pair of crabs—but they knew one another too well for that.

'Jared here has been lecturin' me on the importance of not makin' foreign imports impossible, but touchin' 'em up just enough to keep our own trade buoyant. I tell him, he should be on the Hill, not me.'

'And so the *Washington Post* seems to think,' said the senator smoothly, picking it up and waving it at them. 'It certainly sees you as a team, and a formidable one, I may say.'

Both the brothers laughed. Like Mary they had opened the paper that morning to find that as a result of the Silver Debate, still going on inside and outside the House, there was a cartoon on the front showing Orrin, wildly dressed, riding a bucking bronco, and Jared, civilised, with a desk for a steed, a whip in the shape of a dollar symbol in his hand. The caption said, 'Brothers together: Western silver and Eastern gold. . .'

'I am forewarned, I see,' remarked the senator. 'Joint conspirators as you both are.'

Three-quarters of an hour later, the bargaining over, Mary put down her pencil, and sighed. The deal had been struck, each party to it had pledged the other its vote. Both Bills would go through.

If Mary had been surreptitiously watching Jared, Jared, while keeping his mind on the drift of the discussion, was also admiring the Widow McAllister, her bright head luminous against the dark law books, her hand flying across the paper, and he was also relishing the contrast between her decorative appearance and her obvious understanding of the issues which were being debated. Could his Charlie have turned into this sort of woman? he wondered.

Once, at the senator's request, she pulled down one of the books to identify a disputed citation about bimetallism, the theory which lay behind the Nevadan's determination to make silver equal with gold.

'I cannot say,' finally remarked the senator, after nearly an hour's hard bargaining, 'that you have finally convinced me that silver should be on a par with gold in our currency, and consequently that the government should, in effect, subsidise it, but I think that I have heard enough of the benefits accruing to our economy generally to convince me that your Bill is worthy of support.'

'Likewise,' said Orrin, disdaining as usual, fancy phrases. 'Brother Jared had been givin' me good advice on gold, as well as silver, eh, Jared? All helps me to keep yuh happy, Senator. Yuh may count on my vote.'

Brother Jared had been so busy admiring the Widow McAllister's charming profile that he missed this, had to be reminded by Orrin that he was here on business, not to wool-gather, and finally allowed as how brother Orrin had the right of it.

'And now, gentlemen,' said the senator, going to a sideboard where a tantalus stood, 'let us drink to our deal. I have fine Scotch whisky here, specially imported for me. I know you like rye, Orrin, but do me the favour of trying this without having made up your mind beforehand that you dislike it. Mary will excuse us our tippling, I know.'

Mary smiled. 'I am well aware of the realities of Washington life. If I take a man's job, then I cannot argue that I should not be part of men's affairs, and demand that they should change their habits for me.'

'Bravo,' said Jared, his praise genuine. 'I honour you, Mary. Your logic is impeccable—dare I say masculine?' And he raised his glass to her, his smile a little impudent, and certainly inviting. He could not help himself, the Widow McAllister was having such an effect on him, and by her answering amusement he was having a similar effect on her.

'Perhaps one day,' she said slyly, 'though not now, it will not be considered wrong for a lady to take a drink of whisky with you. A small one, that is.'

The three men laughed with her, and not at her, and Jared leaned forward to say, 'For that, my dear Mrs McAllister, I shall certainly take you riding. Will the afternoon of the day after tomorrow be suitable? I am sure that the senator does not slave-drive you every day.'

His manner was almost conspiratorial, despite the presence of the others, and the senator's eyes were hard on them both. So, at last a rival for his tardy son, and a formidable one. Boyce had dangled after the desirable widow for too long.

'How can I refuse such a gallant offer?' was Mary's answer to Jared, and again, when he took her hand and kissed it, that *frisson* of delight ran through her, reminding her of another time, of another passion felt.

'Soon, then,' he said, before dropping the favoured hand, and if he saw the senator's eyes hard on him he did not let that worry him. The chase after Mary

McAllister gained added spice if others were after her too.

After they had gone, and she had picked up her pad, Mary stood silent and thoughtful, reviewing the afternoon. But what filled her mind was not the politics and the dealing, but Jared Tunstall. She thought that she had had as strong an effect on him as he had had on her, and that they both knew it—and by their reactions the senator and his brother, too. Well, that could not be helped. Even when she did not look at him she could feel that he was there, as if some invisible cord bound them together.

How strange, after all this time, to meet another man who engaged her so powerfully. The other afternoon, before the Capitol, she had decided to accept Boyce, sure that she could face marriage without passion, marriage undertaken in friendship, and, yes, for convenience, for although Boyce might love her, she did not love him.

Whatever else, meeting Jared Tunstall had put that decision in the gravest doubt. For supposing, after marrying Boyce, that she met someone who called to her so insistently that she could not refuse him, someone to whom she could give her soul as well as her body? How, then would she respond?

A useless question. For she knew, she knew. And what was more important and more disturbing was that although she had only met him twice, she thought that she might have found that man already in the one who reminded her so powerfully of her lost love.

Mary was at home on the afternoon following the senator's meeting with the Tunstall brothers. She was busy writing at her desk when Miss Nessie, an elderly spinster who had been Anna Whittaker's housekeeper and had stayed on to be hers, came in and began bustling about behind her.

Mary smiled to herself. Such behaviour usually meant that Miss Nessie was bursting to speak to her, but would not ask directly. She was a distant, very distant cousin

to both Anna and Mary. 'My grandfather smoked in
your grandfather's back parlour,' she had once said. She
liked Mary, was not deceived by the Widow McAllister's
control of her life and herself. She thought that Miz
Mary was a vulnerable creature, and from sistering Miz
Anna she now mothered Miz Anna's niece—as far as
Mary would let her.

'What is it, Miss Nessie?' Mary asked her gently.

'I've been thinkin'. Iffen you're goin' to marry Mr
Boyce,' she was instantly told, 'you ought to do it
quickly. Neether of you gettin' any younger. Should
start a family soon. Sally-Anne needs brothers and sisters
to share things with. Let me retire at last, when you do.'

'I should be loath to lose you, but if you wanted to
retire now. . .' began Mary.

'Not likely,' said Miss Nessie. 'An' leave you to the
two-legged wolves in this town? No, I'll go when you are
married—not that I'm greatly taken by Mr Boyce
Hamilton, but at least he's steady.'

That seemed to be Boyce's epitaph, thought Mary
sadly. Miss Nessie had broken her train of thought. She
put down her pen, sighed, and carried some tapestry
work through into her front parlour and sat busy with it
as the hand of the clock reached four. No visitors today,
she was thinking, just as there was a thunderous knock-
ing at the front door.

Livvie, the black maid, put her head into the parlour,
blinked at the Missis. 'Gemmun to see you, Mam. Is you
in?'

'As in as I ever shall be. Has he a name?'

Livvie proffered a card. Jared Tunstall. Of course.
Mary's heart began to beat thunderously.

'Show him in here, Livvie, and ask Miss Nessie to
send in herself, and tea, as soon as possible.'

Livvie bobbed an answer, disappeared, then
reappeared, Mr Jared Tunstall, large, in her wake. 'Mr
Tunstall to see you, Mam.'

He was splendidly dressed—no surprise, that—and

yes, harsh though his face was, he was handsome, and power streamed from him like light from the sun.

They went through the formalities. He kissed her hand and again he had that overpowering effect on her. They sat down, and made idle small talk—admired the spring weather, the early show of flowers, spoke briefly of Senator Hamilton, Orrin and the silver question; the new executive office on Pennsylvania Avenue, brashly white in all its Second Empire glory; and how does Washington compare with New York, Jared? All of which for sheer inanity, Mary thought, took some beating.

Miss Nessie saved them, coming in carrying the tea-tray herself. She laid out the china, the silver, small sandwiches and large slices of pound cake on an occasional table in front of Mary, then sat at the back of the room, knitting. Far from oppressing them, her presence seemed to liberate them.

'And that ride, Mary? Orrin says that he has found me what he calls "a hoss of quality," and insists that I shall ride it with his Western saddle. I ask myself which other senator on the Hill when he sets out for Washington packs his saddle first and his Colt .45 second?'

Mary's laugh was genuine. 'You know, Jared, your brother doesn't fool me. I sometimes wonder what he's really like beneath his Wild West flim-flam—and then I think I know. The phrase "solid citizen" was coined for Orrin.'

Miss Nessie's expression at Mary's pleasure was one of complete approval. At last, a man to make her laugh. Not many laughs in Miz Mary's life.

'Oh,' said Jared, looking at her over his china teacup, dwarfed by his big hand, 'and I—do I share in your praise of Orrin's steadiness? Being his brother?'

'You?' said Mary lightly, wondering why his very glance should disturb her. 'But you are New York, *par excellence*. Civilised frivolity on the surface, and steel beneath. What have you to do with Western virtues?'

'How well you read me,' he said softly. He bit into his

excellent slice of pound cake. 'You don't think that
sharing Orrin's life a little might reform me?' His tone
was as light as hers.

'On the contrary, I might be fearful that you
would. . .corrupt Orrin. Except that when I look at
him. . .'

'Now, Mary,' he said, and the eyes on her were
mocking. 'You wrong both of us. Orrin has already
threatened me with a shotgun if I bring my wicked ways
to Washington. I know I'm *his* target; I wonder who he
thinks is mine?'

'Are you asking me for advice on that?' She queried,
amused and, yes, excited to be fencing with a man after
a fashion in which she knew that she would never fence
with Boyce. So one might walk a tightrope over Niagara
with Blondin when talking to Jared. Being with Boyce
was as safe as an afternoon tea party ought to be—and
this was not.

'You think that you are the proper person for me to
ask,' was his reply, conscious that Miss Nessie's eyes
were on them both, and, he could have sworn, registered
approval.

'Oh, you must already know that I am always proper.'

'Indeed. A very book of etiquette, alive and walking,
I am told. Now, why does not that daunt me, as it
should? The challenge, perhaps?'

'But, I challenge no one. You see, you do not know
the first rule of propriety—never challenge; it leads one
into areas not perhaps foreseen.'

'I would not mind if you challenged me, however.'

'Ah,' said Mary, and she could not resist the banter in
his voice, nor refuse to share in the juggling they had
begun, where words were thrown like balls into the air
to be caught, for to drop them might be dangerous. 'But
you—you do not claim to be proper. And I preserve my
propriety by refusing to respond to any challenge you
might make.'

He put his cup and saucer down, leaned forward, and
said, 'Oh, no. I think not. You have already done so, my

dear Widow McAllister. Pistols were at the ready, and swords crossed between us some time ago. I'm sure that you are clever enough to recognise unspoken challenges, as well as those made openly.'

This must end, it really must. Mary looked at Miss Nessie and said, 'It is nearly half-past four. I'm sorry to remind you that Sally-Anne must be collected. I promised the Rutherfords that we would call for her before five o'clock.'

'Sally-Anne?' Jared could not help querying. Was this a sister? He had not heard that Mary McAllister was endowed with one.

'My small daughter,' explained Mary. She smiled. 'The worst tomboy in Washington. Yes, she is,' she added, as Miss Nessie clucked disapproval at her. 'You must allow that she is the liveliest thing going.' But her expression was proud, not at all ashamed.

'I guess,' said Miss Nessie. 'No harm in her, though.'

'Now, you do surprise me,' said Jared, his eyes suddenly wicked again. 'I would have thought that any child of yours would have been a paragon of all the virtues!'

'I am not sure whether that is meant to praise me, or to rebuke,' Mary could not help answering playfully. 'Or Sally-Anne either. My father used to tell me that I was the wildest thing on the block when I was about Sally-Anne's age.'

'But you are making up for it now?'

Mary coloured a little. 'Well, I could hardly turn hand-springs in front of the Capitol, which was Sally-Anne's latest trick last week, when I was trying to show her off as a perfect young lady.'

'Now, that I really would like to see,' murmured Jared. 'You turning hand-springs, I mean, not Sally-Anne. I take it that she is still a small child?'

'You take it correctly,' said Mary. For some reason she did not want to confess her daughter's age and was relieved when Jared said that he was sorry that he would have to leave before Sally-Anne returned, but he had an engagement on the Hill with someone from the Treasury and must shortly leave them to fulfil it.

'I was just passing,' he lied. 'Remembered where Orrin said that you lived, and thought that I would call to remind you that I had not forgotten about our promised ride. You 'will be at the reception for the new French ambassador this evening. You must tell me how Sally-Anne enjoyed her afternoon.'

'As much as I am enjoying mine, I hope,' replied Mary, sorry to see him go, not at all deceived by his falsehood, 'I was just passing'. No one who lived in official Washington could 'just pass' anywhere in the suburb where she lived, unless he was taking a long walk to the Potomac!

No, it was plain that Mr Jared Tunstall was pursuing her, and it was not only his visit. It was the way he was looking at her, the admiration in his eyes, the two-edged conversation with which he was delighted to entertain her, and to which she had so shamefully responded.

He was making no effort to leave. He looked at her piano and said, 'You play, Mary?' He remembered a girl playing to him, and was curious to hear her reply.

'A little,' she said. 'I hardly find the time to play lately, and when I do I'm afraid it's Stephen Foster, not Beethoven. Sally-Anne loves jolly tunes. Minstrel songs and spirituals are her favourites. She had a true voice, and sings along with me.'

Jared said, apparently idly, 'And does she like "Clementine"? It was a favourite of mine when young, I'm told.'

Faintness almost overcame her. Mary felt like clutching at something, to prove she existed, was not dreaming. 'Clementine', of all songs which he could have named! Surely it could not be a coincidence? But he had spoken so idly, and for once the keen eyes were not on her.

'No, not "Clementine",' she said, and would have liked to add, No, never 'Clementine', I cannot bear to hear it, but if he were not Link—how could he be?—he would think her maudlin.

Nothing on his face gave him away. Jared Tunstall was famous throughout the financial world, and the world of pleasure where men played cards for high stakes, for his poker face. Behind it his mind might be racing, as his was now.

But Mary, unknowing of this, had a poker face, too. She would give nothing away—which was one lesson she had learned from what had happened to her eight years ago.

'And you,' she asked, apparently idly, 'do you play a musical instrument—or sing, perhaps?'

His reply was studiedly non-committal. 'No, not now. A little, as a boy.' He pulled out his watch, said regretfully, 'I'm sorry to have to leave so early, but duty calls. I may come again? And you will ride with me, soon?'

'Of course,' Mary said, rising. No, she did not want him to leave. He had behaved very properly, even if his every word, as well as his merry eyes, had told her a different story and the attraction between them was as strong, if not stronger, than ever. He took her hand and kissed it, before he left, and he murmured, 'I shall see you at the reception, I hope, and we shall dance again. You must promise me that.'

'Of course,' Mary murmured. His touch, as ever, had undone her. She could speak to him, just, without betraying her feelings, but what passed between them when he took her hand was—electric, and he knew it. She felt Miss Nessie's shrewd eyes on them both—she had returned from instructing Livvie to collect Sally-Anne.

'So, a rival for Mr Boyce at last,' she said, when Jared had gone.

'Nonsense,' said Mary lightly. 'An acquaintance, nothing more.'

'Don't fool me—neether of you,' said Miss Nessie. 'Watch out for him, though. Mr Jared Tunstall ain't no pussy-cat. Real tiger—or so I've heard.'

* * *

And that was another epitaph for Boyce, Mary thought, later on, when she sat down again at her desk to continue where she had left off earlier. She was busy doing something of which no one in Washington knew, not even the senator. What was more, no one in Washington would quite believe her if she told them.

A few weeks ago, at yet another reception, she had been approached by Garrison Firth, the editor of the *Washington Gazette*, the *Post*'s chief rival.

'Mrs McAllister. A word, if I may?'

Mary had turned her brilliant eyes on him, and he had said, 'I have listened to you talking more than once, and I have heard—do not ask me how—that the reason that Senator Hamilton's speeches are so brilliant lately is that you are writing them.'

Mary had raised her fan, smiled at him over it. 'Come, Sir, you cannot expect me to discuss such a matter with a journalist, of all people.'

'Oh, Mrs McAllister, I know that your discretion is legendary, which is why I have approached you on this matter. I have had in mind a column to be called "A Lady Looks at Washington", to be written by a lady who knows the world about us in its political and social aspects. I think that you could write that column, Mrs McAllister, and I am prepared to pay you handsomely if you agree to do so.'

She considered for a moment, but felt that she had no idea of his exact requirements.

'I could not pen scandal for you, Mr Firth.'

Firth laughed at that. 'No, indeed. I have others to do that for me. No, what I wanted was a serious, but informed, somewhat amusing, somewhat caustic look at the affairs of the great world of Congress and society from someone educated and informed as you are, but most particularly from a woman's viewpoint. Women are the coming thing in our great Republic, as I am sure that you are aware.'

'And that is so different from a man's? The viewpoint, I mean.'

'Perhaps not. But women are excluded from power, Mrs McAllister, and such an exclusion gives you a certain freedom, and the issues which you raise might not always be those which men would consider important. I would preserve your anonymity—again—to add spice, to allow conjecture. And you have a lively mind, I know.'

The unregenerate girl still inside Mary urged her on. Why not? To speak in her own right, or write, perhaps— the pun amused her—not in Senator Hamilton's voice, would be a challenge.

There would be things which she would like to say— to hint at the cauldron which boiled beneath Washington's decorous surface, the dealings and the lies. The editor caught the glint in her eye, and read his woman correctly.

'You will do it, then?'

'Yes,' she said. 'Yes.'

'And I would like some copy by Thursday. You know what a column would require?'

'If I do not, I am sure that you will tell me.'

'Twice a week,' he said, and smiling, conspiratorial, added, 'It must be lively, I repeat. I want it to be such that people will conjecture as to who the writer is, who is this lively lady!'

'Oh, they will think it written by a man.'

'There,' he exclaimed, laughing. 'From your answers I am sure that you will have the right tone exactly.'

Afterwards she was to wonder if she had been wise. But the column had already appeared several times and, as the editor had hoped, had caused much comment. She found that she could write such a thing, and that the writing freed her.

She betrayed no confidences, but wrote wittily and well about the Billionaire Congress—for such it had been nicknamed—and about the robber barons like Jared who lobbied in Washington for their personal gain. There were many who tried to guess who the Lady was, but no one ever put forward the name of the Ice Princess, and she heard some of the comment with well-disguised amusement.

She put down her pen. She had written a witty, gently mocking pen portrait of Orrin Tunstall, in which she had emphasised the brilliant and subtle mind which lurked behind his Western grotesqueries, and contrasted him with another senator, nameless, but immediately recognisable, whose apparently brilliant exterior concealed—nothing.

And now she must prepare to give Sally-Anne her tea, and after that dress for the reception.

The crowd at the reception was basically the same as that at the ball where she had first met Jared Tunstall. She had been escorted there by Senator Hamilton since Boyce was unable to arrive before the supper interval, having been unavoidably detained by the sudden arrival in the capital of an important client—like his father, Boyce had a wide legal practice.

'You look radiant tonight,' the old man had said to her approvingly, wishing for the thousandth time that his son would hurry up and secure this splendid prize.

Mary smiled up at him—he was another tall man— and did not tell him that it was Jared for whom she had dressed herself so sumptuously, not Boyce. She was wearing a gown of deep cream with old rose trimmings. The roses in her crown of blonde hair were silk, but there was one real one pinned to her bosom where any red-blooded male was sure to look and admire—the bosom as well as the rose.

Jared Tunstall was looking, and of his admiration when he finally saw her there was no doubt. He crossed the room to her, an arrow finding its target. She was by then not with the senator, who had been taken to see the President, but was standing a little apart from a group of his political cronies.

'Miz Mary,' he said to her slightly averted head; she had not seen him, and he said it mischievously, in an imitation of his brother Orrin's voice—or was he deliberate? He did not know.

The effect on Mary was electric. She swung her head around, the blood draining from her face. For the voice, although so like Orrin's, in those two short words brought back the memories which she had spent the last few days trying to suppress.

'Jared!' she said, and met his keen gaze.

He laughed a little, took her hand, and bent over it.

'So European!' she said, in an attempt to be light with him. 'What a strange mixture you are, Mr Tunstall.'

She said his name slightly mockingly, in a further attempt to prevent his presence from unnerving her so strangely. But she knew by his expression, the way he retained her hand that fraction longer than he should, the way in which the bold eyes roved over her, approving what they saw, and his comment, 'You are enchanting, Mary. A more beautiful vision than I ever saw in London or Paris, I dare swear. Washington is to be envied,' the impression which she made on him.

And what could one say to that? Mary decided on mystery, smiled enigmatically, opened her fan.

'You are deserted again,' he offered. 'Mr Boyce tardy? Tut, tut. He neglects his duties. And have you no escort for supper, Mary? If not, I am here to provide one.' And he offered her his arm.

How could she refuse? She knew beyond a doubt that she should, if only to resist the all-conquering male animal which she knew he was. Besides, to associate with him again, so readily, would restart the tongues a-wagging. The Ice Princess pursued by the robber baron who had never known defeat where women were concerned.

Delightful folly prevailed. She took the proffered arm and said, still light, 'Yes, Jared. We may share the baked meats together. Although, I warn you, White House suppers are seldom remarkable.'

'Oh, my company is good enough for me; food is something extra, not the real purpose of my evening,' he

said carelessly, leading her towards the supper-room.
'All else tonight, beside yourself, is a bonus.'

Before she could reply—in a similar light vein, Mary
hoped—she saw an unwanted sight.

It was Boyce, arrived early after all, seeking her out,
his expression when he saw her on Jared's arm thunderous, to say the least.

'So, there you are. I thought that you came with the
senator.' He had not even the grace to acknowledge
Jared, who stopped, eyebrows raised, at this peremptory
salute.

Mary was always equal to Boyce—one reason for not
leaping at the chance to marry him, she thought suddenly. He presented no challenge to her, either physically or intellectually. Was that what Jared was? A
challenge?

'So I did—come with the senator,' she moved away
from Boyce; he had put out his elbow, appeared almost
ready to shove Jared away. 'But, as you are well aware,
your father is always in demand. I was temporarily
without an escort, and Jared kindly offered to take me
to the supper-room.'

'Oh, very well,' he said stiffly. 'Good of you, Tunstall.
Well, your task is over. I will relieve you now.'

Mary's eyebrows rose. This was too bad. Boyce was
treating her like a parcel which could be bandied from
hand to hand whether she willed it or not. She knew,
almost without looking at him, that Jared's face was a
picture of grave amusement.

'No, Boyce. I'm sorry, but I've already promised to
go in with Jared. You did say that you would not arrive
until after supper.'

'I left early, especially to take you in. You might at
least have waited for me.' He ground this out, his face
mortified, perhaps a little horrified himself that his
speech was degenerating into a snarl.

Jared had no intention of helping him, or of giving
way; nor, to his inward amusement, had Mary.

'There will be other times, Boyce,' she said, very

much in command of herself. All her earlier flutterings
over Jared and his disturbing presence had disappeared
before Boyce's boorishness. 'And it would be a poor
return for kindness to switch partners for my—or even
your—convenience at the last moment. We were about
to go in ourselves. You will excuse us, I'm sure.'

We! Ourselves! On hearing such words Boyce's
expression grew purely murderous, and if possible darkened even more when Jared said cheerfully, to turn the
knife in his wound, 'My turn tonight, Hamilton. Yours
later, perhaps.'

His bow as he finished was the *coup de grâce*. 'Come,'
he said to Mary and they walked together into the
supper-room, leaving behind a thwarted Boyce and a
covey of amused spectators, who included Sarah Lee.

What next? Was the Ice Princess at last going to give
Washington some real gossip to get its teeth into? Could
even Jared Tunstall have met his match? The possibilities were delightful.

And if Mary was aware of the excited speculation, or
the watching eyes, she did not care at all—no, not at all.
It was not the Ice Princess who had her hand in the
crook of Jared Tunstall's arm, who smiled up at him,
but another girl, a girl she thought had died long ago.

CHAPTER THREE

THE supper-room was already full—a relief perhaps, since Mary could gather herself together, try to restore her usual calm control, not surrender herself to the passing moment, and to the sexual pull of the monstrous pirate by her side. For she must never forget that that was what he was. But—oh, how difficult it was proving to be.

They stood in line for food, both amused at the greedy way the other guests piled their plates high—'Like sharks around their prey,' murmured Jared.

The room was oppressively hot again, but Jared found a glass door into the garden, held it open for Mary and waved an arm to usher her through it. After a second's hesitation she accepted the invitation and they found themselves on a small terrace beneath a silver-gilt spring moon.

There was a wooden bench near the door, and Jared, taking out his unused silk handkerchief, laid it on the seat between them, took her plate and glass of white wine and added them to his on the handkerchief, and they ate their food and drank their wine, while he played the part of an obsequious French waiter, gravely recommending their rather indifferent tipple in a fractured Gallic roar.

'So,' he said, resuming his own voice, and seeking to improve the hour and his own case with her, 'Mr Boyce Hamilton thinks that you are his property. I had not heard that you were engaged.'

Mary coloured. 'We are not, but. . .'

'All Washington expects that you will be. I know that,' said Jared. 'Can it be that, for once, all Washington is wrong?'

'A most improper question, and one you should not ask me.'

'Oh, I have a genius for asking improper questions,' said Jared carelessly. 'Drink up your wine, Mary. Wine by moonlight, like some other things I know of, is one of life's chief pleasures.'

His cunning tongue amused her. She had to be careful how she answered him. Best not to let him know that she had caught his innuendo.

'So they tell me,' she said, trying to make her tone neutral.

'Tell you, Mary? Have you not tried it yet?'

'Few of my escorts,' she said, 'have opened doors for me to a magic night so readily.'

'And would you have followed them so readily if they had?' he asked.

'How can I answer that, seeing that it has never happened before?' she wondered, and then drank her wine slowly, slowly, watching him over her glass, an odd excitement filling her. Was it the moon, or his nearness, the feeling of indulging in a forbidden pleasure, brought on by her defiance of Boyce, which affected her so?

She did not know, only that she was alive as she had not been for years, since. . . And she shrugged away her memories, clung tightly to a new, enchanting present.

They finished their al fresco supper together. He rose, put out his hand. She took it, and, holding her at a little distance, he lifted her from the bench and walked her away from the door to the blank wall of the House, where they merged into its shadows.

Mary's heart began to beat a tattoo, but he still kept his distance. He stopped. Turned. And the distance was gone.

'Why waste moonlight, and pleasure?' he said. 'My dear Widow McAllister, you have the most kissable mouth. Allow me to kiss it. Yes, we must not waste the moonlight.'

'No,' she said, but too late. While she was speaking, he swung her gently around, until she had her back against the wall. He let go of her hand, and, putting his own palms flat against the wall, on each side of her head—but not touching it, or her—he bent his own head and kissed her. The kiss was so gentle and so compelling that although he was not even holding her, not touching her, except with his mouth, she was unable to push him away; nor astonishingly did she wish to do so.

He lifted his head at last. 'Yes,' he said softly, 'kissable, very. How about elsewhere?' and he bent his head again, and, starting with the tiny cleft in her chin, began to kiss her along the jawline until he reached her ear, where his lips caught the lobe, and began to nuzzle it, again with the utmost gentleness.

'No,' she said, her voice stifled. 'No. You mustn't. This is. . .' And, wildly, she could think of nothing to say but, 'This is assault.'

He stopped and let go of the ear, which had begun to send dreadful messages to the rest of her body. 'I think not. You will note that I am not holding you. You could be a little wild, like Sally-Anne, could duck under my arm, and run away, screaming for Mr Boyce to rescue you. Why are you not screaming for Mr Boyce, Mary? Does the other ear wish to be honoured first?'

The laugh in his voice was so manifest, so outrageous that she began to laugh too. 'And if I ask you to stop?'

'Why should I listen? Your tongue says one thing, your body another. On second thoughts, why should your ear by the only part favoured?' And he bent his head still further, and kissed her just above the rose at her breast, lifting his head long enough to say, 'What, no scream? Mr Boyce not wanted?'

But his light words belied his own feelings. It was taking him all his will-power not to remove his hands from the wall and use them to add to her pleasure, and his, but he knew that if he went too far he would lose her.

'I cannot duck under your arm now,' she complained, shivering at the touch of his mouth, just below the point where the cleft between her breasts began. 'And you are fulfilling all of Boyce's worst suspicions.'

'How fortunate for him that he adds fortune-telling to the list of his other boring virtues,' drawled Jared, pulling away a little, all the same. 'Now you should be telling me that we are bound to be missed if we remain here any longer.'

Seeing that this was just what Mary had been about to tell him, she was temporarily deprived of words, but recovered enough to say, 'Your reputation can only be enhanced, Mr Jared Tunstall, if you put my name on the list of your conquests; but what of my reputation? Yours added to; mine ruined.'

He stepped back and put up his hands, palms now towards her. 'Ah, there you have me. One law for gentlemen, another for ladies. Unfair, is it not?'

Mary had the suspicion that this was as far as he had intended to go with her. She stepped around him smartly, picked up her empty plate and glass, heard him laughing behind her as she made for the door.

'Gently,' he said. 'Gently.' And picking up his own used crockery, he followed her in. A pity to stop when all seemed so promising, but there would be another day. Yes, he was sure that there would be another day.

Mary hoped that their prolonged absence had not been noticed, but, as she might have expected, one pair of jealous eyes had noted her disappearance, and saw her immediately she and Jared re-entered the room.

Boyce Hamilton moved forward, and before he could prevent himself said in a choked voice, 'Where have you been, Mary? I have been looking for you everywhere.'

Mary was surprised; her whole attention had been focused on Jared, and Boyce had been right to see the tension between them—she had never been so conscious of another human being's presence before; and that was a lie, but she would not think of that other time, only register that this time something similar was happening to her. She replied with her usual calm, 'I have been enjoying my supper, Boyce. You knew that Jared and I were going in for supper.'

'I only knew that I could not find you. You were nowhere to be seen—not in the supper-room.'

He was unhappily aware that he was amusing Tunstall, who said smoothly, 'I was taking good care of Mary. You need have no fear that I would allow her to come to any harm—and there are few mountain cats prowling around the White House waiting to attack.'

Boyce hardly knew what to say. Tunstall handed his own and Mary's used plates and glasses to a passing waiter, turned to another, who was carrying a tray of drinks, took one himself, and offered a glass to Boyce, with a look of infinite mockery on his face. 'We have indulged, Mr Hamilton. Would you care to?'

'I never indulge,' said Boyce glacially. 'I do not approve of liquor. It is behind half the ills of the nation.'

'Pity,' said Jared idly. 'Like tea, it is a most useful social lubricant.'

'No,' said Boyce, almost fierce. 'On the contrary. It is a prop which is hardly necessary for the rational among us to resort to. I believe that you agree with me, Mary.'

Mary, who was experiencing a Boyce whom she had never met before, a Boyce who was visibly in the grip of a jealous rage, attempted unwisely to placate him.

She was fearful that this new man might provoke a scene, and was guiltily aware that she and Jared had been misbehaving—as Boyce obviously feared. Alas, she was also equally aware that part of her was not feeling guilty at all about the fact that there was something exciting about being the succulent prey over whom two stags were locking antlers.

'It is not like you, Boyce, to be so dogmatic,' she said. 'You have always proclaimed that everything in moderation was your motto.'

'A belief,' said Jared, 'which I would certainly have expected Mr Hamilton to hold. Most proper.'

This apparent compliment, delivered with Mr Jared Tunstall's usual forthright panache, was obviously not a compliment at all. 'To be moderate,' said Boyce, now almost visibly beside himself with frustration and anger, 'does not mean that one is required to compromise one's principles. I am not moderate where drink is concerned.'

Appalled, he realised that he had inadvertently suggested quite the opposite of what he meant. Overset, he added, to make matters worse, if worse were possible, for he was digging his grave with every furious, ill-judged word he uttered, 'No, no. I meant that I am immoderate in my opposition to it, not for it. It is a demon which ruins those who succumb to it, reduces them to the animal, destroys the seed corn of the nation. . .' He trailed off.

His voice had risen to a ranting shout. Mary was gazing at him as though she had never seen him before, and heads were turning, folk were smiling on hearing his speech, delivered in tones more suitable to a Temperance platform in a public hall than the privacy of a decorous White House reception. He fell silent, visibly struggling with himself.

'You were saying?' offered Jared, eyes wicked. Without even trying to, almost without uttering a word, by his mere presence, he had managed to provoke Boyce into making a thundering ass of himself in public, and before Mary, whom he always wanted to impress.

'Nothing,' said Boyce desperately. 'I fear that I am overtired. I have had a hard week. It is perhaps time that I left. You will allow me to see you home, Mary?'

'No need,' said Jared before Mary could answer. 'The night is young yet. I will see Mary home, if she will allow, that is. I promise to take good care of her.'

Mary thought that Boyce would burst. 'No,' he said, a red mist rising before his eyes. 'Not necessary. . . I will take her.'

Jared raised his eyebrows. 'It is for Mary to decide, surely.' His voice was almost impudently indifferent.

'She cannot wish to be escorted home by someone whom she has only just met,' began Boyce.

'No,' said Mary firmly. 'That is enough, Boyce. You

are kind to ask me, but I do not wish to leave yet. Jared's
offer allows you to have the early night you so obviously
need.'

She suddenly had no wish to be alone with the angry
man before her. She was seeing a side of him which she
had not known existed, and, dismayed, she did not like
it.

There was nothing for it. Boyce bowed sullenly.
Without creating a scene which would bring credit to no
one, there was no way in which he could wrench Mary
from the grip of the libertine on whose arm her own
hand was resting again. He was compelled to suffer
agonies of jealousy imagining what Jared Tunstall might
get up to escorting Mary McAllister home. There was
nothing for him to do but say on leaving, 'I shall see you
tomorrow, Mary, I hope,' but her attention was not on
him; it was on the pirate at her side who had blown him
out of the water with such consummate ease.

Mary watched him go. 'That was very naughty of you,
Jared.'

'I?' he said innocently. 'What did I do? It was Mr
Boyce who did all the talking. He has a nice line in
Temperance rant, even if it did not fit the occasion. You
must admit that I said little.'

'I think the fact that you exist at all troubles Boyce the
most,' said Mary wisely. She could feel the strength of
Jared's arm beneath the hand she had placed on it.

He looked lazily down at her, eyes hooded. 'Does it,
indeed? Well, I am hardly about to commit ritual suicide
in public in order to oblige him,' he said with a grin. He
was referring to Japanese honour and hara-kiri which
had recently been the subject of Washington gossip.

Mary began to laugh. 'At the very least that would be
a new sensation for a White House reception to
experience.'

Jared matched her amusement. 'But messy, Mary,
messy. You must admit that Mr Boyce would not like
that. I should have to find a more decorous way to carry
out his wishes.' Their laughter mingled.

Mary had not felt so wickedly irresponsible for years. She was liberated. The chains which had bound her since she had stepped down from the train on to the platform at Washington's Central station eight years ago were falling away, loosened by the Wall Street pirate at her side, whose role appeared to be to free her, not to imprison her.

'You really must stop,' she said at last. 'Most improper of you and even worse for me to be so amused by your wickedness.' But she did not sound at all repentant.

I shall be sorry tomorrow, she thought. I hope that he behaves himself on the way home. At the moment I cannot resist him—nor, dreadfully, do I wish to. What can be happening to me?

He did behave himself on the way home. Jared had already decided that to make haste slowly might be the most profitable strategy to follow with the Widow McAllister. He was a perfect gentleman, as innocuous as Boyce would have been, which should have pleased her, but didn't.

He made light conversation, turning the full power of his sexual charm on her while he did so. Just before they reached her gate, he stopped the carriage for a moment and said, 'I have a favour to ask you, Mary. One I hope you can see fit to grant me.'

'Oh, that depends on what the favour is,' she said, smiling up at him provocatively, astonished yet once more at his power to make her behave out of character.

'It is not an arduous one,' he said, 'and to reassure you, I must tell you that I have the full approval of brother Orrin for what I am about to ask.'

'If Senator Tunstall approves, then who am I to demur?' said Mary.

'We spoke of it only this morning over our coffee, bacon and beans——' He paused.

'A true Western breakfast,' interjected Mary lightly.

'Indeed. I told him that I wished to re-open the old Sheldon house on the edge of Washington, which my mother left me. I am tired of living in hotels and lodgings. It has not been refurbished for these many years. A woman's touch is needed. May that touch be yours, Mary? I would like to take you there, to ask for your advice on re-decoration. Orrin will come with us to see that we behave ourselves. Between you and me, I don't think he trusts either of us to be good. He has promised me that if I as much as lay a wrong finger on you he will blow my head off!'

'Oh, I think I can agree to that,' was her reply, ignoring his gloss on Orrin's beliefs.

'Good. Then I propose to combine business with pleasure. If you are free tomorrow afternoon, will you allow me to take you riding? On the way back, we may pick up Orrin, who has business on the Hill, and we may all visit the house, in perfect decorum.'

This was travelling at speed, but she could not refuse him. 'If Senator Tunstall will play willing gooseberry,' she said, 'then I will expect you tomorrow. At what hour?'

'At two of the clock,' he said, 'if that is suitable; and here we are, at your *pied-à-terre*. I have rarely known an evening pass so swiftly. It augurs well for the morrow, does it not?'

Only at her gate, when he raised her hand to his lips, and she met his ardent gaze squarely, the electricity between them crackled again, with such ferocity this time that she felt almost faint.

She pulled her hand away, stared at him, and he said, softly, not impudently, nothing brash or forward about him, for once, 'So, you felt it, too. Goodnight, Mary McAllister. We shall meet again tomorrow.'

'Goodnight,' she whispered. 'And, yes, it was a good night, Jared.' She did not say, Yes, I felt it, too. That was unnecessary.

'I was wrong,' he said. 'Not goodnight but *au revoir*, Widow McAllister,' he murmured. 'Never goodbye, I trust.' And he drove his untrustworthy self down the road, leaving her to Miss Nessie and her pleased exclamations that Mary had a man to bring her home at last, Miss Nessie not quite seeing Boyce in that light.

Daylight did not bring repentance. On the contrary, far from regretting her decision to further her acquaintance with Jared Tunstall, it reinforced Mary's belief that she did not know Boyce after all. Her decision to marry him should he ask her had been based on a completely different view of him—possibly a wrong one—from the Boyce who had revealed himself last night.

She made ready for the morning at the senator's—she was not due to arrive at his office until ten o'clock—with less that her usual confidence.

Standing before her bedroom mirror, she was adjusting the shining knot of her hair when the door opened, and Miss Nessie, an odd expression on her face, came in.

'You have a visitor, Miz Mary.'

She swung around. 'At this hour? Who on earth is it, Nessie?'

'Mr Boyce, Miz Mary. He said that he needs to see you most partickler.'

'Does he, indeed! You have put him in the front parlour?'

'Put himself there,' said Miss Nessie, her expression still odd.

And what did that mean? Mary walked down the narrow stairs and into the room where she had entertained Jared. Boyce was at the window, staring out. He turned to meet her, without any formal greeting, all his usual grave courtesy gone.

'Mary! I had to see you. I could not sleep.' She motioned him to a chair. He stood his ground. 'No, I don't want to sit. I have something to say to you.'

Strangely, she thought that it was an admonition coming. He had the air of someone about to admonish. He was most unlike himself.

'I must speak to you. Why have I delayed so long? I know my heart. I thought that I knew yours.' He caught at her hand, took it, kissed it. There was nothing there for her, nothing at all. He might have been a stranger, chance met, it had such a small effect.

'Yes, I will say it. You must know how I feel. I am going mad, Mary, mad because I have held back for so long, out of some mistaken consideration for you, modest as you are. Say you will marry me, Mary. You must, I beg of you.' And, improbably, staid Boyce, after blurting this out, wild, discomposed, not behaving at all as he usually did, dropped to his knees, still holding her hand.

Mary attempted to withdraw it, but could not. He clung to it, almost hurting her with the ferocity of his grip. He put it to his cheek. Still nothing. She might as well have been touching a lump of meat.

'Why do you not answer me, Mary? There, you have me, all of me. Why have I delayed? Say yes. You must say yes. I know that you wanted to say yes.'

That had been true, but was not any more. Yes was the last thing which she wanted to say to him. What she did want to say was, I did not know you. I thought that I did. The man I wanted to say yes to does not exist.

'No,' she said, still trying to pull her hand away. 'No, I am sorry, Boyce. But I cannot marry you.'

'You don't mean that.' His voice rose and broke. Still on his knees, his eyes filled with tears, he said, 'Oh, I know that you wanted me to propose. I was sure that you would say yes. Say yes, Mary. Oh, God, say yes.'

Mary thought suddenly that, were it not demeaning to her sex to consider it, Boyce was as hysterical as any silly woman. His lack of masculinity, so savagely pointed up by Jared's almost excessive possession of it, had never been more plain. For the first time she wondered if more lay behind his unwillingness to propose before than she might have thought.

And what could she say? Her thoughts were in turmoil. Yesterday, a week ago, I would have said yes. What has happened to me that I have changed? For it is not only that I did not know you. I did not know myself. I cannot say any of this to him. What can I say? Only no.

Her agony was written on her face. He remained on his knees, abject. Her hand was still trapped. He was raining kisses on it. Wet kisses. Ugh! No, she could not marry him.

Boyce looked up at her. He saw and felt her revulsion at his suit—and at him. For revulsion it suddenly was.

He flung her hand away. To her great relief he rose. 'It's him, isn't it?' he said, face ugly. 'Him. Tunstall. That's why you are refusing me. What did you and he do together when he took you home? Tell me, Mary, What did you do?' And, frighteningly, with one stride he was upon her, hands gripping her shoulders cruelly, his voice rising to a shriek. 'What did you do? Why will you not do it with me?'

'Stop it, Boyce. Immediately. Nothing. We did nothing. He was a perfect gentleman. He did not seize me and hurt me as you are doing. I am sorry to refuse you, Boyce. It has nothing to do with Jared Tunstall. I do not love you, so I cannot accept you. That is all there is to it.'

'No. It's him. I know it is. You were mine, and now you are his.'

'I was never yours, and I am certainly not his. You mistake. I like you, Boyce, as a brother. I do not love you. It would be wrong to marry you.'

'As a brother?' He shook her. 'Not good enough. And let me tell you this. If it is Tunstall you are after, you are very mistaken. I know him, I tell you. All decent society knows him for what he is. He is a lecher, a womaniser. He wants you as a trophy, Mary, as a trophy! Another woman to add to his list of conquests, like a Western cowboy adding another notch to his gun!'

'Oh, you wrong me,' said Mary, panting between anger and fright. 'Let me go, I beg of you. It is nothing to do with him. If you think that I have encouraged you, I apologise. But it would be wrong to marry you, tempted though I am, and honoured by your offer. I do not love you, Boyce.'

He released her so suddenly that she almost fell. 'So

quick,' he groaned. 'You were so quick to refuse me. No
consideration, no time for thought, but a no on the
instant. And I do not believe you over Tunstall. It is his
arrival which has changed everything.'

And that, after all, was true. Until Jared came into her
life she had been prepared to accept Boyce, but now she
knew that such an acceptance would be of the second
best, and she could no longer go through with it.

'I have thought. . .' she began. He pounced on her
words.

'So you were lying when you said that you only
thought of me as a brother. You must have known that I
intended to propose.'

'Indeed, indeed,' she said, frightened that he would
grasp her again, moving away from him. 'But that did
not mean that I would have accepted you, that I would
have said yes, that I have changed my mind.' A lie! She
was trying to soften the blow of her rejection a little, so
that she might not hurt him. A vain hope. He was
wounded beyond measure.

'At least think again, Mary, think again. Do not refuse
me out of hand, I beg of you. From long friendship—
think again. For what you mean to my father, as well as
to me, think again! Above all, think that there is no
other woman I could wish to make my wife.'

If she agreed, then he would go. But she would not
offer him hope. She said gently, 'To please you, I will
think again. Give you an answer in. . .in a month. But
do not suppose that it will change anything.'

He caught at her hand, grasped it again, but gently
this time. 'There is always hope. I am sure that you
would have accepted me without *his* arrival. So, you may
change again. A month, Mary, That is a long time. . .
Less than a month, I beg of you. You owe me that.'

Did she owe him anything? She doubted it, but, all in
all, if she agreed, he would go. He frightened her. Mild
Boyce, whom baffled desire had changed into something
not mild at all. She would compromise, say it might be

less, but at the month's end she would write him a dignified letter, and that would be it.

Or would it? She retrieved her hand. 'I shall try to decide within a month, but I cannot promise that it will be less. And now you must go, or neither you nor I will be fit for the day.'

Once he had left, still cursing the debauched rogue Tunstall, she sank into a chair, shuddering with delayed shock. He had spoken the truth, made her face the truth. Until Jared came into her life she had been prepared to marry him, and whether Jared wanted her, or she him, was immaterial. She could not marry Boyce. She was no longer the Mary McAllister who would have done so, and what she would do now she did not know, for she hardly knew herself.

CHAPTER FOUR

MARY waited for Jared to arrive. She was wearing a riding habit of dark blue serge, a cream silk shirtwaister, or blouse, beneath it, its bow showing, since she had left the top buttons of her habit undone. She had put her little top hat on the console table in her small hall, her whip beside it.

She found herself trembling a little. She reproached herself, Where has all my control gone? I have ridden with men before—but not with Jared. She knew that Miss Nessie's eyes had been hard on her all day. No, that was wrong. She had been watched ever since Jared first came to the house, and particularly after Boyce's early morning visit.

She had said nothing of what had passed, but Miss Nessie had guessed the substance of it all the same. Improbably, Mary thought, it was the sexual adventurer Jared was known to be whom Miss Nessie obviously favoured, not the conventional and respectable Boyce.

No matter. It was she, Mary, who had to make choices, and what had once seemed easy now seemed hard. Best to take each day as it came. Enjoy her afternoon ride with Jared, and be pleasant to Boyce when she met him, if he would let her be.

So pre-occupied was she that it took a series of banging and clanking sounds from outside, coupled with excited shouts, to startle her into awareness of the present.

A moment later the door to the parlour was thrown open and Miss Nessie, eyes wild, appeared. 'It's Mr Jared riding a. . .thing. Thought you said that you wuz goin' hossback ridin' with him.' In her excitement Miss Nessie had returned to the country speech of her youth.

Mary ran to the window and looked out. Jared was riding, not a thing, but something which she knew

66

immediately was one of the horseless carriages of which
he had spoken. It was large, shining and brassy, with
huge spoked wheels, and brass lamps, and a bench seat,
high up with a wheel on a pole in front of him. He
dismounted by two steps, to leave the monster, now
silent, standing at the kerb before her door, a cluster of
street arabs and urchins around it.

She remembered the slightly wicked look on his face
when he had said that he would call on her to take her
riding with him, and now she knew why it was there.
Excited and amused, she shot to the front door, pushing
by the equally excited Livvie and Miss Nessie, and
opened it before he could knock.

'Jared Tunstall! Where on earth did that come from?'

'New York. And across the Atlantic before that,' he
said, grinning at her, teeth white in his dark face, his
own amusement and pleasure heightened by hers.

'Said I would take you for a ride—and here I am.' He
swept off his hat as he was speaking—he was wearing a
grey Stetson, as huge as one of Orrin's, and Western-
style clothes. 'Game enough to come with me, are you,
Widow McAllister?'

'But I'm not dressed for it,' she wailed, indicating her
riding habit.

'Sure you are. Most suitable,' he said, and he ran his
eyes over her with charming impudence. 'Only, ladies
need to wear a veil when they travel on one of these
things, I'm told, and a special hat. So. . .' And he
whipped his left hand from behind his back to show her
an elegant broad-brimmed hat with a large veil.

'Hope it fits, Mary. Milliner said that it was guaran-
teed to fit anyone. Told her that you weren't anyone,' he
added, and his face and his whole body were as wicked
as a man's could be.

Mary took the hat and said, 'But where's your coach-
man? I thought that you needed a special man to drive
one of these.'

'Sure you do,' he said, laughing again. 'I'm the special
man. A chauffeur, Mary—that's what you call the

driver, and I've been trained to drive one. I don't need a
flunkey to run me about. I'm a good red-blooded
American male. Hat on, Mary, and we'll drive to the
Potomac, away from the staring mob.'

He watched her put on the hat, and when she had
finished took the veil from her, and tied it around the
hat and her. 'Pity to hide such a fair sight,' he said softly,
'but you don't want to be collecting dirt and smuts in
those beautiful eyes.'

'You'll take good care of her in that. . .thing,' qua-
vered Miss Nessie. Livvie had been keening gently at it,
hands to cheeks. 'Don't seem natural,' finished Miss
Nessie.

'Sure it's natural,' said Jared. 'Streets will be full of
'em one day—not far off. Make me as rich as Rockefel-
ler, I hope. . . Come, Miss Mary, allow me to help you
in. ' And he handed her up the steps and on to the long
bench for her to sit by the driver, as though horseless
carriages were the most natural things in the world.

Then he cranked the starting handle so that the
monster began to hiss and bang again, Mary giving faint
amused cries and hanging on to her seat. The watching
urchins cheered her, bringing a pleasant pink to her
cheeks. Jared was suddenly beside her, his hands on the
little wheel, and with a great lurch they were off, going
down the road 'like a tea-kettle on wheels', Mary said.

A team of interested spectators ran beside them at
first, shouting both encouragement and derision, to be
left behind at last when the carriage wheezed along the
dirt-road in the direction of the Potomac, as he had
promised.

'Roads aren't made for them,' he said. 'But one day
they will be. Black day for the railroads, too. Horseless
carriage can go anywhere—don't need rails. Oh, their
possibilities are endless.' And then he concentrated on
driving, two large strong and shapely hands on the
wheel.

The blasé, slightly cynical man of the world was gone.
He was as eager as a small boy, and his manner touched

a chord in Mary, brought back again the memories
which she had repressed for nearly eight years, memories
not at all suited to the staid and virtuous Widow
McAllister of whom all Washington knew so well.

They were now travelling steadily along the route
which they would have taken on horseback, finally
arriving at the track which ran by the Potomac—they
were out in the open country, Washington behind them.
But oh, how different their speed was from that of a
horse. Jared slowed down whenever they passed a rider
on one, or a group of them.

'Frightens horses,' he said. 'Have to be careful, Mary.
And we don't want to be thrown either, not at this
speed. And our speed is constant, so long as that thing
works.' And he took his hands off the wheel to point at
the hood which covered the carriage's engine. 'And, of
course, so long as there's gas in the tank. Make Standard
Oil even richer, this will. Horseless carriages don't get
tired, but they do break down. . .'

They were now far beyond the part of the track which
marked the limit normally attained by riders from
Washington bent on a pleasant afternoon, and he turned
his head to smile at her. 'Do we want to break down,
Mary? Would you like to be stranded here with me?
Would you scream for Mr Boyce if we were?'

Mary was breathless with an excitement which was
not all to do with the carriage, although it was as if the
carriage had liberated her. Or was it the man who was
driving it who had this strange effect on her? As though
she wanted to throw her bonnet over every windmill—
not that she wore a bonnet, nor were there any windmills
near the Potomac, but that was her general feeling!

'Not break down, I hope,' she said, and then, danger-
ously perhaps, 'Stop, maybe.'

'Sure,' said Jared with a grin. 'In any case, the trail,
such as it is, is petering out, and will soon not be good
enough for us to drive along.' They had reached a point
where the dirt-road was running among clumps and

stands of trees and bushes, and the Potomac, shining in
the sun, was on their left.

Jared did difficult things with the various brass rods
which reared up before him, and slowed down where the
track almost disappeared into a large flat clearing. He
explained that he could safely turn the monster around,
ready for their return home.

He carried out even more complicated manoeuvres
with the rods, spinning the wheel rapidly, and the whole
contraption, which really seemed the most appropriate
name for it, Mary thought, shuddered and clanked to a
stop, exuding the strangest smell, certainly not at all like
that of a horse.

'Come, my lady,' said Jared, gravely handing her
down, as though she were a duchess, and he her slave,
bowing when her foot touched the ground. 'You may
leave your carriage, safe in the knowledge that now that
the brake is on it will not dash away, to leave us stranded
here. You see what an obliging monster it is.'

'Tell me,' said Mary, 'is it the first such carriage to
reach the States? Are we the earliest intrepid pioneers?'

'Not quite, I think,' said Jared. 'But one of the first. I
persuaded Gottlieb Daimler to send me one over, promising that I would ensure their future sale here. Most
such motor cars, for so some call them, or automobiles,
are bought by the very rich to play with.'

'And you are not very rich?' hazarded Mary.

'Oh, I am disgracefully rich,' said Jared, 'and would
like to be richer. There are infinite possibilities in these
machines—and to be the first in the field would be a
great thing. And we Americans must build them, too.
We must not be left behind by the Europeans.'

'No, indeed,' said Mary, undoing her veil, and removing her hat. 'And in the meantime we are playing with
this creature. Whatever will happen to the poor horses it
supplants?'

'There will be fewer of them, and it is they who will
be the toys of the rich, when this becomes a workhorse
and not a plaything. The horseless machines will do all

the work that horses do, and more quickly. And we shall fly, or our children will. No, this thing will change the world.' And he patted the carriage's metal flank affectionately.

While they had been talking he had lifted out of the carriage a rug and a small picnic basket. He handed her the rug, and said with a smile, 'A short walk now, perhaps.'

Mary took the rug from him, wondering if he had come here before, not with the horseless carriage, and with whom. He took her free hand, and they walked up a slight slope, finally to arrive in yet another clearing, much smaller than the one which they had left.

It was sheltered from the sight of the road by the trees through which they had walked. There was a superb view of the Potomac below them, with some massive falls just before the river made a sharp bend. Heavily wooded country lay around them, with Washington blue in the distance.

'Now, even if the Potomac should suddenly flood, we are safe,' said Jared, spreading out the rug for Mary to sit on, and beginning to open the basket. 'No tea to drink, but something better, perhaps?'

The something better was a bottle of champagne and two flutes, carefully packed in snow-white damask napkins. Also wrapped in napkins were sandwiches—'Rare beef, with horseradish sauce, and smoked salmon,' he said. There were two china plates, with views of Washington painted on them, two separate napkins and a small spray of hot-house roses for Mary to pin to the shoulder of her riding habit.

Finally, Jared, having opened the champagne with a great deal of frothing liquor and laughing man, handed her a flute, sat down beside her and, companionably, they ate and drank.

Each of them was supremely conscious of the other— the open air, the beautiful scene, the wine and the food, little though there was of it, working on them both more powerfully than any artificial aphrodisiac could.

The final thing to crown their pleasure was the knowledge of the carriage below them, waiting to restore them to the mundane world of affairs.

'And now, Widow McAllister,' said Jared, leaning on one elbow after they had finished their meal, 'tell me about yourself, the lady who excites Washington by the purity of her life, and is a leading senator's aide. To have managed the latter without scandal is surely an achievement in itself.'

Mary was suddenly greatly conscious of him. The very relaxation of their mood was almost frightening. 'Oh, there's little to tell,' she said. 'My life has been so uneventful, compared with what yours must have been, that it is you who should entertain me, not the other way around.'

He was watching her while she spoke, and his eyes were hooded, almost wary. He had a decision to make, which she did not know of, and this meeting might—or might not—affect that decision. He must know, he must. Was this woman his lost Charlie? She was so like, he now saw. Deceived by the maturity of her body, the classic face, the calm manner, so unlike his thin and lively Charlie, he had at first thought the likeness a fancy. But the more he saw of her, the stronger it grew. And, most important of all, when he had kissed her at the reception he had been more certain than ever that she was his lost Charlie, so sweet and similar was their shared and gentle passion—she drew him as no other woman had done since Charlie.

Because of that he could not simply say to her, 'Are you my Charlie, once my mistress, my lost love?' for if she were not, what would she think of him for suggesting such a thing? He might even lose her as Mary, so strong was she, and that he dared not risk.

He was aware that the silence had drawn on, and only the languor induced by food and drink excused it.

'Oh, no,' he said, 'you know my life only too well. It is written in the public prints. Now take yourself. . .your late husband, Mary? What of him?'

'My husband?' said Mary, so shocked by this question that for a moment she knew that she had said the word husband as though she were speaking of something strange and odd. She recovered herself. 'Oh, you mean poor James.'

'Yes, poor James,' said Jared. 'Was he a Washington man, Mary? One of the political coterie that haunts this capital?'

Mary prepared to lie gallantly, as she had sometimes done before. She tried to remember all that she had said.

'Oh, no. He was from the West Coast, California. We met in Montana; he was. . .a mining engineer then. He contracted tuberculosis, and died before Sally-Anne was born. I came to Washington after his death because an old aunt left me the house and a small estate.'

'Most convenient,' he said drily. 'And a sad history. You must have been heartbroken when he died.'

'Oh, yes,' lied Mary valiantly. 'It was true love, you see.' And all she had to do to look sad, to conjure up tears almost, was to think of Link, their love, and his brutal betrayal. For a moment she almost disliked Jared because he reminded her so much of that boy and the love she had lost.

And, like Jared, she thought, can it be merely coincidence, this likeness? Or is it that suddenly, after so many years, I hanker after Link again because I can find no man to love, no man to replace him, so that when someone as unlikely as Jared Tunstall comes along I find such echoes of Link in him?

She looked across at him, massive and masterful, at the strong, clean-shaven face, the perfect clothing. Yes, he had laughter-lines as Link had, but he had been so young, so slim, bearded, with his hair in a pony-tail, and his clothing grimy, with the grime of hard living in the desert, far from baths and luxuries, the scented soap, the lemon oil which she could tell that Jared used. She tried to remember him across the years, but could not—except, when they had embraced last night, it had been so like, so like.

'Why so thoughtful? Jared said.

She shook her head at him. 'It is not often that I am so irresponsible, to sit here in the sun, in the afternoon, lazing.'

'Irresponsible!' he said lazily. 'You should be so more often. Allow me to be your teacher. We may idle the time away together. Leave responsibility to poor Mr Boyce. He has grown old before his time nursing it.'

'Oh,' said Mary, suddenly angry with him. 'You are too bad. You speak to me as though I am one of your. . .toys, to be humoured and played with.' She rose. 'Yes, I will come to look at your house. But you may not speak to me as though I were a backward child.'

He lay at her feet and laughed up at her. 'My. . .toys? You mean my women, don't you, Mary? Well, I have never spoken to them as I speak to you.'

'And I do not believe that,' she said, moving towards the carriage. 'You are like the rest. Women are something outside of your real life to be played with, not to be taken seriously.'

He rose, in one cat-like movement, belying his size and strength, reminding her again of *him*. He had been an athlete, and so was this man, despite the difference in their bodies, the one so slim and light, the other so purely massive—with not an ounce of fat on him; like his brother Orrin, he was all muscle. He moved to her, put both hands on her shoulders, but made no further move to hold her or to embrace her.

'I take you very seriously, Mary McAllister. Very seriously indeed. And I am so relieved to find you a widow. God knows what I should have done had your husband still been with us. Packed Orrin's Colt, I suppose, and made away with him.'

Mary wrenched away. 'Oh, now I cannot take *you* seriously for all your fine words. Let us go pick up Senator Tunstall, and perhaps his earthy common sense can prevail on you to behave properly.'

He made no attempt to hold her again in any way, but simply held out his crooked arm, saying, 'But I enjoy myself so much more being improper, you see. You would not have me a dull boy, would you?' and his grin was as charming and impudent as a man's could be, almost disarming her.

Except that he was exercising his charm in order to use her, she was sure of it, as that other had done, and she would not have that, so she flung at him over her shoulder, refusing the proffered arm, 'You sound exactly like Sally-Anne, and since she is only seven years old even you must admit that that is quite an achievement!'

'Rebuked again,' he said, nothing put out by such criticism, and made it his business to see her comfortably settled before they drove off to pick up Orrin.

But he had made his decision, the one which had been occupying him, and, come hell or high water, he was going to find out the Widow McAllister's true history, for even if she were not Charlie he was suddenly sure that poor James McAllister had never existed.

But Mary McAllister existed, sat warm beside him, and, despite her annoyance with his light-minded approach to her, made cool conversation as though nothing had happened, which impressed him the more, but also warned him that, even if she were his Charlie, she had changed beyond belief, so different was she from the effervescent girl of his lost boyhood.

Orrin was waiting for them outside his lodgings, and Mary welcomed him. She found that Orrin's presence was invaluable. The big man—he was even broader than Jared—so solid that he steadied them all. There was an earthy wisdom about him, and if he knew that beyond a doubt something serious was occurring between her and his brother he did not show it.

The Sheldon house had once stood on the very edge of Washington. It had been overtaken years ago by the capital's growth, and now had been swallowed up by it. It was large, built of a reddish-brown brick and was elegant in the fashion of fifty years ago.

It stood in its own partly neglected grounds: no one

had lived there since Jared's mother had died, over ten years ago, Orrin said in an aside to her as they arrived. There were mews catty-corner to the house, and a gravel sweep up to them, and Jared drove them there with a flourish.

They alighted from the horseless carriage. Orrin offered her his arm, and she walked between the two men to where a glassed-in porch gave an entrance to the side of the house.

'It is like walking between Gog and Magog,' she said, in an effort to be light.

'Gog and. . . Who they?' enquired Orrin.

'Two giants, Mr Orrin, who guarded people. Fabulous men.'

'Oh, then yuh are right, Mary,' said Orrin, laughing. 'I would say that I was fabulous, wun't yuh? Not sure about Jared, though.'

'Half-fabulous,' said Jared, grinning at them both. 'After all, we're only half-brothers, so I can claim merely a part-share in your godhood.'

They were laughing together when the caretaker came from the cottage at the back of the house to let them in, to throw open doors, draw curtains, raise the blinds. He and his wife had kept the place in reasonable order, and the three of them looked about it, while he trailed around after them, occasionally making notes of what Jared said that he wanted done.

'It's a museum,' Jared said. The house was still furnished in the mode of the 1840s, the carpets, the paper on the walls, the furniture and bibelots all a mute testimony to a vanished age, faded a little, although the furniture and the china had a solidity about them quite different from the imitation of French Second Empire elegance which was the fashion of the day. Mary particularly admired a walnut dining suite, with an oval table-top and elegantly turned cabriole legs.

'Pity to change it much,' grunted Orrin. 'Never seen this place afore. Takes me back, though. My own grampa had a house like it when I was a little lad.'

'Back before the flood, then,' said Jared mischievously. 'Well, Mary? What's your verdict?'

'I agree with Orrin,' she said slowly. 'And you might like to keep one room intact, just as it is now. But do you want to live in a museum, Jared? Even if you do, you'll need to install modern plumbing and electric light.' She was fingering the elderly fabric on an armless sewing chair. 'And this won't last long if you begin to use it. A few all-male soirées and most of the furniture would rapidly need re-upholstering. Best perhaps to have it done first.'

Her brisk realism amused the two men. 'No fooling you, Mary,' said Jared. 'You know us too well. Let's see the rest of the place before we make any final decisions— find out the full extent of the problem.'

Well, as expected, the bathroom was rudimentary, a stark room with a tin tub hung on the wall, a wooden horse with some threadbare towels, and a plain deal stool. No heating in it, and no plumbing, the copper jug which stood in a china bowl on a washstand apparently being the means by which water was brought up.

'An' all the usual offices outside, one supposes,' said Orrin, staring at a chamber pot, with elegant floral decorations on the side, tucked under the washstand. 'Needed to be tough in them days to survive. Pa used to say that everything liquid in bedrooms used to freeze up in Northern winters when he were a boy. Liked the West because of its warmth, din't he?'

Mary had to agree. The house in its present state would be hard to heat, and hard to keep clean. Few of the bedrooms even had fireplaces in them, and the beds were still piled high with blankets and sheets ready for use. Later, after they had gone downstairs, Jared went off with the caretaker for a private consultation and Mary and Orrin were left together in the large and draughty drawing-room—'Too grand to be called a parlour,' Orrin said.

Idly, Mary began to inspect the photographs and family portraits which were scattered about it. Jared's

mother, Orrin said, had lived and died here, apart from
her husband, who had been over thirty years older than
herself. Surprisingly, perhaps, there was a small oil
painting of him as a young man in his late twenties, over
a sideboard covered in silver.

'Pa,' said Orrin, who had been watching her inspect
it. 'Like him, ain't he?' Mary correctly interpreted this
cryptic reference. Senator Jared Tunstall, senior, at
almost thirty, could have been taken for his youngest
son.

'Jared's more like him than any of the rest of us were,'
Orrin said. 'Four sons by my ma, his first wife, and none
on us really took after Pa—in looks anyways—and then
Jared! An' him with an Eastern ma, too.'

'Four!' said Mary. She had thought, if she had thought
at all, that Orrin and Jared had been the late senator's
only sons.

'Din't you know?' said Orrin. 'Afore your time, of
course. Old story now. People forgit. Jared don't. He'll
never forgit.' Unspoken was that he didn't 'forgit',
either. He paused. 'Ought to tell you, I s'pose. Explains
him a little. Changed him—that, and what happened
afterwards.'

Mary said gently, 'No, I wasn't aware that you had
three other brothers, nor what happened to them.'

'Nasty business.' Orrin's expression was suddenly
stern. 'Jared came to stay with us after his ma died—Pa
bein' his rightful guardian. He'd started at Harvard
early—only sixteen, he was. Bright boy, clever. Still is.
His ma hated the West, never returned after she left Pa,
regretted marryin' him, took Jared away East when he
wuz a little 'un. Pa was good about it, let her keep him,
'specially when it turned out he wuz so clever. Jared
loved the West, loved Pa when he met him—they wuz
very alike; loved the boys, too. I wuz the oldest.'

He fell silent, staring at the portrait, deep regret on
his face. 'I mind that year well. He came to us that
summer for his holidays as usual. He was eighteen, had
jus' finished at Harvard, honours student, athlete, wuz

goin' to be a scholar. That year our ranch, and others, had been havin' trouble with a pack of no 'count rustlers calling themselves cattlemen. Name of Hughes—a big family, lots of sons, like us, but lawless. Robbed the range blind, till Pa went after 'em. Din't get em all, jus' the father, Sam Hughes, and the eldest boy Clay. Had 'em arrested, tried and sentenced.' He fell silent again, sighed, went on.

'Seems as how the judge got it all wrong. Wuz a Democrat, against big ranchers, thought Pa was one causin' trouble, not the Hugheses—gave 'em light sentences. Local folk was furious about the law. Some of the little fellers had a'most been put out of business by the Hugheses; one man had lost a son in a dawn raid. He couldn't prove that it was the Hugheses killed him, but we all knew as how it was.

'A mob stormed the gaol, and lynched 'em both. Pa was away at the time, or he might have stopped it. Wrong thing to do, I know, but folks see things different out West. Rustlin' a breach of trust on the open range. Any road, the Hugheses that was left blamed Pa. Said that but for him their daddy and brother wouldn't have been in the gaol at all. Threatened revenge. Pa's judgement was wrong for once. He laughed it off. Said they wuz nothin' but straw men.

'One day, I took Jared and the other hands out to round up strays. He was a good cattleman by then. The best. Took to it naturally. Great on a hoss. I mind me the day now. Clara, my wife, had tole me the day before that she wuz expectin', and we wuz talking of how to celebrate—we had been waitin' for a young 'un for years.'

His face twisted. He paused for so long that Mary put out her hand to touch his arm. He looked at her, his eyes full of tears.

'We got back to find part of the ranch house on fire. When we finally had the flames under control, we went in. Found 'em all. . . Pa and the three boys. . .all dead. Butchered, Miz Mary. . .and Clara. . .we found her

later. . .in the grounds, dead too, a shotgun by her
side. . .she'd come on them at their wicked work. . .
That's it, Miz Mary. Law couldn't touch 'em.

'Hugheses all claimed as how they wuz innocent. Mus'
have been a band of wanderin' outlaws what done it,
they said. But Barrett Hughes, their youngest, got drunk
one night, boasted of how he'd killed Pa himself. In
detail. And then. . .they disappeared. I think Jared and
I went a little mad for a time. Jared. . .' He paused
again.

Mary, appalled by the story, said gently, 'Don't,
Orrin, don't distress yourself. Oh, I am so sorry. Oh,
your poor wife. How awful for you. What a thing. No, I
had never heard of this before.'

She did remember that once someone had expressed
surprise that Orrin Tunstall, such a good-looking and
vital man, had remained unmarried, and someone else
answering them, saying, 'Not surprising, perhaps. . .after what happened,' but she never heard what
exactly had happened.

Whether he would have told her more Mary did not
know, for they heard Jared's step outside, and Orrin said
urgently, 'No more, now. He won't talk of it, and it
changed him a lot. He'd only jus' found Pa and the boys,
yuh see, and then to lose them so cruelly. . .' He stopped
as Jared entered.

Something in the air alerted him. 'You're solemn,' he
said, smiling at them. 'Museum affected you?'

Mary raised an answering smile with difficulty. Orrin's
terrible story had explained Jared a little more, and
Orrin's insistence that Jared had been crucially affected
by it did not surprise her. Who would not be affected?
She shuddered inwardly.

'It is a little dismal. Everything being so faded does
not help. Yes, I agree with you, Jared; the place needs
brightening, to be brought up to date.'

'That's it, then,' said Jared, looking around briskly.
'Yes, I think that the old house deserves living in. I'll
see the workmen and the upholsterers tomorrow.' He

turned towards Mary and said lightly, 'And now, Miz McAllister, I trust that you will favour me with your woman's eye and taste when we reach the matter of fabrics and knick-knacks. I am afraid that if all that is left to me this place will be more like a barracks than a home.'

His eyes were caressing her again, and surely he must know what he was doing to her? It must be deliberate. And in front of Orrin, too. But she was unaware that her own face was as revealing as Jared's to his watching brother.

'Tired of playin' gooseberry,' said Orrin suddenly. 'Take Mary home in the buggy, little brother, then drive it back for me. Plenty to occupy me here. Yore grampa kept a good library, some fine stuff in it. Y'all both be good, now.'

They were, and Jared particularly. Whether it was the house, or Orrin working on him, he regretted the manner of his last words to her beside the Potomac.

'My thanks to you for coming,' he said, eyes on the road, steering them capably back to her home. 'And you will allow me to take you out again—I have not blotted my copybook too heavily, I hope?'

Of course she would agree to meet him again—how could she not?—and, of course, he would not be serious; for when she answered, 'Yes,' he looked sideways at her, and said, smiling,

'There, I knew that forgiveness would come readily to you, Mary McAllister; you are, after all, not like those of your sex who run around nursing grievances—"A Lady," for instance, in The *Gazette*—now there I am sure is a prune-mouthed creature for all her wit, which I must admit is considerable.'

Mary stiffened. Oh, so he was conventional after all— at least where women were concerned, despite his claims to a kind of Bohemianism. One part of her wanted to bridle at his dismissal of 'A Lady,' the other, the unregenerate part of her, wanted to giggle wickedly at her secret knowledge that she, whom he was pursuing so assiduously, was the prune-mouthed creature about whom he was so dismissive.

What would he say if he knew the truth? She kept her voice steady, her eyes on the road, and said smoothly, 'Oh, but even you must admit that she puts her finger on a number of issues about which we should be concerned, but which most men would prefer not to see aired—low pay for working women for one.'

'True,' he said carelessly. 'And, while I admire clever women, I am not sure how much I admire seeing them display their cleverness in the popular Press. The *Gazette* is a scandal sheet after all.'

'But "A Lady" does not peddle scandal,' she offered, enjoying this opportunity to be two-faced.

'No, I grant you that—if she did I might think that Sarah Lee was responsible for the column, and not, as some aver, no lady at all, but some male hack pretending to be a female to gain sales.'

'Of course,' murmured Mary, still wicked, 'I had not thought of that, I must confess.' Not so liberated, eh, Mr Jared Tunstall?

And, what was more, there could be no question now that she might ask him whether or no he was her lost lover. Respectable women, 'Ice Princesses', had no business having lovers, straying and ending up. . . Forget that. No, that was reserved for men, who might say what they like, behave as they pleased, the obloquy for licence being reserved for the women who were their partners. Now *there* would be a column for The *Gazette*, and she would write it, would she not?

By now, they were home again, and he handed her down, watched from the window by Miss Nessie, and a highly interested Sally-Anne, whom Miss Nessie had to restrain from running out to inspect Mama's new gentleman and the horseless carriage.

'Lord, no, child, not yet. You'll meet him soon enough, I reckon.' For it was plain to Miss Nessie's eyes that Jared Tunstall was much occupied by Miz Mary, but how seriously only time would show.

Jared was very serious indeed. As proof he made his way to Willard's Hotel that evening, and was shown to a quiet bedroom at the back.

There he briefed his agent, a Pinkerton man whom he could trust absolutely, on his new mission, which was to discover exactly who Mary McAllister was, where she had come from, and everything about James McAllister, Sally-Anne's supposed father, which he could possibly find.

'Spare no expense,' he told him. 'Act with the utmost dispatch as is consistent with accuracy, and, above all, be as discreet as the grave. The moment you have discovered the truth about her, whatever that truth is, contact me at once.'

If his agent wondered why the man of power opposite him, who could have any woman he pleased, should want this woman so badly that he needed to know her entire history, he said nothing of his surprise, merely nodded curtly and said, 'Understood. It should not be a difficult task. Sounds from what you say as though the lady covered her tracks carefully, but you'd be surprised how difficult it is to suppress everything.'

'Yes,' agreed Jared, who had covered a few tracks of his own in his time, and hoped that they remained hidden, but feared that the past might catch up with him yet.

Would it catch up with Mary McAllister? And, if so, what was he likely to discover when the agent finally handed in his report?

Almost he decided to retreat, to cancel his orders. And then he shook his head. No, he must find out the truth about her, and if to track her down was the action of a cur, then so be it. For never since that far distant day had he ever felt for any woman what he was now beginning to feel for Mary McAllister.

He was not the only man in a ferment about the Widow McAllister. Boyce Hamilton was pacing his room. His father had spoken to him that morning.

'A word with you on a personal matter, son.'

He had followed the senator into his office. It was one of the days on which Mary did not attend.

'I don't like to raise this with you, but I must. I had hoped that before now you would have had the common sense to propose to Mary McAllister. You need a wife. She would make an excellent one. I would lose the best aide I have ever had—but no matter. I cannot understand why you are so dilatory. You will lose her if you don't move soon. Other men can see her excellence, too.'

'None of your business, sir,' said Boyce stiffly, and then, seeing the pain on his father's face, 'I have proposed, but. . . I am to wait for an answer.'

'So, you have waited too long to ask,' said the senator sorrowfully. 'I have said nothing to her, you understand. That would be wrong. You should have asked her long ago. I cannot understand why you delayed.'

But he knew, he knew. He had feared that his son was nothing but a. . .half-man, would never be able to have a proper relationship with a woman, and he had hoped that Mary McAllister might be his salvation. The delay was Boyce's ambivalence towards women, and it was a tribute to Mary that she could interest him at all. But not enough, perhaps.

'I should have asked her before *he* came on the scene,' said Boyce savagely. 'I know. Hindsight is a great thing, Father.'

The senator did not need telling who 'he' was. He had seen for himself—saw more, perhaps, than his son thought.

'Then you must be aware that Tunstall has many attractions. How serious he might be, given his reputation, is another matter. But she is a pearl of great price— clever, beautiful, and a good woman; all three attributes seldom come together. She is a free agent, and I know her judgement to be good. It is yours that I know to be faulty. Never more so than now.'

Boyce glared at him. 'No need to tell me what I already know. I only know that now I want her to be my wife, unreservedly. I shall go to see her the moment when the month I gave her is up.'

'I would wish to see you settled. Married with a family.'

'Settled! Married!' said his son, his face ugly. 'I sometimes think that you would wish to see me married to a pie-faced hag, so long as you could say that I was married. It is Mary—or no one. You had better hold on to that—for that is all that there will be.'

The senator stared after him, his face sad. It had been his dream for Boyce to marry Mary, for her to redeem him, to prevent him from living the life he might live if he renounced normality and women forever. He had tried not to manipulate them, but thought now that his son had missed his one chance, and, whether or not Mary McAllister married Jared Tunstall, he feared that Boyce had lost her.

CHAPTER FIVE

'MAMA,' said Sally-Anne, 'do you often go there?' She was standing on the Mall before the Capitol, one small hand in Mary's, the other pointing to the dome before them. Quiet for once, she looked enchanting in a cream silk dress reaching to just below her knees, a sash of deep blue satin, matching her mother's walking dress, tall white socks, polished bronze pumps and a tiny, lacy hat, its blue ribbons tied under her chin.

In looks she was completely unlike Mary. Blue-black hair, in ringlets, framed a heart-shaped face, her eyes were dark, and she possessed a lively piquancy quite different from her mother's calm aloofness. A changeling, Mary often thought, except that in many ways she resembled her unknown father, especially in possessing his bubbling energy.

'Yes,' she answered. 'Or, rather, I do go there, but not often. It depends on what is happening, how much the senator needs back-up.'

It was a Sunday afternoon. The Mall was filled with people, for once not moving purposefully, but walking idly, wearing their best and most elaborate clothes. To their left, carriages moved in an endless procession in front of the museums which formed part of the capital's heart.

The weather had turned sultry, and Mary's dress was almost too heavy; a light perspiration stood on her brow, loosened the hair above her forehead so that it sprang in curling tendrils beneath her fashionable hat with its giant pale blue bow.

'Shall we sit for a little?' she suggested. 'You could roll your hoop. But try not to annoy people.'

Sally-Anne was carrying a hoop and a cane, and had been promised a run if she consented to wear her best

Sunday go-to-meeting clothes, which she hated, and walk decorously with Mama before and after her treat.

'Swell,' said Sally-Anne inelegantly, and then ran off, leaving Mary sitting there, her parasol unopened beside her, happy to relax in the sun, trying not to think of Boyce, who had adopted a wounded expression whenever he met her, or of Jared, whom she had not seen for nearly a week, but who was constantly with her in some mysterious fashion.

Yesterday morning, opening the *Graphic*, she had found there another cartoon of him. This time he was depicted seated in the horseless carriage, dust balls springing about him, a group of street arabs apparently staring and hallooing, the Capitol's dome at his back.

The caption beneath said, with a pointed question mark at the end, 'Nuther Tunstall drivin' into Washin'ton?' They had made him look rakish, piratical, with a flag showing a skull and crossbones flying from the front of the carriage.

Musing so, almost as though she had conjured him out of the ground, she heard his voice. 'Dreaming, Mary? And alone?'

She looked up. He stood before her, head slightly bent, dark eyes gleaming—was that possible? Dark eyes could not gleam, surely? His tall person was, as usual, elegantly clad. He, too, was alone, joining the Sunday parade walking in the balmy air, anonymous among the crowds, belying the importance given to him by the cartoon.

She made to rise, but he put a hand on her shoulder. 'No,' he said. 'Allow me to sit with you. So public an occasion must enforce propriety.' And there he was, beside her, head half turned to look at her, to admire her, so *à point* was she, so controlled, so perfectly turned out and presented.

'I have missed you,' he said, 'but duty called, and I was compelled to answer it—Refurbishing the house, helping Orrin with his campaign on the Hill. Not that he really needs help—he merely feels that he ought to

keep me busy. "Satan finds some mischief still for idle
hands to do" is a Tunstall motto. My father hated to see
us idle.'

Mary nodded. 'You came in your German monster?'
she queried. It seemed something safe to say.

'No, alas. Two days ago, I cranked her, but Lo!
nothing happened. She remained mute and motionless.
Her mechanic and shuvver——'

'Shuvver?' Mary could not help asking.

'Oh, that is Orrinese for chauffeur—the proper word,
you remember, for the man who ought to be driving the
carriage for me? He glowered at me every time I took
her out, was happy to have her break down so that he
could demonstrate his versatility and his ability to do
what I could not. He's surly when I try to get him to
explain her innards—doesn't want me to penetrate his
mysteries, you see. But I shall overcome. If I am to
promote the thing I must know exactly how it works, be
able to repair it myself.'

'How very Yankee you are, Jared,' she could not help
saying. 'I'm sure that a European aristocrat would not
deign to know of such things. He might get his hands
dirty!'

'True. I am not really a swell at all, either European or
Stateside. You see before you an imposter. My spiritual
home is the workbench. All the fault of Pa again. He
would not have his sons ignorant and idle gentlemen. I
understand Orrin—he has decided to be a Western
workhorse, makes no concession to Eastern gentility, but
his way is not mine. In the end the East Coast always
claims me. I was bred there, if born elsewhere.'

'But you are both true Americans.' She hesitated.
'Orrin told me a little of. . .how your father and brothers
died, and poor Clara. Such a dreadful thing.'

Jared's face shuttered. 'Worst of all for Orrin. He
loved Clara so. . . He was broken for a long time
afterwards. He changed. He was not at all like he is
now. . .' He fell silent. Mary remembered that Orrin
had said that Jared had changed, and it seemed that both

brothers had been permanently affected, which was not surprising. She thought fit to leave such a painful subject.

'Shall you be at Sarah Lee's ball?' she asked. She had been invited, along with Boyce, which surprised her a little, although if she married Boyce it was natural that she would become part of Sarah Lee's orbit, her husband being the senator's political ally.

'Who could doubt it?' said Jared with a smile, and at that moment he received Sally-Anne's hoop against his immaculately trousered leg, and Sally-Anne, breathless, unable to stop herself, crashed into him, excited and rosy, a second later. He put up a hand to check her, saying, 'Whoa, young lady.' Mary had been monitoring her erratic progress while she talked to Jared, but this sudden arrival took her by surprise, too.

'Oh, dear,' said Sally-Anne repentantly. 'I hope I didn't hurt you. I wasn't really being wild, Mama. It got away.' She turned her astonishing eyes on Jared, who was staring at this small and delightful vision. The colour in her cheeks, her animation, added to her charm.

'Mama?' he said, eyebrows lifted.

'My daughter, Sally-Anne. Curtsy to Mr Tunstall, my love, and apologise for your rough behaviour.'

'Oh, I will,' said Sally-Anne fervently, curtsying as she spoke and giving Jared the benefit of her most dazzling smile. 'I'm truly sorry—but I didn't hurt you, Mr Tunstall, did I?'

'No, indeed,' said Jared, his voice husky. He cleared his throat. 'Most pleased to meet you, Miss Sally-Anne McAllister.' And he spoke no less than the truth.

Sally-Anne regarded him reflectively, the hoop and cane forgotten in her hand. 'Was it you who took Mama riding in a horseless carriage?'

'Yes,' said Jared, his mind in a whirl, almost refusing to admit the effect which the piquant little face was having on him.

'When I grow up,' said Sally-Anne, 'I shall have a horseless carriage and I shall drive it myself.' She lifted her hoop up before her face, looked through it at him, and the smile which she gave him was heartbreaking. 'You know, I wish that I were a boy. Boys have all the fun. I'm sure that I shall be told that girls aren't allowed to drive them. But I shan't take any notice of *that*.'

'Well, that won't be surprising,' said Mary cheerfully, 'seeing that you never take any notice of anyone or anything. Mr Tunstall will think that you are a proper hoyden.'

Sally-Anne turned to look at her mother. Some instinct, some message received from the posture and attitude of both of them, informed her, young though she was, of what lay between Mary and Jared.

'That's because I haven't got a father. Miss Nessie says that Mama needs a husband, and that I need a father.' She looked again at Jared, who had been strangely silent since her arrival. 'Why don't you be my new papa? I'm not greatly fond of Mr Boyce. He thinks I'm a hoyden, too.'

'And I don't?' said Jared gravely, his eyes avoiding Mary's. Her face was rosy with embarrassment. 'Now, how do you know that, Sally-Anne? I might be a regular tyrant with little girls.'

She put her head on one side and considered him seriously. 'No. You took Mama out in your new carriage, and, besides, you don't have that *look*.' Bored with all this, she said in a quaint mimicry of adult manners, 'You will excuse me. I don't often get the chance to play with my hoop.'

'Certainly,' said Jared, as solemn as she was. 'No point in passing up an opportunity for fun is my motto, too.'

Struck by this, not fully understanding him, but pleased that he did not talk down to her as Mr Boyce did, and knowing all the same that she was approved of, Sally-Anne dropped her hoop, saying confidentially to her mother, 'You see, I'm right, Mama. He's not at *all* like Mr Boyce,' and, with a wave of her hand, she ran gaily off.

Jared watched her go. It was as though a whole series

of possibilities had come together in his head to create a
certainty. This enchanting child, Mary's child, but so
physically unlike her, was like someone else.

Yesterday, sorting through memorabilia in the
Sheldon house, he had found a large photograph album
full of tintypes of his grandparents and his mother when
they had been young and his mother a child.

Staring at him out of the faded prints, sepia against
lemon, as he turned the pages, had been the double of
Sally-Anne's face and figure: his mother. Roaring
through his head, stunning him, making him almost
incapable of coherent speech, was now the near certainty
that Mary was Charlie, improbable though that seemed,
and her child—was it possible that she was his? He no
longer regretted setting his agent on her trail, although
the action was almost unnecessary, because even more
now he needed to know, to be sure, for now he had a
daughter to gain.

And Mary, sitting beside him so calmly, speaking to
him in her cool, level voice—could it possibly be that
she did not know him? Surely the feelings which had
struck him with such force when they had met again,
must inform her? But that composed, beautiful face told
him nothing.

Whether she was so superb at masking her emotions
that she would have made a poker-player extraordinaire,
or whether she had not seen behind the sophisticated
cosmopolitan man he had become from the wild boy he
had once been, he could not tell.

More, what did that inform him of the woman his
Charlie had become? A woman, he suddenly knew,
whom he would have to court and to win all over again.

She was speaking. Distracted, he tried to listen. The
poker face which wheeling and dealing had given *him*
came to his aid at this crisis in his life. He wanted—
what did he want? He wanted to say, Exactly who are
you, Mary? But he could not do that. Suppose that he
was mistaken? Suppose that Mary McAllister was not his
lost Charlie? What would it do to her for him to say. . .

in effect. . . Were you my long-lost love, my mistress? Is your child illegitimate, and, if so, is she mine?

He would lose her, he knew, if he were mistaken, if she were what the world thought her—if once there had been a James McAllister who, by chance, had fathered a child who looked so remarkably like Jared's own mother when she had been Sally-Anne's age. And was *that* why Charlie had disappeared?

So practised was he in deception that Mary, chatting to him, had no inkling of what was racing through his head. 'She is not at all like you,' he said, watching Sally-Anne tear round the green, bowling her hoop between amused or annoyed spectators.

'No,' said Mary, 'not at all.'

'Takes after her father, then,' said Jared, apparently idly, his eyes anywhere but on Mary's face, for which she was thankful. She had never been more relieved that she had concealed the true facts about Sally-Anne's birth so well.

'No—his hair a little, perhaps,' she shrugged. 'Miss Nessie calls her a changeling. But even if she does not look like me she behaves very much as I used to.'

She wished that the conversation were about anything else, but sooner or later Jared had had to meet Sally-Anne, and, feeling as she did about him, she had no wish for him to discover what a light woman she had been. He might not be her lost lover; either way he might despise a woman who had borne an illegitimate child—even if that child were his. She knew only too well how the world wagged.

Oh, she had no illusions about men; however dissipated they were themselves, they expected their women to be virgins when they married them, or, if they were widows, chaste.

'Now, I find that difficult to believe,' said Jared lightly, his eyes on Sally-Anne, who was dashing along, hair flying behind her, almost the light of battle in her eyes, narrowly avoiding bowling over anyone in her headlong path, missing them at the very last moment.

'So staid, so proper as you are, my dear Widow McAllister. The senator's aide, so severe and learned that you might almost be a senator yourself—if the law permitted, that is!'

A spasm of anger passed over her. She thought the compliment two-edged in the way that men's compliments often were, praising in one breath, taking it back in the next, as though the hearer could not guess what was being done—an elaborate form of patronage, no less.

'Oh, you are as light-minded as most men are where women are concerned. You see us as having no existence in our own right, living only to minister to you, or to entertain, never as independent souls who might wish to fashion our own destinies, live our own lives, choose what to do with them—as men do.'

'But your destinies are different from ours,' he replied. 'You bear children, guard the home—that valuable refuge. . . What you do with the senator is worthy enough, I grant, and you do it as well as—or better than—any man; but women can do what men cannot— secure the race. What nobler role than that? What higher duty?'

'And that justifies oppression?' she said. 'But what of the dual standard—the demand that women live up to what men need not——? You, of all men, must be aware of the reality of that.' She turned away from him, gazed blindly at the Capitol's dome; such considerations had never troubled her when she had been a heedless girl, but she was now a woman who had suffered, and had thought deeply about her own condition and that of the exploited millions. She was only too troublingly aware of how fortunate she was—reputation saved, supported by an inherited income and a privileged education which enabled her to earn a good living.

'I may not want to be a senator myself,' she said, 'might merely wish to support one, and write his speeches——' that flew out without her meaning to say it '—but other women might, and why should they not?

And if I marry I should expect to be my husband's partner, not his slave, the occupation of his idle hours, his sometime plaything.'

It was a declaration; they both knew that.

'Even so, and, I agree, a true wife should be more than a plaything,' he said, and that was a surrender of a sort from a man who had, notoriously, only played with women. 'But I am unregenerate enough to think that we cannot deny nature.'

This should have annoyed Mary, but didn't, for he had spoken as though he took her seriously, and to some extent she agreed with him that woman's biggest problem was that of the need, as he had said, for the race to continue, and to that degree women were tied to the home. Perhaps, one day, things might change. . .

She smiled, the unease, the tension between them relaxed. 'Some might say that your view of nature was wrong.'

'And do you say that, Widow McAllister?' And although his words were light, the look on his face was such that she knew that he was taking her seriously at last.

'To the extent that I think that women ought to have the vote and be allowed to develop their talents seriously, as men do, yes.'

Mary could see that he had never thought to have such a conversation with a woman, and waited for his reply with some amusement. Only Sally-Anne, who had given her hoop such a blow that she had lost control of it, sending it towards them, arrived breathless, immediately after it had struck Jared on the leg again, and died at his feet.

Playfully he caught her small hand, and pulled her towards him. 'And would you like to be a senator, Miss Sally-Anne McAllister?'

'I'm not sure,' she said, smiling up at him. 'I think, if I were allowed, that is, I might quite like to do what Miss Nessie says you do—make lots of money and employ people to run things. If horseless carriages are here to stay—and Mama says that they are—I should like to own a factory where they are made. That would be more interesting than all that boring talk on the Hill. On the other hand, I wouldn't mind being President. It would be so nice to tell everyone else what to do, instead of being ordered about all the time, as I am now.'

Jared's amusement was patent. 'Oh, I think that it will be some time before a woman becomes President, Sally-Anne. Your granddaughter, perhaps.'

Sally-Anne could imagine being a granddaughter, even though all her grandparents were dead, but she could not imagine having one.

'Too long,' she said, trying to peer into the impossible future when she would be older than Miss Nessie. 'Please, I think I would like to be President *quite soon*.' And she bounded away again.

'Time to go home,' Mary said. 'I really ought to fetch her back.'

'And I may escort you both.'

'But it is so out of your way.'

'You are never out of my way, Mary,' he replied gently. 'And, now that I have seen her, neither is Sally-Anne.'

Jared only knew one thing. He wanted, against all the odds, Mary to be Charlie, and her enchanting child to be his. And as for Sally-Anne, she was quite won over by him, to her own and her mother's surprise, for up to now she had always disapproved of her mother's suitors. But Mr Jared now, as she told Miss Nessie later, well, he was quite another thing.

CHAPTER SIX

'DEAR BOYCE,' wrote Mary, then paused. She had begun the letter several times, and each time had torn her efforts up. Since Jared had seen Sally Anne on the Mall of the Capitol, he had visited her on several occasions, not in the horseless carriage—that, he informed her, was under repair—which was a great disappointment for Sally-Anne, who ever since she had met him had been dreaming of a ride in it.

There was no doubt of the reality of his pursuit of her, or his apparent seriousness: Washington gossip buzzed with it—and Boyce visibly suffered.

And still she was not sure of him—or of herself. Was she a trophy? Boyce's words rang in her head. For sure the burned child that she was feared the fire. Besides, his very masculinity, the confidence which he always displayed—that he had merely to crook his finger, and she would, in effect, like any other woman, come running—alienated her a little.

She found herself, against her will, trying to recover her lost past, the memories which she had for so long suppressed, in an effort to remember *him*. Surely, more than any physical difference, the one that was between the joyful boy and the hard, cynical man who was Jared Tunstall was the most striking, and caused her to question the certainty that he was the Link whom she had thought he might be since she had seen him and Sally-Anne together.

For that day, in front of the Capitol, standing together, the similarity was not so much to the Jared he was, but to the boy he must have been—and that boy was Link.

Consumed by doubt and hope, her once secure life now shaken to its foundations by Jared's arrival in it, she had allowed the time when she should have given Boyce his answer to pass.

Once, he had stopped her on the stairs at his father's home, an unspoken question on his face, and she had said hurriedly, 'Soon, soon. You shall have your answer soon.' He had nodded only, not spoken, and the constraint between them had been so great that she wondered that she had once thought she might marry him. For she knew the answer she wished to give him, but her heart failed her in the giving.

Once, Washington society had seen them as a pair, and now they were separate, and the sly talk was all of Tunstall, and whether he was serious in his pursuit of the widow, and which would win the war of the sexes which existed between her virtue and his reputation as a philanderer.

She stared unseeingly out of the window and then began again. Of one thing she was sure—the letter would be one of refusal. The knocker sounded, and a moment later Livvie was in the room.

'Mr Boyce Hamilton to see you, Miz Mary. Is you in?'

He could, quite rightly, wait no longer for her dilatory answer. He had come in person to receive it. She must be in, must see him. To do otherwise would be unfair. She had kept him dangling long enough.

'Send him in, Livvie.'

'Shall I ask Miss Nessie to bring in tea?'

'Not today, Livvie.'

Boyce was pale, but otherwise seemed quite normal. The look on his face was one of determination. He came to the point straight away—which was unBoycelike, but not surprising.

'You promised me an answer within the month. You have had six weeks. Even Congress is not so slow in its deliberations.'

This, too, was unBoycelike. She said, 'I am sorry, Boyce. It has been unfair of me to take so long, I know, and I have found it hard to write an answer which would not give you pain. I was trying, even as you came.' And she pointed to the half-written letter on the desk before her chair.

His face twisted in anguish. 'You intend to refuse me, then?'

'Yes.' Mary would not, could not, elaborate further. There was no point in doing so. She had spoken the truth; she should not have given him the month's grace, for, in doing so, while trying to spare him, she had merely inflicted further pain. Having done so, she should have replied promptly to him.

Boyce bowed his head, then raised it, his eyes fierce. 'No hope for me at all?'

'No,' she said steadily, hating what she was doing to him, but compelled to hold to her decision. 'It would be unfair of me to offer you any.'

'As I thought,' he said, adding, 'I have seen you with him.'

Mary, unwisely, elaborated after all. 'You are wrong. My decision has nothing to do with Jared Tunstall.'

To name him was enough to enrage, to inflame. 'Nothing to do with him, indeed! Until he came to Washington you had never looked at a man—other than myself. Your reputation was spotless. I honoured you for it. I was even foolishly pleased that you were cool with me. And now. . .now you have destroyed my life.' Dreadfully, Mary saw that he was near to tears.

She rose, walked to the door, and held it open. 'No, Boyce, this must end, before you say something that you will regret. I am truly sorry not to be able to give you the answer you wished for. And you will be sorry if you say more to me.'

'Sorry? I am only sorry that, after all, you are nothing but a whore, only too willing to be seduced by such a villain as Jared Tunstall, whom every decent woman ought to abhor. Sorry! Perhaps I should be pleased that I found you out before marriage, instead of unhappy that you have refused me.'

He moved towards her, his face savage, quite unlike the mild Boyce whom she had always known. 'Oh, my darling, what am I saying to you? He will never marry you, will never offer you what I am offering—a husband for you, a father for Sally-Anne.'

And then, almost rejecting her again, even as his hands grasped her shoulders and began to pull her towards him, his eyes cruel, he added, 'And who is, or was, her father, Mary? Tell me that! Tell me that!'

'Enough, Boyce,' she said, trying to pull away from him, near to tears herself. He was touching on the one thing, the one secret which she could not confess. Baffled desire was revealing to him what his love for her could never have told him.

'All women are the same,' he railed on. 'I should have learned my lesson from the failure of my first love. You all prefer the rake and the seducer to the decent and honest man. Would you have accepted me if I had defiled every woman I had met? Would you? Would you?' And he began to shake her.

'You must leave,' said Mary desperately, fear for herself replacing pity for him. Who knew what this changed Boyce might do? She did not wish to ring for Miss Nessie, to create a scene. . . 'This is not worthy of you, Boyce. When you are calm again, you will regret what you have said.'

'Never. I shall never regret anything again. Only that I did not learn my lesson earlier and ask you to marry me before he arrived to tempt you, the serpent who has destroyed my Eden.' He flung her violently away from him. 'Go to him, Mary. Add yourself to the roster of his conquests—be deserted—and then you may be sorry that you turned me down!'

He had reached the door, at last. 'How could I have been so wrong about you? To give my love to an unworthy object? My father respects your judgement. Your judgement! What happened to that when *he* arrived. . .?'

He was through the parlour, still cursing Jared and herself. She shut the door and leaned against it, almost fainting.

She might have married him! At least she now knew what seething passions lay behind his calm mask. What sort of husband would he have made? Jealous and demanding, no doubt. What kind of marriage would she have shared with him? Better by far to have discovered in time that her view of him, and their future together, had been a mistaken one. Sally-Anne had never liked him. In her innocence she had seen the true man.

Sally-Anne! His slur against her had been frightening. Did many think that? Was there a general suspicion that Sally-Anne had no real legitimate father? That the Ice Princess was not icy at all? She put her face in her hands, for, of course, all Boyce's suspicions were true.

For eight years she had almost believed herself that James McAllister had existed, that she had married him, and that he had fathered her daughter, and then had died before her birth. She had pretended that Sally-Anne was not the illicit result of a passion so strong that it had almost destroyed herself as well as her virtue.

Shivering and shaking, she rang for Livvie, said that she had been taken suddenly ill, and was going to her room, and was not to be disturbed for any reason.

Once there, she recovered herself and sat up, cold and proud. She would not allow him to disturb her, to destroy what she had so patiently built. She was now a woman of such probity that none dared question it, and the few men who had tried had retreated, ashamed, before her.

She was the virtuous Widow McAllister again, Sally-Anne's mother, who would even fight off and reject Jared Tunstall for whom she was beginning to feel what she had never thought or hoped to feel again—she dared not call it love—if he crossed the line which she had set for herself in her relationships with men.

And she had another duty, a sad one to perform. She could no longer remain as the senator's aide after Boyce's behaviour.

* * *

Mary had wandered on to Philadephia Avenue, her thoughts anywhere but on the busy life before her. Her occupation gone, her once placid life in ruins, she must face the necessity of rebuilding it. For the moment she did not wish to think of either the present or the past.

And that was not true—she could not help but think of Senator Hamilton, and she remembered this last interview with him with pain. Part of her life, an important part, had ended, and she could not simply dismiss it.

She thought of what he had said to her when she had finished speaking.

'I cannot say that I am not sorry to lose you. But if you feel that you must give more time to your child, Miz Mary, then so be it.'

He had gazed keenly at her. She had sat before him, looking pale and a little ill. She had not told him the true reason for her resignation: that, by refusing Boyce, and by his response to her refusal, she had made it impossible for herself to continue at his side, working where she might meet Boyce every day.

Her resolution had been strengthened that morning. Coming in, she had met Boyce in the hall, and he, looking more ill than she did, had pushed by her, wordless, not acknowledging her presence by more than a curt nod.

She was aware that she had not deceived the senator. He had known quite well why she was going, but had given no hint when he answered her.

'I will not pressurise you to stay,' he said. 'You have been a good aide—the best—and I shall miss you sorely. I shall not find a replacement of your calibre. A man of your attainments would be a representative already. You see, I am admitting that women are held back—and that that has been to my benefit.'

Mary nodded. Regret was rendering her almost speechless.

'At least, then,' she managed, 'I have achieved your

respect as well as having enjoyed myself working for you.'

She rose to go. For the first time the old man made a move towards her, and said something of what was in his heart. His regret was for himself, not his son—as though, now that she was leaving him, he realised that it was not for Boyce that he wanted her, but for himself. A regret that he had let the years between them hold him back—and now it was too late. He had seen her with Tunstall, and, wise in his knowledge of men and women, he knew where Mary McAllister's heart was given.

'Forgive me,' he said, and he kissed her on the forehead. 'I had hoped that you might be my daughter. I wish you well in the future, and. . .' He hesitated. 'I must say it. I hope that you have not made a mistake. . . If you have, you know where you may always find a friend and an adviser.'

'I hope so, too,' said Mary steadily. For the first time she asked herself whether, if the senator had proposed to her—before Jared had arrived—instead of Boyce, her answer would have been different. However much she respected the old man, she could not marry Boyce to please him, regardless of what might lie between herself and Jared.

Her walk had taken her almost to the British Embassy, and she smiled to herself ruefully. She knew why it had done so. The Ladies' Club had been planning, with the help of the ambassador's wife, a garden fête in the embassy's grounds, the proceeds to go to the aid of fallen women. Her duties with the senator had precluded her from taking part in it, although she had sent a tapestry cushion which she had worked to be sold or raffled.

Well, her first free afternoon might be spent there, in an effort to forget what had passed. She might even give a hand at one of the stalls, although she doubted whether, in her present turmoil, she could make change successfully. She even savoured, walking through the gates towards the bustling scene, all fashionable Washington being assembled there, the exquisite irony of such a fallen creature as herself taking part in a charitable event devoted to those who had broken society's laws as she had done!

She strolled down a small avenue lined with stalls, examined some second-hand books on one of them, bought a battered copy of John Stuart Mill's work *The Subjection of Women*, which seemed, in the circumstances, an appropriate purchase, and then sat down on an iron bench under one of the trees.

'I had not thought to find you here,' said a man's voice, 'seeing that this is one of the days on which you work for the senator; but, having found you, I hope you will allow me to shelter from the sun with you.'

It was Jared. She looked up, smiled at him, a little ruefully, and said, 'I had not thought you likely to attend an event of such exemplary innocence—one intended for pussy-cats, not lions,' but she patted the seat beside her with her gloved hand to indicate that he might join her.

'Oh, Orrin brought me,' he said. 'He is over there, buying up one of the stalls, all part of his senatorial duties, you understand. The lady running the stall has a husband Orrin wishes to win over for something or other and you do not need me to tell you that, if some political dealing is done in smoke-filled rooms over Bourbon whisky and poker, it is also performed at such sedate gatherings as these. I wonder what Orrin is going to do with all the embroidery and knick-knacks he is collecting? Give it to his widow, I suppose.' He looked wickedly at her. 'Strange that we should both be pursuing widows.'

Mary knew that he referred to Nella Murphy, with whom Orrin had lodged for some years, and also knew that gossip said he was about to make her the second Mrs Orrin Tunstall.

'Perhaps not strange,' she said, 'seeing that you are both above the common age of marriage.'

'The common age of marriage,' he said gravely. 'Is that what I have reached? It makes me sound moth-eaten, rather than romantic.'

'Oh, you must take it as you please,' replied Mary, feeling suddenly that when with Jared she either flirted with him, or reproached him. 'But remember—if you feel moth-eaten, what does that make the widows you and Orrin pursue?'

'So,' he said, 'you admit that I am pursuing you.'

'I cannot do anything else, seeing that, at the moment, we are the subject of considerable interest, and it cannot be because of any intellectual challenge we pose.'

'Hardly,' he murmured. 'And, of course, I am pursuing you—most desperately. I think that you understand that we were fated to come together. Something pulls at us, Mary. You are my magnetic North—and I am yours.'

She remembered her lost love's Texas drawl and his earthy wit, so different from the sophistications of the man sitting beside her. He had played with words in another sense, far removed from Jared's literate use of language; but both had used words to confound, to amuse, to express love—and to betray?

She would not be played with—or betrayed again—by him, or by any man.

'Very pretty,' she said, her tone almost acid, the book in her lap reminding her of the drawbacks of being a woman. 'And how many other women have you said that to? It may be forward of me, but I should like to know.'

'And you,' he said, going on the attack. 'You accuse me of being the same to all women, but are you not the same to all men? The Ice Princess, who offers a little, only to retreat. Are you playing with me, as you play with Mr Boyce? Have you given him your answer yet?'

He had no right to ask such a question, and in such a cavalier manner. All the ease between them had disappeared again. She temporised. 'How did you know—that he awaited an answer?'

He smiled, his whole mien suddenly lighter. 'Oh, Mary, all Washington knows, and is agog. You may not be easy to read, but poor Mr Boyce is. He carries his fate on his face.'

'Unlike youself, of course,' she flashed.

Jared became easier still. To fence like this, with a mind as keen as his own—and as fearless—was one of the benefits of knowing her. She would not simper at him, offer him a false deference—oh, she was a delight in every way. 'And are you, Mary? Easy to read, that is? You see, I do not know what your answer is. . .' he paused '. . .although I am sure by your manner that you have made it.'

Mary looked away from him. Well, he had read that correctly, if nothing else. 'I think that you do know. The very fact that I am here, instead of in the senator's office, tells you that. You see, if we are to play games with one another, it must be on equal terms. As in every other respect, you must not toy with me, as you do with other women. And then I ask myself, Are you ever serious, either with men or women?'

He was silent at that. Her shaft had struck home. If he were honest with her he would be compelled to admit that he was contemptuous of most of those with whom he met and dealt, and because she had seen that he was compelled to give her an honest answer.

'You have reached the heart of it. Yes, I do play games with people, but I do not play them with you, for the very reason that since you can see through them—why, then, they become worthless.'

Silence reigned between them. When he had finished he looked away from her, and then, 'A confession,' she said at last. 'For that I will be truthful with you. I have refused Boyce—and I have lied to him—which, I suppose, is a form of playing with people. I said that you were not the reason for my refusal of him, and that was not the truth. Or not the entire truth.'

'So Mr Boyce will be even more hangdog than he has recently been. He wears his emotions on his face, unlike his father—who is a master at playing the game of life. Mr Boyce should never play poker.'

'Boyce does not approve of poker—or the people who play it,' was her answer to this.

'You need not have told me that. Now you, Mary,

would be a masterly player, if your skill at the game matched your ability to control your facial expressions and your knowledge of human beings. You should not reproach me for playing with people, for I think that you play with all of us.'

Beneath what he said lay his assessment of her—that he had absolutely no knowledge from anything which she had said or done of whether, like himself, she thought that they had met before. Her self-control was absolute.

Mary looked hard at the dome of the Capitol, half hidden by trees, and not at him, made him no direct answer, but said instead, 'I have resigned from Senator Hamilton's employ.'

'Oh, you are so upright. You reproach me. You reproach us all!'

Mary swung round to face him, and oblivious of the curious stares of those who passed them, said explosively, 'No! You are mocking me, as you mock Boyce. What are *you*, Jared Tunstall? Do you believe in anything—except yourself, that is? After all, Boyce is an honourable man, and if he does not drink, gamble, or womanise, is any of that cause for shame? Can you say as much?'

His eyes on hers were rock-steady. 'You know that I cannot. I come before you with all my sins upon me. Morally, I am dirt beneath Boyce Hamilton's feet. There is hardly one of the seven deadly sins which I have not committed—except that I have never been deliberately jealous, or treacherous.

'Only, I live in the world of reality, what *is*, rather than what should or ought to be. I have no inflated expectations of how men and women ought to behave. I think that you live in my world, Mary, not his. That admirable reserve which you so carefully display is there to protect you from the jungle in which we all roam. And because you know and recognise that jungle, you too know what *is* and behave accordingly, to preserve yourself, the excellent Widow McAllister.'

Oh, he had read her so correctly. She knew now why he was a man of power, had made himself rich, would be even richer and more powerful, and if he became a senator would be one of the masters of America's Manifest Destiny.

Jared saw her face change, and knew that she acknowledged the truth of what he had said. He spoke again. 'My dear Widow McAllister, I only wished to point out that you and Boyce are oil and water, and that the senator wishes you to marry him because he knows that you would provide for him everything which he so conspicuously lacks, and which the senator possesses— masculinity, steel, a sense of purpose. He would sacrifice your happiness to make a man of his son.'

'No,' said Mary. 'He did nothing to influence me in Boyce's favour.'

'No?' said Jared—they seemed doomed to repeat the negative in this conversation. 'But he wanted you for Boyce, all the same. He would have been a fool else.'

'And you?' said Mary, a little angry.'What do you want?' And then, rapidly, 'No, do not answer me. I would not push you into a corner. Besides, I know already—the pleasure of the chase. Am I not correct? To master the Ice Princess? Is that your new aim, Jared? To help you pass the time pleasantly in Washington? To keep boredom at bay?'

Their eyes locked. A strange look, almost of pain, passed over Jared's face. He was about to answer, almost to say something irrevocable, to make a declaration to her, to commit himself to a woman at last, without knowing, or even caring whether she were Charlie or no. For Charlie had gone, and Mary was here, living and breathing.

So intent were they on each other that the world around them had disappeared. Yet the world, after all, was still there, and now broke harshly in on them.

'Jared, Mary McAllister! The embassy and the Ladies' League are alike honoured.'

The mocking voice was Sarah Lee Chase's. Parasol in

hand, a group of fashionably dressed women behind her, released for a moment from their duties, she had come up on them unseen, eyes hard and curious.

Jared rose, and bowed. Whatever else, his manners were always impeccable. Mary rose, too. The masks which society's demands imposed on them were firmly in place. Both of them appeared quite unruffled, as though the unspoken passion which had flowed between them had never existed.

Sarah Lee's eyes were inimical. Something vibrated in the air and disturbed her.

'I had not thought you so inclined to the conventional, Jared, as to enjoy such a session as this is like to be,' Sarah Lee said, her voice satiric to a degree.

'I once said that you hardly knew me,' Jared replied, and his usually clipped speech had slowed to a drawl. 'I see that I was right.' He had completed his polite formalities to the other women, and their looks at him and Mary were as avid as Sarah Lee's, if less openly curious.

She took Mary by the arm to draw her away, leaving Jared to entertain her courtiers.

'I see that you are willing to brave Boyce's displeasure, my dear,' she drawled in her turn. 'Pity to risk that, you know. Attractive Jared Tunstall may be, but faithful——' And she shrugged. 'Whereas Boyce——'

Mary broke in, her lovely calm, which for some reason Sarah Lee always wanted to smash, unmoved, 'Oh, Sarah Lee, I am not Boyce's property, and do not wish to be Jared Tunstall's—or any man's, for that matter. Such delightful weather that we are experiencing, are we not? Warmth, without overmuch humidity. Quite remarkable. One hardly knows how to dress.' And her cool eyes roved across Sarah Lee's purple face and her ample, over-upholstered body.

There, she thought, that should hold you a little. Her expression had not changed as she spoke, and Sarah Lee, infuriated that her darts were failing to pierce Mary's iron self-control, was ill-judged.

'Oh, but I think that you really ought to consider a little, Mary. Such open preference must hurt not only Boyce, but the senator. Is it really wise?'

'What a fortunate thing, then,' said Mary coolly, 'that circumstances have compelled me to resign as the senator's aide. That consideration will no longer trouble you, Sarah Lee. You may sleep easily. I should not like to think that my affairs disturbed your peace of mind.

'And now, forgive me, I must leave you. Resigning my duties will leave me more time to spend with Sally-Anne. Adieu, Sarah Lee, ladies and Jared. I suspect that we shall meet again soon, when you can favour me with more of your advice Sarah Lee. You should set up as the correspondent on the Women's Page of the *Post*—society's loss would be journalism's gain. Only think—you might even rival "A Lady Looks at Washington".' And she was gone, straight-backed, graceful, walking slowly away, down the drive towards the gates, and ultimately home.

Sarah Lee's purple face had turned almost black. She had caught Jared's amused and mocking eye on her. Doing two things at once, he had overheard Mary's demolition of her, while mouthing social nothings at fools—for so he thought the women before him.

Oh, yes, Mary McAllister was a jewel of price. Anyone who could put Sarah Lee in her place. . . And his inward laughter was almost audible to Mary's victim.

'Come, Sarah Lee,' he said, offering her his arm. 'Allow me to escort you wherever you wish.'

She pushed him away. 'No, I have no need of you. Go and charm others. You will not charm me.'

'No?' he said. 'A pity. Then you will excuse me. I must collect Orrin before he expires beneath the burden of all the purchases he has made.' And he bowed himself away to where Orrin was booming genially at several senatorial wives, for despite his years he was, like his brother, a man who attracted women to him, as moths were drawn to a flame.

But Jared's thoughts were not on Orrin, or the latest

gossip from the Hill, but on Willard's Hotel, where he had learned that morning that his agent would be awaiting him with the news about Mary McAllister which he so urgently required.

CHAPTER SEVEN

'SO, YOU'VE finally given Mr Boyce his marching orders,' said Miss Nessie, clearing away the luncheon things two days after Mary and Jared had sparred outside the Capitol.

'Yes,' said Mary briefly. 'And that is why I shall be working for Senator Barton Graves instead of Senator Hamilton—and for fewer hours. I must not neglect Sally-Anne; she is growing quite wild.'

Miss Nessie said nothing for a few moments, then at the door offered Mary her parting shot, 'And does that mean we shall all be seeing more of Mr Jared? You know how much Sally-Anne has taken to him.'

'And what is that supposed to mean?' said Mary, sighing a little. 'Off with the old, on with the new; is that it?'

'She needs a papa more than she needs anything else,' said Miss Nessie, 'and it's time you gave her one, that's all!' The latter was said triumphantly, and she closed the door behind her before Mary could answer.

All Washington would like to see me married off, she thought ruefully, taking up her pen, and beginning to write a scathing attack on the scandals surrounding the politicking involved in promoting the proposed Anti-Trust Bill, which was aimed at such pirates and entre-preneurs as Jared Tunstall. 'A Lady' might have some-thing trenchant to say about the dollars changing hands on the Hill to bring about the desired result for them—that should set the cat among the pigeons and cause a few feathers to fly about.

She had finished the article, slipped it into a large manila envelope and gone upstairs to dress herself suit-ably for the short walk to the *Gazette's* letter-box, where she hoped to post it discreetly—first making sure that nobody was about to see her—when Miss Nessie knocked at her bedroom door, calling, 'Miz Mary,' while she did so.

'Yes,' Mary said impatiently. 'What is it now?'

'It's Mr Tunstall, Miz Mary. Here to see you, looking so worried. I put him in the parlour. He wouldn't take coffee nor nothing.'

Mary unpinned the hat she had just put on, and laid it carefully on the bed. It was a more frivolous thing than usual: cherries and their leaves fruiting around the brim. She wondered what he wanted, to come calling at such an odd hour.

For some reason her heart was hammering a little when she walked into the parlour. Jared had his back to her. He was examining her bookshelves. Her sensitivity to him, which had increased on their every meeting, told her from his pose, and the way in which he swung around at her entry, of his tension, of some anxiety, of emotion strongly felt, barely contained, although his face was as impassive as usual.

Seeing her, Jared hardly knew how to begin. He had lived in ferment since his agent had arrived the previous evening with his report, both written and verbal. He had listened to him, read the report, and his control had been so consummate that the man might have thought him disappointed in what he heard.

At the end Jared had poured the agent a whisky and said to him, 'And you have been discreet?'

'As the grave,' was the reply.

'And you will remain discreet?'

'That is why you pay me so highly,' said the agent steadily. 'For my discretion, as well as the work I do for you.'

'Well, I depend on your continuing discretion. You will not report any of this back to your superiors. Tell them nothing of what I wanted to know. Say it was—routine—about mining operations in the area to which you went.'

'Indeed—seeing that you pay me to be discreet with my employers, too.'

Jared rose and handed him a pile of greenbacks in a plain envelope, which the agent put in his pocket without counting them—he knew his man. He also knew that for some reason the news he had brought had hit Jared Tunstall hard.

There was a good fire blazing in the hotel bedroom's grate. Jared threw the envelope containing the papers which told him, beyond doubt, that Mary *was* Charlie, and that Sally-Anne was his daughter, into the flames and watched them burn.

He also knew, again beyond a doubt, something which had long puzzled him, which had originally almost destroyed him—why his Charlie had deserted him; and the knowledge had hit him so hard that when he reached the Sheldon house, now being restored after Mary McAllister's suggestions, he could neither sleep nor rest, only wait for the next day to arrive so that he might see her again, and try to turn back the years. . .

Only, when she walked through the door, her very presence overwhelmed him. She was wearing a soft green dress, with a collar up to her chin, the skirts subtly draped, the fashionable bustle minimal. The waist was highish. A cream silk shirtwaister, what the British called a blouse, was revealed beneath the dress's bodice, and its short wide sleeves. The shirtwaister's sleeves were full, and tightly gathered at the wrist above her beautiful hands.

His Charlie! And yet not his Charlie. Her woman's taste was so impeccable—the mature Mary, deep-bosomed, was even more desirable than his charmingly boyish Charlie had been.

How could he not have known her? He should have recognised her from the moment he had seen her, seated on the Mall. She was his Charlie, found at last.

'Mary!' he could not help exclaiming. 'You look more beautiful than ever.'

Only his speech told her how powerfully he was

disturbed, so powerfully that when he strode towards
her, his eyes suddenly glowing, his whole face soft, as
she had never seen it, she almost retreated. His next
words caused her to stop, to stare at him, her face losing
its delicate colour, growing ashen as the import of what
he said struck home.

'Forgive me for bursting in on you without warning,
but I had to see you. Oh, Mary—no, Charlie, my
Charlie—you surely know why I am here.' He put out
his hands to take hers, to try to pull her towards him.
'After all these years, to find my lost Charlie again in a
woman I can admire, as well as love!'

So! She had been right to see her lost Link in Jared.
How could she not have known him through all the
disguises which time and chance had put upon him—as
on her? What struck her the most, however, was a most
astonishing grief—the grief which the abandoned Charlie
had felt on the day when she was sure that he had
betrayed and deserted her. How could he come to her
now, with a smile on his face, expecting her to welcome
him?

Should she be pleased at what was, by his manner, a
courtship renewed, his desertion of her now doubtless
regretted? Did he expect her to forget his treachery
simply because eight long years had passed, and now he
knew who she was—and had seen Sally-Anne—he had
changed his mind and wanted her back again? And how
was it that he was so certain that he knew her?

'After all these years,' she repeated, pulling sharply
away. 'A fortnight gone, or a little more, you said.' Her
voice was ice, and the pain which knifed through her
was as much for the loss of Jared as of Link.

'Forever and a day,' she flung at him. 'That was what
you said, the day you deserted me. At least the last two
words were true.'

Her voice was cold and rejecting, her face a mask of
remembered pain, the hurt as great as though the last
eight years had never been.

In his eagerness to see her, to claim her, now that he

had found her, and knew the reason for her disappearance, he had been clumsy, Jared suddenly realised. To her he was the faithless lover who had deserted her, left her to face a hostile world, pregnant, saved only by the chance of the unexpected Washington inheritance from ruin and shame. And Sally-Anne, his daughter, also saved only by chance from ruin and shame.

Eight years later and nearly two thousand miles away, they had met again, to be attracted again, but to Mary the years and the miles were as nothing. The past she had denied, had blotted from her memory, was as real as though it had been experienced yesterday. Anguish overwhelmed her.

She had retreated from him, was pushing him away. Her hand was rising to pull the bell, to dismiss him from her life. He had no business in it.

Jared suddenly realised what she was doing. The look she gave him had nothing of love in it, was implacable, laced with pain. He cursed his precipitate self.

'Oh, my dearest love, my Charlie!' he exclaimed, moving towards her to prevent her from rejecting him, possibly permanently. 'What you do not know is that I truly meant to return to you within the fortnight. It was ill luck which delayed me, caused me to be so late returning, so that I missed you, destroying all our hopes and the future which we should have had together.' But still she retreated before him, pushing a chair between them so that he should not touch her.

'I am not your Charlie,' she said coldly. 'Charlie Nelson died of grief on the stage from Heyes Landing. I am Mary McAllister who never knew Link Travis, and does not wish to know Jared Tunstall now that I know that they are one and the same. You had better leave at once. I shall ring for Miss Nessie to see you out, and I do not wish us to meet again. Let us be as unknown to each other as we have been for the last eight years. You say that you were delayed. What delay could there be sufficient to excuse you for not returning to the girl you had seduced and said that you loved? Please leave at once. You left me easily enough before.'

Mary could not believe either the depth of her own grief and sense of loss—as strong as it had been on that long ago day when she had finally come to terms with his betrayal—or the shock and pain which filled his face at her words.

How dared he? How dared he, after his callous desertion of the loving girl she had been? The calm composure which she had shown for eight years still ruled her face and body, but inside she was screaming as the young Charlie had done so long ago. Twice! I have lost him twice. Once as Link, and now as Jared, for much though I know that I have come to love Jared Tunstall, and partly because he reminded me of him, I dare not, I will not, risk being betrayed by him again.

'No,' he said, his hand on hers, as she found the bell at last, and began to pull it. 'You must listen to me. . . Affairs went wrong after I left you, and I was prevented from returning. . . I had been ill, and when I finally reached Heyes Landing it was to find you gone. I thought that you had deserted *me*. It was not until I met you again, thought that I recognised you, finally saw Sally-Anne, that I understood why you had gone. For eight years I thought that you preferred not to wait for me, had gone without a word, treating our love as the mere idle pleasure of a summer's day. Sally-Anne is my child, is she not, and the reason for your flight?'

The room swung about Mary. She feared that she was about to faint. She steadied herself with difficulty, and said brokenly, 'I cannot put on one side what happened between us. You say that you could not return in the fortnight that you promised me, but even in Arizona Territory there was a post, means of letting me know that you were delayed, but. . .nothing. . . And I waited for you until it was almost plain that I was carrying Sally-Anne. I still find your explanation of your delay unconvincing. And what were you doing in Arizona Territory, calling yourself Lincoln Travis, speaking in a Texas

drawl? My name truly was Charlie Nelson then, but who
and what was Lincoln Travis, that Jared Tunstall should
call himself so? It may be wrong of me to ask such
questions, to be suspicious, but the burned child fears
the fire. How can I trust you? I trusted you once before,
and only great good luck saved me from ruin.'

Jared's face showed that he was now in agony, as well
as Mary. 'I cannot,' he began, 'tell you why I was calling
myself Link Travis, nor even why I was late back, nor
why I left you. God knows, I did not want to. I had, or
thought I had, a duty to perform, and a duty of which I
have never spoken to anyone, not even Orrin. I would
not add that burden to that which you have carried since
the day I left you. Believe me when I tell you that only
the direst necessity kept me away so long—and ill luck,
too. I only know that I loved you truly then, and love
you truly now, that you are even more beautiful than the
girl I remember, and that you are so completely what I
have always wanted in a woman, but thought that I
should never find, and that I want you most desperately
for my wife.'

Mary seized on one phrase he had used. 'The day you
left me,' she said slowly. 'Since then I have been my own
woman. From the day that you rode out of my life I have
been in charge of my destiny, and Sally-Anne and I have
forged a new life here in Washington, a life I do not wish
to share, unless it is with someone I can truly love and
trust. Can I truly love and trust you? After all, what is
Jared Tunstall but Link Travis writ large, the most
notorious womaniser of his generation, the man everyone
assumes is pursuing the Ice Princess because she presents
a challenge to him, not because he loves her? Why
should I trust that man? Tell me that.'

She had sunk into a chair, and he had fallen on his
knees beside her. He took the hand which lay lax on her
lap, bent to kiss it. Mary looked down at him, at the
blue-black head which lay in her lap. Age had dimmed
the lustre of his hair a little, fashion dictated its short-

ness. In every way he differed from the slim pony-tailed boy of her memory.

'Oh, Charlie—Mary—I hardly know what to call you. Believe me that I loved you then, and, if possible, love you even more now, with a man's love, not a boy's. I could not sleep last night after I learned the truth.'

His Mary was so quick, so quick. She pounced upon what he had said, and the bitterness of betrayal was thick in her voice.

'Learned it?' she said. 'Learned it? How did you learn of me? Yesterday? Oh, never say that you set a detective on my trail! Is there no end to your treachery? Can I believe a word you say. . .about being delayed? Is it possible that, having betrayed me and thrown me on one side as Charlie, you decided that you wanted me as Mary, and used the memory of our old love to win me back again? Or is it for Sally-Anne that you want me?'

'No,' he said, looking up at her. 'You wrong me—as we both thought that we had been mutually wronged. It is you I want. Charlie Nelson. Of course, I want Sally-Anne, too, as who would not? And after all she is mine, as much as she is yours. And yes, I hired a detective to find out whether or no you were my Charlie. It was a brute thing to do, but I had to do it.

'Think how you would have greeted me, if after all you had not been Charlie, if I had asked you whether or not you were the girl I had loved, made my mistress, if only for one afternoon, and that Sally-Anne was the result of that love. Such an insult—for so it would have seemed to you—I dared not risk, loving you as I do, hoping to make you my wife—as I still hope to make you my wife.'

Mary had lifted her hand away from his head; at his last words she replaced it.

'All my certainties have disappeared,' she said, voice low. 'And I have to face the fact that you have still not fully explained why you were late, why you needed to be Lincoln Travis, a desperado so unlike the Harvard scholar that Orrin said you had been. You are avoiding

that. Unless there is truth and trust between us, how can
we take up where we left off that morning when you
rode away?'

'No,' he said determinedly. 'You cannot refuse me.
Had I not found out who you were, you would have
accepted Jared Tunstall—that I do know; for we are as
happy together as we were when we were boy and girl.
Why turn me away now? You know that Sally-Anne is
mine, that she came to me as willingly as a child can
come to someone she does not know. She deserves a
father as well as a mother, and she is already beginning
to love me. You are still my Charlie when all is said and
done.'

'Oh,' said Mary, 'what can I say to that that does not
sound selfish? You say that I am your Charlie, but I am
not. She is long gone. And what are you? What did I do
to you when you found me gone? What Jared Tunstall
has been these last eight years is so little like my lost
Link—as little as I am now like Charlie.'

Jared had never foreseen an outcome such as this. He
had visualised them falling into one another's arms,
almost boy and girl again. He knew that much of what
Mary said was true. He thought bitterly of the amoral
life he had lived since he left her, a life so different from
Mary McAllister's.

'No,' he said slowly. And then, 'Yes, you are hardly
the Charlie I loved and lost either.'

He stood up. He pulled her, unresisting, to her feet,
and swung them both round to face the mirror over the
hearth.

'Look,' he said. 'The boy and girl are gone. I admit
that. There is no going back. But did either of us possess
the strength and maturity of the man and woman we
have become? We stand among the ruins of the past and
present. Cannot we build something on that? I am sure
that we can still love one another greatly. Why refuse
happiness when it comes at last?'

Mary was still in a state of acute shock—the shock of
learning that her suspicion that Jared might be Link was

true; the shock of learning that Link had returned for
her after all. She conceded also that, had he come to her
as Jared only, and not as re-found Link, she might well
have accepted him, even despite his reputation.

A paradox. Because she had loved him so dearly once
that she had surrendered herself, she was hesitant now.
The shadow of her belief in his falsity, his desertion, the
lost eight years, could not easily be forgotten.

She looked away from the handsome and dominant
pair in the mirror, so different from the boy and girl
they had been.

'Until a few minutes ago I lived with the knowledge of
Link Travis who had callously seduced me and deserted
me. I had built a new life and a new self on that belief—
as you changed, because you thought that I had betrayed
you. And now everything has changed again. There are
no foundations to my life. My beliefs may have been
wrong, but they sustained me. You must give me time
to think. I cannot simply pretend that what happened
did not happen. We are not living in a fairy-story where
present, past and future have no meaning.'

How, Jared thought wildly, could he have believed in
a simple, happy ending? The complex man he had
become should have known better. Falling into one
another's arms! What stupid fantasy had he been weav-
ing? Desolation enveloped him. Charlie—Mary—and
his daughter were slipping away from him.

'Sally-Anne,' he said hoarsely.

'Oh,' said Mary sorrowfully. 'I must consider her, too.
Time, Jared, give me time.'

'Time! We have lost eight years. Can we afford to lose
more? And wait. You said that to Boyce. You were
deceiving him to delay giving him pain. Are you deceiving me?'

'No,' she almost keened. 'No, never that. You cannot
expect me to fall into your arms, hand Sally-Anne over—
it would be wrong. We cannot pretend that the past is
dead, or that it never happened. I do not want to carry
my resentment with me into a marriage. We cannot

lightly expunge from our memories what we so wrongly thought of one another. I do not want them to be ghosts that we carry with us to rise again so that we might yet come to reproach one another. I you, for making love to me when I was an untried girl—and then leaving me, regardless of possible consequences—and you hating me for being weak and flying before you returned. I must think. Can we, indeed, be truly happy together?'

He caught her to him again and held her against his heart. He put his arms about her, began to kiss the beloved face, and, against her will, she began to respond.

'You see,' he said into her neck, 'It is there between us still. Always will be. Stronger than life or death. How can you refuse me?'

She pulled away reluctantly. 'I know, I know. But mere passion is not enough. There is also the ordinariness of living and the strength of the web of deceit which I have created to save myself from ruin, the kind of woman I have, in consequence, become, the Jared you have made of yourself. I must think and you must leave me to do it. I must keep you at arm's length. Heedless passion, no thought for the morrow, destroyed us once before. . .'

'No, not that, but chance. . .'

'No,' she said, turning away from him still further, bright head bent. 'If I have learned anything from what happened to me, there, in the Territory, it is that payment is always required of us for what we do. We cannot take what we want, as and when we want it. This time I must do what is right, Jared, not what I like or what is expedient. I have learned that, if nothing else. That is why I refused Boyce. I could not marry him on the lie that I loved him. Marriage exists to sanctify love and should not be entered into as some form of expediency, or to gratify an empty passion.'

'But you do love me. No lie there,' he said, only to meet her shaking head.

His Charlie! Found and not found. The slim, eager girl had become a woman whose strength of mind and character he coveted as well as her love. But that mind and that character might not allow him her love. The lost years, and what they had done to each other, stood between them still, a chasm he could not cross.

'I only know that I love you,' he said simply and humbly. 'And I love you now for your strength and your integrity. I must respect you. But oh, it breaks my heart, the thought of losing you again, the more because of Sally-Anne, the child I might never call mine.'

Her eyes filled with tears again, but the power of her will prevented them from increasing. 'You are as strong as I am. You will be strong, will you not, Jared? Mere desire to please your body will not rule you, I know. The mind and heart must be satisfied, too.'

'One thing I must ask of you,' he said. 'That you will not drive me from your life. You acknowledge that Sally-Anne is mine, and you must also agree that she needs a father. Will you allow me to visit you both, to. . .court you again, this time as the Jared Tunstall who wishes to make you his wife, give Sally-Anne what is hers, to try to persuade you that, after all, we may share our lives?'

'No,' she said slowly, 'I cannot deny you that. Yes, you may visit us, and see her, and perhaps—I only say perhaps—we can build a new future together. But you must be honest with me, and I fear that you have not been totally so—over your failure to return, and why you were in Arizona at all, posing as a desperado——' for she saw how he had evaded giving her a true explanation for that '—and we must be careful to say and do nothing to cause gossip. I do not want either of us to be prey for such as Sarah Lee.'

Face to face, almost heart to heart again, but oh, so far apart. The few yards which she had put between them were as fatal as the few weeks by which he had missed her in Heyes Landing. The yards might as well have been miles, as the few weeks were an eternity.

Jared bowed his own head. 'Mind and heart, Mary, mind and heart,' he said at last. 'Above all, remember that you possess mine, they are already yours, do not have to be won. The body is only a vessel which holds them, and through which we sanctify them.'

He had deliberately used the word 'sanctify', which she had earlier employed, and he saw her face change as he did so. . .and he risked one last plea, and one he thought was powerful.

'Remember this,' he said slowly, 'as you remember those few happy weeks we spent together. I never married. You destroyed all other women for me, and if I lived the life I did it was because, God help me I wanted and want no other woman but you.'

CHAPTER EIGHT

JARED had gone. She was alone again, sitting as he had said, in the ruins of her life.

For eight years she had almost believed herself that James McAllister had existed, that she had married him, that he had fathered her daughter, and then had died before her birth. She had pretended that Sally-Anne was the legitimate result of a happy marriage, not the product of a passion as powerful as it was illicit.

Lately, even pretence itself had disappeared. The lie had become the truth. She had refused to remember her real past so successfully that she had barely been able to recall it. More truthfully first she had not wished to recall it and then it had disappeared from her memory as though it had never been—until she had met Jared Tunstall at the ball.

And then, this afternoon, when he had walked towards her, calling her by the name she had been known by in that lost time, it had suddenly risen before her, the colours, the scents, and, yes, even the feel of those few brief weeks when she had known him before.

It was though he had turned a key in a door, flung the door open, and told her to live again in that desert country where he and she had first met.

Shuddering, Mary rose to her feet. She must be alone, somewhere where no one could disturb her, somewhere where she could remember. He had used the word so many times, and perhaps he was right. She must remember—what had happened and how it had happened, and then, perhaps, she might know how to act.

She rose, met Livvie in the hall, told her that she had been taken suddenly ill, was retiring to her room, and was on no account to be disturbed.

Once there, she sat on her bed, compelled, by what

she did not know, to recall what she had never recalled
in all her time in Washington. What good it would do
her, she did not know. She only felt, quite deeply, that
she might come to know her true self if she could recover
that girl, the girl to whom Boyce Hamilton would never
have proposed, the girl whom he had begun to suspect
was hidden behind Mary McAllister's mask of virtue.
The girl who would have accepted Jared Tunstall gladly
and without question, who would have given herself to
him as joyfully as she had given herself to him in his
other identity—and what was he doing in Arizona under
a false name?

No matter. All that was nothing. She lay down on the
bed, closed her eyes and gave herself up to her past. The
years rolled back. Time turned in on itself. She was
nineteen again, living under a desert sun, her very name
a different one; she was a girl who did not know
Washington, or politics or the social etiquette of the life
which Mary McAllister lived. The life of the girl who
had been Charlie Nelson. . .

'Charlie Nelson,' said Mrs Potts despairingly. 'You'll
never catch a man dressed like that.'

'Don't want to catch a man,' said Charlie.'What would
I do with him? Or him with me? I'm happy as I am.'

'That's now,' said Mrs Potts wisely. 'What about *then*?
When you can't run round Arizona Territory dressed
like a boy, and packing a gun.'

'Don't do it for fun,' said Charlie, wise in her turn,
her pert, pretty face turned towards Mrs Pott's worn,
middle-aged one. 'A girl has to live and protect herself.'

'A girl could be a man's wife, not running a general
store in the desert. Particularly a pretty one like you
used to be. Why, I remember you when you wore skirts.
Men don't respect women who wear pants. Think you
fair game.'

'I was a lady when Papa was alive,' said Charlie. 'Now
I've no one to protect but me. Wolves—that's what the
men are around here. Chase anything in skirts—that's

why I don't wear 'em. A single girl ain't safe for all their talk about respecting women, particularly when the Bar Y gang come to town. Cowpunchers,' she said scathingly, 'villains to a man. Not that they've been in lately, thank the lord for small mercies.'

She was talking to Mrs Potts, the wife of the town's carpenter and undertaker outside the store she ran in the main street of Heyes Landing, in Arizona Territory, not far from the border with New Mexico. The pitiless midday sun shone down on them, and on the town, relentlessly revealing the false fronts above Charlie's General store, and Mr Potts's shop next door.

The only genuine two-storey building in the one long street was that of the Aces High saloon—which no decent woman ever entered—upstairs being a lodging house, and 'something worse', as Mrs Potts was wont to say, genteelly closing her eyes.

Charlie was wearing men's faded blue trousers, a plaid open-necked shirt rolled up to her elbows, men's high-heeled black boots, sported a short-barrelled Colt Peacemaker .45 on one slender hip, and had her blonde hair cut short for convenience and easy care, as well as against the excessive heat of the desert which surrounded the town. She had just dismounted from a fine chestnut horse which had a Winchester 44.40 rifle in a scabbard on the saddle. From the rear she might almost have been mistaken for a boy; from the front, despite Mrs Potts's strictures, no one could ever have taken her for anything but a girl.

'Preacher Mason has given you more'n one look,' said Mrs Potts. 'Now there is a man for you. You could talk books to him, too.'

'Don't want him, either—to talk books to, or anything else. I am,' she said firmly, 'happy as I am, and now I must open the store again.'

Her firmness did not offend Mrs Potts—she knew her Charlie. 'Mr Right ain't come along yet,' she said. 'When he does. . .' And she paused significantly.

'When he does!' said Charlie. 'You mean if he does.

Anyone visiting me here will be a hairy monster two jumps ahead of the law. I'm minded to buy a shotgun as well, but Pa allowed as how they was mean things.' In her daily life about the town she spoke as the locals did, and now when she went indoors there was no one waiting there to speak to her in the accents of the late nineteenth-century American East, of books and music and art.

The piano stood mute. Since her father's death she could not bear to play it. Even the many books which filled one wall of her living-room had lost the savour they had once possessed, now that there was no one to share them with.

She could almost feel Mrs Potts sigh as she entered the store, pulled up the blind, left the door invitingly open and waited for customers. Five years ago, her father Robert Nelson, a one-time Professor of Philosophy from Boston, Massachusetts, had come West in search of health, bringing his motherless only child, Mary Charlotte, always known as Charlie, with him.

The locals thought him what they called a lunger, consumption being the disease which usually brought Easterners to the hot, dry desert, but Robert Nelson's illness was a different kind of slow wasting away and his emigration to the West was a last hope suggested by his physician rather than a conscious belief that a cure awaited him there.

'I don't know what is wrong with you,' the doctor had said frankly. 'One day we might know, but not now. I think that dry air might help you—living here in the damp certainly doesn't.'

'And I am growing incapable of carrying out my duties at the university,' Robert Nelson had said coolly. He had thought a moment, then added, 'I can afford to sell up. It's Charlie, Mary Charlotte, my daughter, I'm worried about.' He brightened a little. 'But she's an adaptable child.'

He had said this to her more than once in the years which they had spent at Heyes Landing, running the store which he had bought from its departing owner shortly after they had arrived there.

For a time he had undergone a brief remission, had almost believed that coming to the desert had saved him, and then, slowly, his illness had taken hold again, and it was Charlie who ran things, as well as nursed him with the utmost devotion.

First she had been his scholastic pupil, continuing her academic education in the desert, then she had been his help, and finally his mainstay.

'I have been selfish,' he said, not long before he died, 'to bring you here, away from civilisation. To die and to leave you alone in the wilderness, a boy now more than a girl.' For in her father's last illness she had begun to wear boy's clothes all the time, finding them more practical than her skirts in her hard-working life.

'Nonsense,' Charlie had said briskly. 'I love it here,' which was true. She would not have exchanged the garish desert splendours for all the delights of Eastern urban civilisation.

'You should have a husband and children,' he had said. 'And I am leaving you here, alone and friendless.'

'Nonsense,' Charlie said again. 'Nothing I want less than a husband—or children.'

'One day,' he said, repeating what Mrs Potts and others said, often and often, 'you will want them, whatever you think now. Remember what I said then.'

She was recalling this while she unpacked the boxes and stores which had come in on the stage from the railhead, thirty miles away, the spur which ran from the Southern Pacific, that long snake-like link with civilisation. She was laying out and counting pairs of denim trousers, preparatory to stacking them on the open shelving, when the quiet peace of the afternoon was shattered by the thundering of hoofs, men's voices shouting and laughing, dogs barking, and the occasional pistol shot.

Although she did not know it, Charlie's uneventful

life was about to end forever. Curious, she walked to the door, and looked out.

A horde of men on horseback, hairy monsters all, were milling around before the Aces High saloon. Her heart sank. It was the ruffians from the Bar Y, the ranch which lay to the west of the town, and which took in a large part of the desert, a few mangy cattle being the ranch's supposed herd.

The ranch's owner, Garrity, and his men had stayed away from Heyes Landing for some months, spending their leisure time at Fort Pendleton, neglecting Heyes Landing to the relief of everyone there except the saloon owner and the livery man.

Even the money they spent in the store was hardly worth the nuisance of their presence. They might call themselves cowboys, or vaqueros, in the picturesque Spanish of the Old West, but the ranch was a blind. They were outlaws who came here to be away from civilisation and its laws, to hole up when their usual haunts had become too hot to hold them, or the US law was pursuing them with more than usual venom. Arizona Territory offered them a lawless sanctuary.

They usually stayed in town for the best part of a week, turning night into day, troubling innocent citizens, fighting and drinking in and out of the saloon, and on the streets. Sometimes the fighting turned ugly, ended in gun play, with one or more body to be buried in Boot Hill, the cemetery on the edge of town.

She wondered what had brought them back again, and what Jim Tatum, the town marshal, would make of them. Little, probably. He was in the pay of Heck Warren who owned and ran the saloon, and the town as well.

Heyes Landing had been built and settled in the days when copper had been found—bonanza days, in Mrs Potts's fond memory—but the big lode had run out early, and now offered little for the remaining few miners who worked the hole and the galleries which did not need a deep shaft.

No one remembered who Heyes had been, and the town's name was a joke, for the dry wash near by was a river only once a year, when the rain came, and the waters rushed down, before disappearing again. True, there was a small wooden landing at the wash's edge, but it, like the river, was also a joke. Supplies came in by stage. Some wag had painted a crude sign and erected it on the landing—'No fishing from this stage'. It stood in silent mockery above the desert sand.

Most of the townsfolk were white; the few Indians were long gone, like the US army garrison at Fort Pendleton, deserted now that this part of Arizona was peaceable.

The other visitors who kept Heyes Landing alive were the small ranchers, farmers, and their hands from the countryside around, genuine ranchers—unlike Garrity—improbably trying to make a living on the few fertile patches of this wild land, although herding cows in this climate and on this terrain seemed the chanciest business in the world to Charlie.

The noise of the milling men increased; the largest and brawniest, Garrity himself, had dismounted. He went over to one of the riders, who was the loudest in joshing him, pulled at him by one leg, while shouting jovially himself. The rider, a lean, dark young man whom Charlie had never seen before, obliged him by falling off his horse—on top of Garrity—all done with a neat acrobatic movement, and then they were scuffling and wrestling in the dirt of the street.

Many dismounted, some more ran whooping out of the saloon, into the street, to form a loose ring around the combatants, taking bets on the outcome, most favouring Garrity.

They were wrong. The wrestling had become serious, and the dark young man, pinioning his larger opponent's face to the ground, arm wrenched behind his back, was suddenly sitting on Garrity. He was laughing while restraining him, not easily, but holding him down nevertheless.

'Liam's lost. Ain't champ no more. All bets due. Right, Liam?' His drawl was thick Texan, but the tone of his voice was light and mocking.

'Right,' gasped Garrity. 'Damn yuh, Link Travis, get off me, boy. Yuh'll break my back.'

Still laughing, Link obliged him again, rose lithely and moved away. But Garrity had one more trick left in him. As Link turned towards his horse again—another rider had been holding it for him—Garrity seized him by the ankles and threw him down on to the street, so that he slithered almost to the watching Charlie's feet, dazed from the unexpected fall.

'So, who's won now?' roared Garrity. 'The ole bull knows a few tricks. That'll larn you to turn yore back on me.'

Travis, gasping now himself, looked up at Charlie's booted legs and put out a hand. 'He'p me up, boy, so's I can show Liam what's what agin.'

Charlie looked down at a tanned and mocking face, dark blue-black eyes, long, blue-black hair tied back in a pony-tail, and grimy blue-black, stubbled cheeks and jaw. Perfect teeth—something of a surprise—flashed at her as he spoke.

He was the exact image of every reckless desperado who roved the Territory. She heard herself say primly, 'Not likely, Link, whoever you are. Ain't helping anyone to brawl in the street. Save it for the saloon.'

Hearing her voice, and looking at her carefully for the first time, Link's grin grew broader. 'Oh, beg pardon, mam. Din't know yuh wuz a lady, mam. Purely deceived me, but a nat'ral mistake, as yuh'll shorely agree, mam.'

His voice took on an even more mocking note, parodying what he doubtless imagined was gentlemanly speech. 'Pray assist me up, mam, of your Christian charity. Wun't like to leave me in the dirt, shorely, mam?'

'Shorely don't mind where I leave you,' said Charlie, unmoved by the ruffian's appeal. 'But, yes, I'll give you a hand, if only to get rid of you. Garbage shouldn't be

left lying in the street.' She was certain that he was
perfectly capable of rising without her help.

He was. He took her offered hand lightly, rose in one
graceful movement to his over six feet of height, and
then, before she could prevent him, he took her gently
by the shoulders and said in a voice filled with laughter,
'Thanks due to yuh, mam, yuh bein' so gracious an' all,'
and he bent his head, tightened his grasp, and kissed her
full on the lips. No light kiss this—a true kiss, forcing
her mouth open slightly, so that the tip of his tongue
met hers, teased it, and then withdrew.

To the sound of cheering from the watchers, for
Charlie's resolute untouchability was a local legend, he
stepped back, still laughing. 'Shorely a pleasure to thank
a purty young lady,' he observed.

'Oh, damn you for an insolent bastard,' blazed
Charlie, and struck him fiercely across the face, which
hurt her hand more than it did him, and did no good at
all, for he took the striking hand, twisted it gently, but
firmly, behind her back and said,

'Badly want another, d'yuh, mam?' and before she
could wrench her head away favoured her with another
kiss, longer and fiercer, the searching tongue more
insistent, so that to her horror she found her body
responding. Her senses, starved for so long of affection,
were asserting themselves, demanding satisfaction.

He let her go as suddenly as he had seized her, so that
she reeled back. 'Enjoy garbage, after all, d'yuh, mam?'
he said, grinning. 'Yuh know where to find me if yuh
want more.' And he turned back again to his horse, to
redoubled cheering.

'I shall set the marshal on you for assault,' she raged.

'Don't trouble, mam,' he said, without even doing her
the courtesy of turning towards her. 'I hear as how he
ain't much of a feller with a Peacemaker, and I ain't
breached no peace. Yuh was the one makin' all the noise.
Shorely quietened yuh, mam, for a moment at least.'

Charlie, suddenly realising that virtually the whole of
Heyes Landing was staring fascinated at the fracas

between herself and Link, stamped her foot, and
retreated into the store, banging the door so fiercely that
the glass pane in it nearly shattered, and turned to watch
through it Link Travis, surrounded by his fellow outlaws, being slapped on the back by big Garrity, then
making his way into the saloon.

Charlie could imagine what he was saying, she having
repelled him and his fellow outlaws successfully more
than once—only to meet her downfall at the hands of a
tall boy of her own age.

Mrs Potts put her head round the door. 'Tole you you
needed a man, Charlie Nelson,' she said reprovingly,
'someone to protect you from Bar Y scum.'

'I should have shot him,' said Charlie grimly. 'And, if
he touches me again, I shall.'

'And where did *he* come from?' said Mrs Potts. 'Ain't
seen him afore.'

'From some open sewer east of El Paso,' blazed
Charlie. 'Never met a decent woman, and sure has no
idea of how to treat one.'

'It's them pants you wear,' said Mrs Potts righteously.
'Cain't blame a feller for mistaking what you are when
he sees you in 'em.'

'Well, I don't mistake what he is.' Charlie was fierce,
and, looking through the door at the mountains beyond,
she blinked tears from her eyes. How could everywhere
be so beautiful, and men be so vile? Doubtless they were
all drinking themselves stupid in the Aces High, and
laughing with her tormentor about silly Charlie Nelson,
who wore men's pants, kept the store and despised men,
but couldn't stop an impudent boy from kissing her.

Most shaming and distressing of all was the memory
of how, at the last, she had melted in his arms, had not
only welcomed the kiss, but had begun to return it!
Where had all Charlie Nelson's virtue and resolution
gone to then?

And that was how it began. Nothing warned her of what
was to come. She realised that it was with hindsight that

she now understood that he was only a boy, barely twenty himself. Then, he was simply another of the hairy monsters who pursued her, and for whom she had no time. Mary McAllister, eight years later, mourned for that lost girl, tried to recall what had happened next.

Surprisingly, she had no difficulty; the very sights, sounds and, yes, the smell of that desert land were in the bedroom with her, and *him*. Yes, she wondered now at how easily she had forgotten him—and herself—but, of course, she hadn't. Always behind the proper creature who was Mary McAllister wild Charlie lived and breathed—and Link Travis with her. . .

Later that same day Charlie was behind the counter in her store. She had had to endure a series of customers this afternoon, who had come, not to buy, but to commiserate with her over Link's behaviour. That was on the surface; secretly they were highly amused that hoity-toity pants-wearin' Charlie Nelson had at last received her come-uppance. The only thing which she got out of all this was that she sold several reels of cotton, two packets of pins, and one of needles—all excuses for coming in.

She was perched on a stool replacing a box containing lace trimming, which her last visitor had refused after she had brought it down from the top shelf, when she heard the door open and shut behind her. She turned— to see that it was *him*. Standing there, as large as life, his greasy hat in his hand.

Rage mounted in her. What had he come back for? To annoy and to assault her again? Her hand dropped to the gun on her hip, drew it, pointed it at his middle, and she said, 'Out! Out at once. Before I let a hole in you.'

Sheer amusement crossed Link's face at the sight of her standing on the stool, face rigid with anger, the heavy gun pointed at him at short range.

'Come now, mam. Yuh won't shoot me, shorely. Ain't done nothing yet.'

'Shorely will, Link whoever-you-are. Jus' try me. One wrong word and you'll not jump on a girl again.'

'Came to apologise, mam, for a-teasin' of you. Not to have a hole blown in me.'

'Apologise?' She waved the gun at him, which made him bob and weave and caper, an absurd expression of feigned alarm on his face.

'Woah, now, mam. Hold that thing still. Might go off accidental-like. Take my head with it if yore not careful.'

'No, it won't,' said Charlie angrily. 'I know exactly what I'm doing with it. And I meant what I said. Out.'

'Well, now, mam,' he said, still laughing, face alight with mischief so that she suddenly saw that he was, as she had suspected, not very much older than herself, the grime and stubble deceiving those about him as to his true age. 'D'yuh treat all yore customers like this, mam? Shorely not, or yuh'd never make a livin'.'

The gun was growing heavy in Charlie's hand. She holstered it and stepped down from her stool to stand, businesslike, behind the counter. It was then she discovered that she had lost her advantage, since she had to look up at him, he being so much taller than she was.

'Say your piece and go. I've still a mind to blow a hole in you for the wind to whistle through.'

'Not now,' he said, still grinning at her. 'Parm me, mam, for sayin' so. Could outdraw yuh any time. Not very gallant, but the truth.'

'You said that you wanted to apologise. Do it—and go!'

'Shorely will,' he said, imitating her own speech of a moment ago, and, spurred on by the mixture of annoyance, and, yes, almost amusement at his impudence on her pretty, lively face, he dropped on to his knees, raised his hands, lightly clasped them together, like an actor in a melodrama, and said, 'Fergive me, mam! Oh, pray, fergive! I promise yuh I'll never kiss yuh agin. Unlessen yuh ask me, that is.'

Despite herself, Charlie began to laugh. Her life since her father died had been so harsh and joyless, the men

who had approached her had been so intent on themselves, had so little of worth to say to her, and humour
had had so small a part in it, that the gaiety of the
impudent wretch on the floor before her melted her
anger at his careless public handling of her.

'Oh, do get up,' she said briskly, unable to be cross
with him any longer. 'You'll have rheumatics in your old
age something desperate if you go on like this. If you
promise to behave yourself in future, I'll promise not to
shoot you dead the next time I see you.'

He hung his head, said 'Oh, mam. Yuh've shore made
my day,' lifted it again, and rose to his feet in one
graceful movement—he was as lithe as a cat—put his
elbows on the counter, leaned forward, and added, with
the utmost seriousness, 'A Bible, mam? Yuh have a Bible
for sale?'

'A Bible?' said Charlie, taken aback by such an odd
request. 'For why a Bible, Mr Travis?'

'Link,' he said. 'Not Mister. We've gone beyond
Mister, mam. Or may I say Miz Charlie? Or even
Charlie, perhaps? No? I thought as how a little study of
the Good Book might reform my character as well as my
manners. Do yuh recommend any partickler part of it,
mam?'

Charlie gazed at him, fascinated. Such effortless impudence, combined with—yes, she had to admit it—such
effortless charm, she had seldom encountered before.
And certainly not in the roughnecks who rode into town
behind Garrity.

'Mr Travis,' she said repressively, 'it seems to me that
nothing you read in the Good or any other book, could
possibly improve your manners or your character.' She
had reverted without thinking to the Eastern and educated speech of her life with her father, and she missed
the sharp way in which her tormentor registered this,
being so preoccupied with her own strange reactions to
him.

'Not a friendly act, mam,' he said, 'towards a seeker
after salvation. First yuh want to shoot me, and then yuh

bar my road to reform. He'p a pore wand'rin' sinner, mam. Take pity on me, I beg of yuh.' And he turned his eyes on her so earnestly that she began to giggle against her will—she, Charlie Nelson, who hated gigglers.

Encouraged, he continued, 'Save the pore sinner from his sin,' and then, without changing his manner, added, 'Oh, and by the by, I need me a new bandana. This 'un I'm wearin' is full of holes.'

'Oh, you're impossible,' said Charlie, still overcome. 'And which do you want first—the Bible, or the bandana?'

'Leave that to yuh, mam. Whichever yuh think I need to rescue the most—my appearance or my soul.'

'Both beyond rescue, Mr Travis,' she said, fetching out a cardboard box, and beginning to pull out bandanas, all new and all garish.

He picked up a flaming red one, with large white spots. 'This 'un'll suit my complexion, yuh think?'

He lifted it until only his wicked eyes showed over the top. 'An improvement, Miz Charlie?' And his eyes defied her to tease him back.

'Even better if I couldn't see you at all,' she said severely, quite aware that she was treading on dangerous ground with such a cheeky ruffian. Why, he might even try to kiss her again. And suddenly, improbably, she knew that she half welcomed, but was half fearful of such an outcome.

As though he knew her thoughts, he lowered the bandana, leaned forward and said softly, 'Another one, mam? Yuh'd like another kiss?' and very gently he kissed her again, this time on the cheek—a kiss for a child, and not a grown woman, nothing offensive in it, except that when he withdrew his head and she put her hand to the spot which he had saluted his eyes were dancing.

'Shoot me now?' he invited softly.

Charlie jerked awake suddenly as though he had mesmerised her until that moment.

'Wouldn't waste bullets,' she snapped.

'Oh, never say that, mam. Fergiven, am I? Din't really mean to shame yuh so publicly. Only my fun. Went a little far, p'raps?'

'Fun!' she said, angry all over again. 'Are you taking the bandana, or not?'

'Takin it,' he said, and then put it to his cheek, head on one side, still smiling at her. 'Yuh had it, mam, and now I do. A bond between us. Yuh still haven't said that yuh fergive me.'

'Oh, you've quite worn me down with your nonsense, Mr Travis. Of course I've forgiven you. And now, if you pay me and leave, I can get on with my work.'

He looked around the store, face puzzled. It was empty but for the two of them.

'An' what work is that, mam?'

'Accounts,' she said, lying rapidly. 'Stocktaking.' And she took the money he held out, made change, gave it to him, and as he backed towards the door said, 'The Bible, Mr Travis; you've forgotten your Bible.'

For a moment he looked puzzled again, then gave her his brilliant white smile.

'Ah, yes, mam. The Bible. Wrap it up nice and purty, and I'll call for it on the way out of town. Wun't do to let my friends know I'd got religion. A secret between us, Miz Charlie. An excuse to come in agin. Another kiss when I do?' And his white smile stayed in her memory long after he had closed the door gently and gone.

Charlie sat in the large comfortable living-room at the back of the store. She had drawn the curtains against the desert night, lit the lamp, darned a pair of socks, and then had taken down one of her father's books and tried to read.

He had continued her education until the day he died, and she sometimes thought that she must be the most learned person in the Arizona Territory—even if few knew that; and what good it did her she hardly knew. The book was poetry, *Idylls of the King*, and anything less like the lords and ladies of Arthur's court than Liam

Garrity, Link Travis and the rest of the outlaws from the Bar Y she could hardly imagine.

Faintly, from across the street, came the noise and music from the saloon, and once or twice brawling cowhands fell into the street to continue their quarrel in the open. King Arthur and his knights failed to hold her. She put the book down and thought of the past, of the mother whom she hardly remembered, the little house on Boston Common, the quiet world in which she had lived until she was fifteen.

Finally, she thought of her loneliness, and how cut off she was from civilisation, and that really she had no one to talk to as she had talked to her father.

She remembered the regret which he had expressed when he lay dying—that he knew that she would be alone—and she knew, at last, why he had worried about her. Until Link Travis had come into the shop, she had hardly spoken to anyone of near her own age. He might be uneducated, but he was articulate, and the young men of Heyes Landing were not even that.

How stupid, she thought fiercely, that a pair of wicked dark eyes, a white smile and a mocking tongue could upset her so.

She suddenly wanted all the delights of a normal girlhood which she would have had back East. Pretty dresses, giggled confidences with other girls, beaux, bouquets, skating parties on a frosty winter's day—she remembered them dimly—where young people gathered together. Not trousers, a six-gun, hard work and a blazing sun in a perpetually bright blue sky—everything which she had come to know and love since she had arrived in Arizona with her father suddenly seemed strange and alien.

'Oh, damn you, Link Travis! Why did you have to arrive here to upset me?' She thought of the Bible, neatly packed, and awaiting his return. Was the hairy monster right? Was she really desperate for a man to kiss her, and that man him?

She caught sight of herself in the flawed mirror over

the empty hearth, short fair curls, worried face and the blue bandana knotted inside her shirt—like a boy, like him.

'No,' she said to herself, but to what, she hardly knew, and opened the book and addressed herself sternly to Tennyson, but the words flew away. She was in the street once more, and a laughing face was looking into hers, refusing to be resisted—and kissing her.

Abruptly she rose, went to the kitchen, pumped cold water into a bowl, splashed it over her hot cheeks, held her hands in it. She told herself, he is an outlaw, a rogue, a criminal, unwashed, not properly shaven, wears his dirty hair long, is doubtless sitting in the saloon at this very minute. . .one of. . .those girls on his knee, or is gambling, and boasting about his women. . .about me? But then he made me laugh, several times. . .and I can't remember when I last laughed.

Charlie drank hot milk, tried to compose herself for sleep, retired to her little room at the side, where she lay down and, despite her fears, went to sleep almost immediately, tired out by the conflicting emotions of the day. . .

To be awoken by music and laughter in the street outside, and a man's voice singing. She lay quiet until she thought that she recognised the voice, sat up, looked at her watch—two in the morning!—and sighed. Garrity's mob frequently made the night day.

A guitar began to play, and then the voice, a pleasant if untrained baritone, began to sing a love song, a plaintive Mexican ballad, recently translated, a favourite of the locals, about a lovely, dark-eyed girl—'La Paloma', the dove. The throbbing music—for the touch on the guitar was expert, and it was being played with Latin flourish—was coming from immediately outside the store.

Charlie lit a candle, slipped out of bed, pulled on her long man's top-coat, and walked into the shop, pulled up the front window's blind, and peered out.

Link Travis, head bent over his guitar, sat cross-

legged on the pavement opposite, singing. 'La Paloma'
ended in a flourish of grace notes. He paused, swept his
hands across the strings, and began another song, a
memory of an old rebellion in England—'Charlie is my
darling'—and Charlie knew, beyond a doubt, that he
was serenading her. Windows had begun to open along
the street, the noise waking up the inhabitants of Heyes
Landing.

A mixture of rage and amusement swept through her.
Once, he looked up at the store window, the moonlight
plain on his face. The song ended, and the group of
outlaws who were lounging in the street with him,
enjoying the joke, applauded him, and called for more.

Rage won: discretion lost. Shaking—but even now
her temper was laced with amusement—Charlie opened
the door. He had begun to play 'Juanita', another
sentimental ballad, his voice wobbling and throbbing as
though he was in the last throes of lovesick passion. Her
voice as severe as she could make it, she called to him,
'Link Travis! What in the world do you think you're
doing?'

Obligingly he stopped, looked up at her, his hand
motionless on the strings. 'Thought that was plain, mam.
A serenade in yore honour.'

'At two in the morning,' she said, as repressively as
she could, and then carelessly, as she was immediately
aware—for he was as quick, witty and feral as a mountain cat—she added, 'Go to bed. You'll wake the whole
town.'

'Too late, mam. Whole town awake already. And my
bed's a lonely one, mam. Take pity on a poor lonesome
cowboy, mam, even if yuh don' like my singin'.'

All the outlaws were laughing and joking, the sally
about his lonely bed being greatly appreciated.

'Not in the middle of the night, I don't,' said Charlie,
wondering how on earth to wrongfoot him verbally. 'Not
at any time.'

'Mus' purely take some more lessons, then, mam.

P'raps a wrong choice of song. Have a favourite, do
yuh?'

'There is no right choice,' she raged, suddenly realising that she had been unwise to come out at all; there
was no holding the man. He had uncoiled himself
rapidly, rose, and walked across the street to her, guitar
loosely held at his side.

'Shore about that, mam?' he said softly. 'No right
song? No song that we could sing together, p'raps?'

'I knew that you were impossible this afternoon. At
two in the morning you're insufferable. Of course there
is no right song.'

'In-suff-er-able,' he said, eyes dancing, dragging the
word out. 'That shore makes me sad, mam. Purtier than
ever in that get-up, mam. Deserve ever' word I sang.'

By now the outlaws were hallooing encouragement at
them both, and Link and she were standing close
together, so that she could see the laughter-lines on his
face, feel the warmth from his body, and almost drown
in his eyes, which were hard on her. Oh, God, what was
happening to her? She wanted to put out a hand to touch
the smiling mouth, saw that he knew what was troubling
her. . .

A window flew up, a head came out. Mr Potts. 'Some
on us has work to do tomorrer. Get the hell out of the
street, an' do the billin' an' cooin' indoors,' he shouted,
and the window flew down again.

'Good advice,' said Link approvingly. 'Yore keepin'
the whole town awake, mam. Shame on yuh.'

'And shame on you, Link Travis,' she said fiercely.
'Aren't there enough girls in the saloon for you? Go and
enjoy yourself there.'

'Don' want no saloon girls, mam.' And he lifted the
guitar as though he were a Mexican musician, high on
his shoulder, and played, gently, the first bars of 'Charlie
is my darling' again. 'Found yuh, haven't I?'

'I was never lost,' she blazed, and then, as if seeing
the boggling spectators for the first time, so much had

he engrossed her, rage, a delightful one, with erotic
overtones in it, overcome her again.

'No use to appeal to your better self, I see. You don't
possess one. I'll leave you to wake the town on your
own.' And she turned to enter the store again.

'Meant what I said, mam,' he called after her. 'Purtiest
sight I ever seen. Purtier still in a temper.' And he
played her a final riff on the guitar, full of flourishes and
stamping feet, with his fellow outlaws clapping and
cheering in unison, so that no one was left asleep in the
whole town.

The noise accompanied her, the banging of the store
door being her only riposte, which she did so fiercely
that the glass in it nearly fell out.

Once in her room again, she sank on the bed, cheeks
hot and scarlet, her body aflame. For the first time in
her life it was awake, and ripe for love, so stirred by the
monster outside that, had he been with her, the good
Lord knew what she might have done with him. No
need to call on God—she knew herself! And what she
wanted could not be admitted by a decent, untouched
single girl.

And at whom should she direct her anger—him or
herself? Every time she saw him a strange excitement
gripped her, to be exorcised only by being annoyed with
him; otherwise. . . Otherwise what? Mr Potts had said
billin' an' cooin'. Was that what they were doing, she
and Link? Of course it was! A sensible girl would not
have opened the door to bandy words with him, to
encourage him—would, on the contrary have ignored
him.

Are you a sensible girl, Charlie? she asked herself—to
receive back the message, Face it, Charlie, face it. You
were flattered, weren't you, to be serenaded by a young
ruffian, who, to be fair, played the guitar so beautifully—
and all for you? What can be wrong with you, to be
seduced by a gun-slinger and an outlaw—one of Garrity's
mob, whom you have always despised?

'I'm lonely,' she admitted aloud. 'And he's young,

and has an artful way with words, for all his other uncouthness. He can't be much older than I am, if at all. And all the other men here are so dull. Link Travis isn't dull. . .and he makes me feel alive.'

The music had stopped once she had left the street. Outside all was quiet. Was he with one of the girls whom she had recommended to him so savagely? Oh, she did hope not. Her body, which had come to life today, told her that she could not bear to think of him enjoying himself—like that—with one of them.

'Oh, you're an idiot, Charlie Nelson,' she said aloud. 'What else would he be doing? How can you be mesmerised by such an. . .oaf? Go to sleep, do.'

But sleep was long in coming, even though the night was now quite silent, and the day seemed like a far country whose shore she would never reach.

CHAPTER NINE

MARY McALLISTER, sitting on her bed, uncounted miles away from Arizona, eight years later, wondered at the girl she had been, wondered at her own ability to recall what she had for so long denied had ever happened. Had she truly been that wild creature, passionate, vibrant and forthright, ready to fall into the arms of a charming rapscallion? Memory said yes.

And the next morning? What had happened then? Mrs Potts in the store, severe. 'You'd best not encourage that scallywag who's jus' joined Garrity's lot, Charlie. Not like you to bandy words with such good-for-nothings. Ignore them. That's best.'

Hers was not the only voice Charlie heard that day, saying similar things. It was as though it were she who had sat in the street singing, waking up the whole town, she thought resentfully. As though she, Charlie Nelson, were to blame, and not Link Travis.

Around midday Garrity's mob wandered out of the saloon, blinking their eyes at the sun. They were obviously ready to leave. She wondered whether Link would call for the Bible which he had so improbably bought. Just when she had decided that he had given up on her, the doorbell went and he was in the store.

'Came for the Good Book, mam. Seem to need its teachin's.'

'You shouldn't make fun of the Gospel, Mr Travis,' she said severely, handing it over, trying to avoid his merry eyes.

'Oh, not the Book, mam. Wun't make fun of that. It's me, yuh see. Want to do what's right, but Satan's allus whisperin' in my ear.'

'Like last night, you mean,' she said, unwise again.

'That's it, mam. Got it in one. Seemed a good idea at

the time to serenade my girl. Fergot that it might upset others. Troubled yuh today, have they? Not yore fault.'

Charlie noted the penitence in the last sentences, but seized on an earlier word.

'Your girl, Link Travis? Whatever should make you think that I'm your girl?'

'No one else's girl, are yuh, mam? Sad, that. Right purty young lady like yuh should be choosing from her beaux, not lookin' for 'em. Men 'round here blind?'

'Oh. . .' said Charlie, exasperated all over again. 'What business is it of yours?'

He leaned forward over the counter, holding the Bible in both hands, and before she could stop him she received yet another kiss, on the cheek this time.

'So soft,' he said admiringly, 'so soft,' and gave her another, lightly, like a butterfly landing.

'Yuh see. That's why it's my business. Cain't resist yuh, can I? Don' go round kissin' every girl, mam.'

'Well, you can for me!' She blazed at him, her treacherous cheek telling her that it liked his repeated salute.

'Now, mam, yuh don' mean that. Hear as how there's a dance here on Saturday in the church rooms, mam. An' a box supper. Share yore supper with me, mam?'

'I don't go to dances,' she said repressively.

'Well, yuh jes go for once, mam—an' wear a skirt, fer me,' he said, his white smile flashing again. 'Purty gal like yuh needs some fun in her life.'

'Mr Travis,' she said, floundering a little at failing to deter his naughtiness—that seemed the proper word, somehow, 'your friends seem to be about to leave. They will go without you if you dally here any longer with me.'

'Dally, mam? Is that what we're doin'?' And his eyes twinkled.

'No! It's what *you're* doing. Oh, take your Bible and go. Read it when you get to that hell-hole Garrity calls a ranch and mend your manners.'

He bent his head to look at it, and said meekly,

'Fergive yore enemies, it says here, mam. Fergive me, will yuh?'

'If you'll only go, I'll forgive you anything.'

'S'pose that'll have to do, mam.' He walked to the door, his Stetson, which he had lain down on a barrel lid, in one hand, and the Bible in the other. 'See yuh on Saturday, mam. Save a dance fer me.'

He was gone. And the room seemed empty without him. She saw him walk over to his horse hitched to the saloon rail, carefully put the Bible in one of his saddle-bags—what could he want it for?—and then mount in one easy movement.

He was as lithe and acrobatic as most of Garrity's men were heavy. They all milled around in the street for a moment or two, some of them shouting to Link, who shouted back—about herself, probably—and then they thundered off. They had seen the elephant—for so they called a rowdy night in town, after the elephant painted on many saloons' external walls—but would probably be back again for Saturday's dance.

She sighed. Mrs Potts bounced in. 'I saw him come in, Charlie. What did he want this time?'

'He called for the Bible he had bought,' said Charlie truthfully. 'That's all.'

'His Bible? Fancy that! He can read.'

'Yes,' said Charlie—she suddenly knew, beyond a doubt, that for all his rough exterior Link could read. The agile tongue betrayed that.

'But a Bible! Why should he want a Bible?'

'To improve his manners,' Charlie almost snarled, tired of Mrs Potts's well-meaning inquisition.

'Book of etiquette better for that.' Mrs Potts sighed. 'Sounds like an excuse to talk to you, Charlie. You mind what I say; don' go hankering after fly-by-nights like Link Travis. You'd be better off with Preacher Mason.'

'Don't want either of them, do I?' blazed Charlie, trying to forget impudent eyes and butterfly kisses. 'And now, if you'll excuse me, I've work to do in back.'

Which was a lie. But she had to get rid of old Mother

Potts somehow. Was everything she did watched, criticised and gossiped about? Go to the Saturday night dance, indeed! Not she!

But she did, and in skirts, carrying the boxed supper which she had made up herself, to sit among the ranchers' and miners' and shopkeepers' daughters, and the rest of the respectable town girls in the church hall, her cheeks flaming, ignoring the whispered comments of the town's elders, disliking the approval of the town's matrons, who were pleased that she had resumed a decent woman's garments at last.

Charlie genuinely had no idea of how pretty she was. The older Mary McAllister remembered that with a rueful smile. She had tied a broad blue band around her curly blonde hair to disguise its shortness. Her dress was an old blue and white gingham one, with a deep blue sash to match the band. It was a little short—but that merely provided an excellent view of her shapely ankles and small, slender feet, the latter in elegant black slippers, for all the men to admire.

Preacher Mason came over and made a fuss of her, and all the old biddies looked rancidly at poor Charlie for apparently removing a desirable man from their daughters' reach. Fancy the preacher favouring a girl who cut her hair short and wore men's trousers! There were some who regretted that she had abandoned them. She looked far too pretty in skirts.

'You will do me the honour of a dance, Miss Charlie,' said the preacher, and led her on to the floor. He eyed her box supper, and Charlie was suddenly aware whose supper the preacher was going to buy in the raffle. She quite enjoyed dancing with him.

'So glad that you have decided to honour us with your presence,' he said in his stiff, formal way—no dreadful jokes and snatched kisses were to be expected from the preacher.

'Yes,' said Charlie. 'I thought that I was spending too much time alone.'

'You should join our sewing circle,' said the preacher kindly. 'I gather that new fingers are wanted.'

'Keeping the store doesn't leave me much time for that,' said Charlie, desperate to do no such thing. She was surreptitiously looking around to see if any of Garrity's men had arrived, but there was no sign of him—or them.

Next, Chet Potts, the gangling Potts heir, favoured her. She knew, dismally, that Mrs Potts would like the store, as well as herself, to be part of the Pottses' small empire.

'Say, Charlie, you look real swell tonight. Skirts suit you.' He blushed when he had said this, thinking it perhaps not proper to remind a girl that she wore pants. 'See you brought your supper box along. Ma says you make great cookies.'

As conversation this could hardly be thought exciting either. Chet held her as though she were china and would break if held too hard—amusing, thought Charlie cynically, who knew what he got up to with the marshal's daughter; she wondered if his Ma knew. Link had been teasing her, she decided. Of course he wouldn't come to a church supper. She didn't know whether she was glad or sorry at his absence. Yes, she did. Sorry, sorry, sorry! She was aware that Chet had asked her a question, and had no idea what it was.

'I'm sorry,' she said, 'I didn't quite catch that,' which had been just as well, she thought as Chet launched into a windy description of his prowess in riding some of the wild broncos which Garrity kept at his ranch to sell to legitimate ranchers when he had broken them.

Next it was Preacher Mason again, asking her to step out. His interest worried her. She quite liked him. He was not a bad-looking man, and talked to her about books, although he thought that she really ought to read the milk-and-water stuff most of the girls in Heyes Landing read, and cried over, like *The Wide, Wide World*, and was quite shocked to learn that she liked Dickens and Thackeray—particularly Thackeray—

'Such an immoral cynic, Miss Charlie.' She had a dreadful mischievous desire to ask him an intelligent question about Plato. That would put him off for good, she thought.

He held her a little more tightly than Chet, and his conversation was certainly more cultured, if dull in a different way. All the novels she had read, and the whispered comments of the girls she had associated with, told her that if you really like a man you felt a special thrill when you met and talked to him. There was no special thrill for her in the preacher's company, although by the way he looked at her, and squeezed her hand when he spoke to her, she was certainly doing something to him.

And now she didn't know what *he* had been saying to her. So she nodded and smiled, and said, 'Yes, indeed,' because those were the two words most men seemed to expect from her, and she hoped that she hadn't agreed to anything irrevocable.

A terrible thought struck her, so that she stopped dancing, and the poor preacher fell over her feet.

'Oh, I am so sorry,' she said, wailing a little. 'I can't imagine what came over me.'

Oh, what a lie that was! She had suddenly remembered that she certainly felt a thrill when that dreadful boy Link spoke to her. Dear lord, was *that* what the novels meant? That excitement which she felt in his presence, which was making her look about for him now? The disappointment she felt at his non-arrival? How could a pony-tailed rapscallion make her feel like that, and the preacher such a kind, good, well set-up man, make her feel nothing at all? She must pay attention to what he was saying.

'I own it is un-Christian of me,' said Preacher, 'but I am so pleased that Garrity and his men are not honouring us with their presence tonight. We can hardly keep them out. Our Lord would not approve of me, I know, for thinking so, but they come here reeking of drink. . .and the places where they have been.' He could not say saloon to virtuous Miss Charlie. 'They set such a bad example to the young.'

'But our Lord says, "He that is without sin among you, let him first cast a stone",' Charlie could not help saying.

'Oh, but that was in quite a different context,' Preacher replied swiftly, and then flushed scarlet to think that he could refer, however indirectly, to fallen women—and that Miss Charlie should have brought them into the conversation. . .! Respectable young ladies should not know about them.

Charlie saw his confusion and was sorry. Was this the man whom Mrs Potts thought, after Chet, she ought to marry? What a choice! Dismally she was aware that if this was truly all that there was for her, and if she showed interest in his tedious courtship, she would go to the altar and emerge as Mrs Preacher before he had laid so much as a respectful finger on her. She didn't want his fingers—respectful or disrespectful—but at least his intentions were entirely honourable——What on earth were Link Travis's?

The dancing stopped. Everyone looked expectant, and all the girls were picking up their supper boxes since they were rapidly nearing the point when the boxes would be auctioned off to the highest bidder, and their owner with them, to enjoy a joint meal, the money raised going to the church's funds. And, of course, the way things were going, she was about to share her supper with the preacher, who was giving her a look so soulful that she felt that she really ought to start singing a hymn.

Everyone would be pleased if she accepted Preacher—except Charlie Nelson. Papa would have been pleased. Mrs Potts would be pleased. Heyes Landing would be pleased. Charlie Nelson tamed and settled down at last. She tried to visualise her life as respectable Mrs Preacher, but couldn't. Oh, why was she such a restless, flighty thing?

Mr Potts, the senior sidesman, rose importantly, his gold watch-chain strained across his fat stomach, to raffle

off the boxes. The other girls began to giggle. Charlie
hated gigglers. That was why men thought women were
silly. She never giggled, and wasn't allowed to give a
good hearty laugh—ladies weren't supposed to do any
such thing.

One by one the girls, boxes and men were paired off.
Mr Potts was going clockwise around the room. Her
turn soon. She clutched the box to her, saw the preacher's eye on her, smiling. No, I don't want him, I want to
go home. No, what do I want? she moaned silently.

'Now, Miz Charlie, seein' as how yuh've finally consented to come. . .' boomed Mr Potts, reaching her at
last. She stood up, all eyes on her, so engrossed by her
coming, unwanted fate—for every man left would hold
back for the preacher—that she failed to hear the door
open, and a fresh, noisy party arrive.

As she had expected, everyone did hold back, and
Preacher made his modest bid—all of five dollars,
enough to discourage anyone else, nearly half a cowhand's wages for a week—and Mr Potts was about to
declare that Charlie was Preacher's for the rest of the
evening, when a new voice broke in.

'Jes' a moment, Mr Potts, sir. Can take a new bid,
cain't yuh? No boxes reserved beforehand, are they?' It
was Link, with some of Garrity's gang behind him. It
was they who had entered just before the bidding for
Charlie's supper had begun.

'Well. . .' said Mr Potts.

'Very well,' said Link. 'Ten dollars I bid for Miz
Charlie's supper.' And he grinned at Charlie holding her
box and the preacher standing beside her, ready to take
her hand. Link was as disreputable as ever, his pony-tail
even longer, clothes even shabbier. By rights it should
have been no contest over whom she preferred—
Preacher Mason should have won hands down. But that
odd, strange joy seized her again.

The preacher looked at Charlie, looked at Link. Miss
Charlie could surely not want such a desperado to share
her supper and the rest of the evening? He gulped, and

said in a brave voice, 'I bid twelve dollars.' He could hardly believe that it was he who was wagering such an immense sum.

He need have had no fear that he was in danger of having to hand it over, even though Mr Potts looked at Link, convinced that Preacher had won; but Link had other ideas.

'Well, now,' he drawled. 'A brave bid. But not enough, Preacher, not enough. I bid forty dollars. That should do it, wun't yuh say?'

Forty dollars! A cowhand's monthly wage, the cost of a good saddle, or four horses! And all for Miz Charlie and her supper. That settled it. Preacher Mason helplessly watched Link paying over his greenbacks. He should have been pleased to see his church funds so swelled, but he wasn't. And Charlie and her supper were Link's, and improbably her heart was singing.

They walked towards each other, all eyes on them. The preacher knew that he had lost her—but then, he had never really had her. They were both, he suddenly thought, so achingly young.

Charlie knew nothing of this, and the mature Mary had a brilliant flash of total recall. She saw again the tall boy, bending his head gravely towards her in quite a solemn bow, not at all the jesting man he had been the night he had serenaded her.

'Miz Charlie, allow me,' he said, and he took the box from her. Unknowingly, her face blazed its new message at him. Link took her arm, and, realising that they were being watched from all sides by prurient eyes, walked her away from them into the shadows.

Charlie walked beside him as though she were in a dream. Almost as though he knew this, he whispered in her ear, 'Outside, Miz Charlie, there's a moon, and we can be in the open air.'

Caution said, no, safer to stay inside, although she knew that several couples had already slipped out of the hall to be alone. But to be alone with Link? Would that be wise? What was wisdom? Unresisting, happy not to

be stared at, she allowed him to lead her through the
door.

Outside, no one was visible. Muffled giggles came
from the lee of a small shed where another pair of
lovers—was that what she was, one half of a pair of
lovers?—were enjoying themselves.

Link was right. The moonlight shone on the desert
which was all about them, once they moved even the
smallest way away from the homes of men. Strange
shadows from rocks, cacti and the occasional twisted
Joshua tree fell across the pebbled floor. They slowly
mounted a short slope to come to a plateau, where below
them Heyes Landing lay, its feeble lights pale imitations
of the stars beginning to appear above them.

The moon had not long risen and the mauve sky was
still full of banners of colour, ranging across the whole
spectrum of the rainbow from violet to red, with turquoise predominant. Link put down the box, removed
his slicker, put that down, too, and invited Charlie to sit
on it—'So's not to spoil yore purty dress,' he said.

Still unwontedly silent, still under the spell of some
strange compulsion, Charlie did what he asked. He sat
beside her, opened the box, and found the filled rolls,
the cookies Charlie had baked that morning, the two
oranges, part of a consignment which had come in on
the stage from California a week ago, and the little screw
of candies.

'Oh, my,' he said, his eyes shining in the moonlight. 'A feast, Miz Charlie.' He had stopped calling
her mam since he had bid for her, and he handed her a
roll, adding slyly, 'Purty, ain't it?' pointing at the
heavens above them. 'Would have missed this, wun't
you, if the preacher had won you? Still be down in that
dusty hall.'

Charlie spoke at last to say, 'Yes,' and looked from
him to the opalescent sky. They were quite private, she
realised. The others had stayed close to the hall. He did
not speak again while they ate, except to commend the

quality of the cookies, asking gravely, 'Home-baked, Miz Charlie?'

To which she answered a dazed, 'Yes.'

'Can allus tell,' he answered her. 'Now, Cookie at Garrity's can jes' about manage bacon and beans. Shorely do miss home cookin'. Lady of all the talents, Miz Charlie. Pack a gun and cook as well. Tapestry work, too?'

'Yes,' she said, reduced to the monosyllable by the magic of the night and the magic of—face it, Charlie—him.

'Mus' pay yuh for this banquet,' he said, eating the last candy and adding, 'Home-made, too? Now, what kin' of payment would yuh like, mam?' He was teasing again. 'Mam' was for teasing, 'Miz Charlie' for serious— she had worked that one out, at last.

'No need for payment, Link.' There, she had said his name at last, without scolding him.

'Oh, I mus' pay, mam.' He leaned over—they had been sitting side by side, a little apart—and he kissed her cheek, just as he had done earlier in the week, quite gently. He sat back, gave her his white smile again—his teeth were noticeably better than those of the other men she knew—and added, 'Not enough, mam. More, wun't yuh say, mam?'

'No—yes,' she said idiotically, mesmerised.

'Oh, Miz Charlie, you shorely are so purty.' And this time when he leaned forward he put his hands on her shoulders and first kissed the other cheek—'No favourites,' he said, surfacing for a moment—and after that transferred his attention to her mouth, which, unresisting, allowed him to do as he pleased with it.

The Mary McAllister remembering all this now realised how gentle he had been with her—that he, despite his youth, recognised the inexperience of the girl he had been dealing with, the vulnerability behind the tough image which she presented to the world, and had treated her accordingly.

She remembered, too, how sweet that first short

passage of love had been, the shock of understanding
that this was what she had wanted from him ever since
their first clash in the street, that something lay between
them, the boy and girl they had been, more powerful
than anything she had ever known, or was to know again
until she met Jared.

Link had known it, too. He had pulled away after a
time when the kissing and embracing had grown a little
more passionate—he stroking her breasts through her
clothing—and she, shivering with delight, had pressed
herself to him, not knowing what to do with her own
hands, until he said gently, 'Enough, Miz Charlie. More
for another day.'

Shamingly, she had not wanted him to stop. She had
always thought that when he came her lover would be
like the engravings of Prince Charming in her book of
fairy-tales, smooth, and sleek, not a wild, unshaven boy,
the grime of outlaw-living on his clothes, his blue-black
glossy hair not cut short and carefully groomed but long,
tied by a raw-hide strip into a pony-tail which hung
down his back.

She wanted to undo the raw-hide, let the long hair
free, especially when she realised from the smell of him
that, despite the grimy clothing, the body beneath was
clean, and the hair had been recently washed.

'Time to go back,' he said. 'Wun't want to ruin yore
reputation. Bad enough I court yuh at all, I s'pose.'

'Court you'? Was that what he was doing? Courting
her? Could he conceivably be serious? He was on his feet
again in one of his graceful movements, the empty box
and discarded wrappings in one hand, his other held out
to her as he stood, tall against the night sky.

She took the offered hand, rose, and he pulled her to
him and said, 'Look at the stars, Miz Charlie,' and when
she did, lifting her head to see them, shining grave above
them, he kissed her exposed throat and delight shivered
through her.

'Yuh too, Miz Charlie,' he said softly into her ear.
'Yuh feel the magic of the night too.' And he kissed the

ear for good measure, before helping her down the
hillside to return her to the hall.

Charlie knew that she might as well be wearing a sign
reading 'I have been soundly and thoroughly kissed',
and she was not far wrong. Loving and being loved had
made her face so soft and sweet that belligerent Charlie
Nelson seemed to have disappeared for good, and more
than one young man wondered what he had missed by
overlooking her. Preacher Mason's glance for her was
sorrowful, but in her new-found joy his sadness hardly
registered with her at all.

The rest of the evening passed like a dream. She drank
lemonade, only with *him*. Danced, but only with *him*,
sat in a corner, only with *him*, her hand warm in *his*. *He*
walked her home, and she ignored Mrs Potts's shaking
and warning head when she left, and *he* kissed her again
at the door to the store and stood there, keeping guard
until she let herself in.

His last words were, 'Go ridin' with me tomorrow,
Miz Charlie? In the evenin' when it's cool. Be ready for
me, will yuh?'

'Yes,' she had said. 'Yes.' And even now, eight years
later, a sadder and a wiser Mary McAllister could
remember that happy girl going to her bed thinking only
of. . .*him*, of course.

CHAPTER TEN

STILL back in the past, Mary remembered that, true to his promise, Link had come to her the following evening, walking into the store in the middle of Mrs Potts's objurgations to her to avoid all such fly-traps as Link Travis was.

He was carrying his guitar, and gave Mrs Potts the benefit of his charming white smile, so that she could suddenly see why Charlie was so drawn to him.

'Arternoon, ladies. I brung my guitar, Miz Charlie. Thought you might prefer to hear it in the day, rather than the night,' he said, before Mrs Potts had bounced out, after giving Charlie further meaningful looks.

He sat on one of the barrels, and played and sang Spanish love songs for her, while she tidied the store and made up the books for the day as her father had taught her.

'Tea?' she said questioningly, to receive the reply,

'Make a nice change from cawfee, mam,' and he followed her into the room at the back.

Charlie had worried about asking him in, but he sat there as good as gold, the teacup in his hand, his face angelic—if a hairy desperado's face could be angelic, that was—eating sandwiches and then cookie after cookie: his appetite was enormous.

They even made small talk. Charlie could not ask him about his past, and never did so, either then, or in the following six weeks of their time together, while he carried out his courtship of her—for courtship it was.

'And do you like the desert country, Mr Travis?' she began.

'Link, mam, Link,' he answered. 'We've gone beyond Misters, shorely.'

'Link, then,' she said shyly.

'I must allow as how I do. Thought I might not like it so dry, but it shore is beautiful.' And he gazed hard at her face when he spoke, so that she blushed, and looked even prettier. Always now his face told her how pretty he thought she was.

'Father said that it was the night sky which was the finest thing,' Charlie said, 'after the natural beauties, like Oak Creek Canyon, which we rode out to see once.'

'Yore pa died not long ago, they said, mam. You must miss him.'

'Oh, I do.' Charlie's face grew mournful. 'Poor Father. He was better for a short time after we reached here, but then he failed very rapidly.' She thought it might be safe to ask after his father. The unwritten rule about not quizzing Westerners about their past did not extend, she thought, to such an innocuous question as that.

She was wrong. The merry face opposite her darkened, his whole manner changed completely and he said, shortly, 'Dead, mam,' after a fashion which discouraged further questioning.

But his untoward seriousness did not last long, and presently he rose, insisted on helping her to wash the dishes, and then went out back, and saddled her horse for her, the stern look which had passed briefly over his face gone so completely that she thought that she had imagined it.

The rest of the evening was a delight. They rode into the desert together, and when they dismounted he put down a blanket, fetched out his guitar, and played and sang to her. The mature Mary now realised that much of what he did was to shorten the time when, as was inevitable given two healthy young bodies in propinquity, they began to kiss and cuddle.

He obviously knew what dangers lay in too much of *that*. But gradually their lovemaking went further and further, extending beyond the exchange of innocent kissings and strokings, although he always ended it before they went too far.

Their excursion was the first of many. Once, they

went off for the whole day, carrying food and water, into the foothills of the mountains which surrounded the hollow in which Heyes Landing lay—mountains which were the colour of milk chocolate, rather than the usual blue, and which in the evening turned a burnished red-gold.

Together, they watched them change colour more than once, lying back on the blanket, only their hands touching in silent communion.

On the first whole day together alone they rode to one of the few natural lakes in the entire Territory, and picnicked on its shores. Afterwards they had sat talking together. 'So's our grub can go down,' he had said, and then he had pulled her to her feet, pointed to the lake, held her close to him, looking into her eyes, his own merry, 'Skinny-dip, shall us, Charlie?'

She avoided the eyes, flushed scarlet, shaking her head, frightened a little—not of bathing naked, but of what might happen afterwards.

'No?' he said. 'Another time, p'raps?' And he had not forced her, or tried to persuade her otherwise, but merely laughed, and then had run her to the water's edge, where they had paddled, boots and socks off, trousers rolled up, like two innocent children.

She remembered that his patent love of natural beauty, in one so apparently ignorant and uncouth had surprised her, although looking back, with her greater knowledge of the world, she realised that many times he had said and done things which betrayed a wider background than a raw boy of no family or education might have been expected to have.

He went so slowly with her. After the aggressive caresses of their first encounter, his later holding back, his care not to take her further than they ought to go, was another surprise.

All the same, Heyes Landing was shocked at her capitulation to one of the rowdiest of Garrity's gang. He fought and frolicked and swore as much and more as any of them when he was not with her, but he avoided the fancy women in the saloon, whom once he might have patronised. Charlie, and Charlie alone, was his girl, and so he told her.

She knew that he had once gone with the soiled doves in the Aces High, because Mrs Potts took care to inform her so. 'Shouldn't encourage him, Charlie,' she said severely, 'but I must allow that he's been a good boy since he met you, Potts says, so there must be something to him.' And then, 'Biding his time with you, prolly. You be careful, miss.'

Did she want to be careful? Not when she was with him, that was for sure. There were days when she did not see him. Once, he disappeared for a whole week, and when he returned he sat in her parlour, tired and grim-faced, all his jokes missing, and Charlie said nothing, leaving him to himself, while she tended the store.

An odd thing. When she returned to the parlour, he was reading, and he put the book back without saying anything when he saw her. Later, curious, she went to the shelves to see what had interested him. He had pushed it back among its fellows, but she knew it, had recognised the purple and gilt binding in his hands, and had thought, No, he could not be reading that, not that. It was Kant's *Critique of Pure Reason*, and she wondered what on earth he had made of it. Simple curiosity, perhaps.

Link had brightened again, and he took her hand, pulled her on his knee, and began to kiss her, murmuring, 'Sweet Charlie, dear Charlie, you perfume the whole landscape.' Surely *Kant* hadn't inspired him to that! She kissed him back, and then cooked them supper. 'Useful, as well as beautiful,' he said, leaning against the wall, his face soft again.

Afterwards he walked her out, hand in hand, quite proper, Heyes Landing's eyes on them, and the people making comments like, 'Shore no good could come of this. Who'd have thunk it, Miz Charlie caught by a wild, young gunslinger?' and a train-robber and bank robber, too, for that was what Garrity's mob had been up to the previous week.

The preacher stopped her one day, his face sad. 'Are you sure that you know what you're doing, Charlie? A girl of good family like yourself to take up with such a rogue. If you need help or advice at any time, you know where to find me. The Lord's arms are open wide.'

And so are yours, Preacher, for me, so are yours, thought irreverent Charlie, but said aloud, defiantly, 'Yes, I do know where to find you, and no, I don't require any help or advice.'

That Sunday she took Link to church, where he behaved himself, was meek and quiet, only saying afterwards, somewhat surprisingly, 'Preacher shorely took the wrong text—"Love thy neighbour". Should have used "Vengeance is mine; I will repay, saith the Lord"—except, of course, He never does, leaves it to us to do His dirty work.'

His voice was harsh and mocking, quite unlike its usual light tones, as though he was teasing not her, but the whole world, and it was true that the good burghers of Heyes Landing didn't find him sufficiently respectful to them, something which they constantly told poor Charlie—not realising that opposition and criticism simply made her love him the more.

The days streamed by, so fast, where once they had previously crawled so slowly. Such a vital part of her life to have gone like a dream, Mary McAllister thought. And when the end came she was not ready for it.

It was a Sunday. A hot day. The air was like crystal, the sky a heavenly blue. He had said that they would spend it together, go to the lake again, and she had prepared food for the day. He would come early, had been his last words to her, and she watched for him through the store window.

She saw him ride in, heading for the store like an arrow from a bow. His face, as he dismounted, was shuttered, closed. She could believe the stories that he was deadly, with his gun as well as his tongue, and that, for all his youth, it was he who had organised Garrity's recent successful raids on the bank, over to Bisbee, where the mining company kept its money, and on the train, carrying gold and greenbacks to it.

But, when he entered, he was the Link whom she loved, joking and laughing, Link at his maddest. He strode towards her, put his two hands around her tiny waist—yes, it had been tiny then—and swung her into the air, laughing and squealing.

'Put me down, Link! Whatever are you at?' But, of course, she didn't want him to put her down, wanted him to go on with his jesting play.

He perched her on his shoulder, said, 'Top shelf, Charlie. Need me a new string for m'guitar,' and, seated there, she opened the box near the ceiling, fetched out the rarely asked for strings and handed them to him.

Link put her down, went outside, fetched the guitar in, and, sitting on the counter, began to restring it.

'What payment now, mam?' he said, lifting his head, which had been bent over his work, his clever fingers having finished their task. He was neat and perfect in all he did, despite his wild appearance, and she loved him for that, too.

He lifted her up again, beside him on the counter, and he swung into 'Clementine', playing it as he did for Garrity's gang, giving the words a faint mocking intonation, but the eyes on her were loving, and instead of Clementine he sang, 'Oh, my darlin', oh, my darlin', oh, my darlin' Charlie girl,' and ended the song with the fiercest kiss he had given her for some time.

It seemed particularly reckless to be embracing him, there in the store, where she was usually proper Miss Charlie Nelson, surrounded by canned tomatoes and beans, salted bacon, yard goods, coffee, sacks of flour, hardware, a roll of barbed wire in the corner, and boots, standing on their cardboard boxes beneath shelves filled with the working clothes of the West.

He broke off the kiss, saying, 'More later, mam,' and

together they collected the impedimenta for a trip to the
lake. But there was something on his mind, she was
sure. His gaiety was a little wild and forced, but gradually, after their ride, and later, sitting on the hillside, he
steadied down, was his usual easy and happy self again.

Link spread a blanket on the stony ground. Strangely,
Mary remembered the blanket clearly. It was an Indian
one, with faded pinks and turquoise patterns on it, and
a dark, rich brown background. He had bought it in
Tucson, he had said, one of the few times when he had
referred to his past. She still had no idea of where he had
come from, and who, or what, his family was—or even
if he had one, and was not one of the nameless orphans
who had found a home in the south-west.

With his eyes on her, loving her, they ate their food,
and drank from their water bottles, the sole wine they
had, and then Link walked her down to the lake, and
pitched stones in it. 'Watch, Charlie!' he shouted, before
showing her how to make the stones skip in and out of
the water several times before they disappeared into it.

Link loved to teach her to do things. He had shown
her how to play chords on his guitar, and she could
pluck out 'Three Blind Mice'. After throwing stones, he
said, 'Come on, Charlie, target-practice time.' He was
educating her in the proper use of the Colt revolver she
wore on her hip.

He set out their targets—stones and empty cans which
he had brought with him—teaching her to do a fast
draw, and then turn and whirl, firing the gun while
pointing it as though it were a finger. When she was
successful, her reward was more innocent lovemaking.
That day, she remembered, she had done very well, and
with a shout of joy after five cans out of six flew away he
had pulled her to him and kissed her.

Apart from that, from a distance, they were two boys
larking, but later, when the sun began to decline, and
they had tired of active play, seated, and then lying, on
the blanket, they were not even boy and girl, but man
and woman, embracing together.

He said to her suddenly, in the middle of teasing kisses, and embraces growing bolder and more daring, 'I have to go away for a little, Charlie, leave yuh for a fortnight, mebbe. I have a duty, yuh see.' He did not tell her what the duty was.

A duty. Charlie wondered what it could be. He didn't explain, merely added—and even after all this time Mary was sure that what he had said next she had heard correctly—'I don't want to go. But I must.'

There was grief in his voice, but then he said, more brightly, 'But I shall come back for yuh.' She was sure that she remembered that aright.

He bent his head, and kissed her, and she kissed him back. The kisses became deeper, more passionate, and the caresses rapidly went beyond the half-innocent ones of the past, and on that day, because they were so soon to part, even if only for a little, the constraints which had operated between them began to disappear. They needed to prove the depth of their love for one another.

She could not remember when they passed beyond the line between affection and passion. She pulled undone the raw-hide strip which bound his long hair, and ran her hands through it—as she had long wanted to do—and he unbuttoned her shirt for the first time, to caress her revealed little breasts, instead of stroking them through the fabric.

Charlie gasped as he did so, but, rather than push the intruding hands away, she held them to her, and his thumbs caressing her nipples quickened them, so that she cried out, and thrust the rest of her body at him.

Link's breathing shortened to match her gasping, and he removed her shirt completely, so that his hands and mouth could rove over her whole torso, and his shirt followed suit, and almost before they knew it they were naked together on the blanket, nothing to stop them from exploring and loving each other's bodies thoroughly.

Mary remembered it all. The whispered endearments, his hands on her back, his mouth travelling down her body, a body which ached and quivered and constantly wanted more, even, than he was offering. Her hands pulled him tighter and tighter to her, her body lifting itself, legs parting so that he might enter her, because that was all she wanted—to have him, all of him, as he wanted her.

And the stab of pain was followed by such intense pleasure, for, moving together, they achieved a final and perfect consummation. Oh, such joy! And he had called her name aloud, drowning her own cries at the moment of final pleasure, as though they had exchanged identities, had become one another.

She was old enough, and wise enough, now, to know that the only surprising thing was that two such healthy young bodies, full of the joy of life, had taken so long to reach the final rational consequence of love and proximity. What had triggered it was his coming departure.

Afterwards, they lay quiet in one another's arms, and then he had started to his feet, pulled her up, and, hand in hand, they had run down to the lake, and played, naked, in the water, laughing and shouting their mutual joy.

Charlie could not swim, and Link had begun to teach her, the occasion for more handling, caressing and loving. She could remember no shame, no remorse, and after their play they had gone back to the blanket, and made love again.

He had said, after their second joyful climax, holding her to him, and stroking her short curls, 'Oh, I was wrong to let this happen, Charlie. I tried not to. But oh, I love yuh so. Yuh do believe me? And when I come back I shall take you home, and we shall be married.'

To the happy girl she had been, sated, replete, wanting only to hold the body which had pleasured her with such mutual love and affection, none of this mattered, except, 'You do love me?' she whispered into his long and glossy hair, loose about her.

'Yes—oh, yes, so much. I love yuh. . .' and he sought for words '. . .I love yuh forever. . .and a day.'

He wore a battered gold ring, and he slipped it from his finger as he spoke. It was too large for any of hers, but she took it, and kissed first the hand that gave it, and then the ring.

'Keep that,' he said. 'My pledge. Yuh are my wife already in the eyes of God. The eyes of men must wait a little.'

His words were as cunning in love as they had been in play. 'I shall not be away long, I promise,' he said between more butterfly kisses, sweet in the aftermath of loving. 'And when I return I shall claim yuh for my own. Oh, Charlie, I cannot lie to yuh; I have been a bad boy with the ladies—but not since I met yuh—and never again, I promise that, too.'

She could forgive him anything, anything. They were sitting up now, and she was plaiting his lustrous hair—'They will think me a squaw man at Garrity's,' he laughed, but made no attempt to undo it, and she tied it firmly with the raw-hide strip—such a thing to remember, grooming him, and loving him while she did so. She only knew that she loved him—and that he loved her.

They rode back together, and ate supper in her little room, and made love again, on her bed this time, and at the end they had clung together, like two children lost in a storm. He had not wanted to leave her at the last, renewed his promises to her, and she had believed him. Could not believe that such love could be followed by treachery.

Through the store window she had watched him ride off, the ring clutched warm in her hand. A fortnight, he had said, perhaps a little more. What was a fortnight? An eternity in one sense, nothing in another.

But it wasn't a fortnight. The weeks, and then the months, started to go by. And she was so alone.

Every cruel eye seemed to be on her, some in pity, some in amusement. Link Travis had disappeared, was gone as suddenly as he had come, leaving Charlie Nelson alone, deserted.

'Told you not to trust him, didn't I?' said Mrs Potts

shrewdly, coming in one day when he had been a month gone.

'He said that he would come back,' asserted Charlie defiantly, although her heart was growing cold and afraid.

'Oh, they allus say that. Don' mean anything.'

'He promised.'

'He said a lot of things. Potts says that he betted with Garrity that he would get into your pants. A joke, it was. They all knew.'

No! He could not have said that. Not Link. No!

'Hope you weren't a fool girl with him, Charlie Nelson. Seen the last of him, you have.'

But she had been a fool girl. Very much so. And the worst had happened, the very worst. The fool girl she was, was carrying the consequence of one afternoon's loving. The strained white face and hollow eyes were caused not only by a dreadful fear that he would never return, but by the beginnings of pregnancy.

Every morning she woke up praying that it was not so. She was merely late. But she began to be sick and felt faint, even later on in the day.

'Stomach trouble,' she told Mrs Potts one afternoon when she came in to find Charlie vomiting, face yellow, purple smudges under her eyes. She hardly knew, or cared, whether Mrs Potts believed her, she felt so ill, between betrayal and her changing body.Had he bet on destroying her virginity? Had he? And had he won his bet and taken his winnings before he left? She was beginning to believe anything as her secret Calvary wore on.

She had put Link's ring on a ribbon around her neck, wore it under her clothes. She fetched it out when she was alone. Surely he had meant what he had said? He had given her his ring. Said that he would claim it and her.

'Still poorly?' asked Mrs Potts later, in the street, talking to her cronies, and eyeing Charlie shrewdly, and Charlie said cheerfully,

'Can't seem to throw the bug off—must be the weather.' She was screaming inside, for soon the day would come when her condition would be plain to see and no lies would help her.

She met Preacher Mason after church one Sunday. He was saying goodbye to his morning flock at the church door. She had begun to feel better. Her colour had come back, and her figure was gaining a new roundness before it finally burgeoned into betraying life.

'Miss Charlie,' he said, sure that now that detestable rogue had deserted her she would have time for a good man. 'Happy to see you looking better. We are having a little hoe-down at the church hall this weekend. I would be so pleased for you to be my partner.' His eyes on her were anxious, but welcoming.

What could she say? Had she not been pregnant she might in desperation have turned to him after all. But she could not encourage him, knowing what she did. She rebuffed him.

'Thank you, but no. I have no time for dances, Preacher. New stock came in on the stage, and I haven't unpacked it yet.'

What would she have said, if she had told him the truth? I cannot accept your kind offer, for now you cannot want me. I am ruined; I was a light woman and I have paid the price for it. I am carrying my faithless lover's child. He has deserted me, and shortly all Heyes Landing will know, and what shall I do then. . .? Who will cast the first stone? How far will *your* Christian charity extend, Preacher Mason? I am curious to know. And then, But not yet, God; please, not yet. Leave me a little time, and perhaps. . .perhaps. . .*he* might even return, and take me away.

One morning she rose—and could hardly fasten her trousers. Even she could see how rapidly her appearance was beginning to change. The suspicion that Mrs Potts might know grew stronger, but she would say nothing until she was compelled to.

And then salvation came. The stage brought in the

mail one day when she was nearly three months gone, and no word or sign from him. It had all been a lie—to enjoy her, there on the blanket, and in her room before he left for good.

Silly deserted Charlie Nelson—the ring had been given to deceive her, to make her lie with him again. She took it off, stared at it, and put it in her workbox. It seemed to weigh her down, burn her skin.

There was a letter postmarked Washington in her mail, which was otherwise all to do with running the store. She read it, and a vast relief consumed her. Her mother's cousin, whom she had never met, had died. She, Charlie, was her sole remaining relative, and she had been left everything: a house and a reasonable income, enough to keep her and the child in modest comfort.

Charlie stared out of the window on to the blank street. She could sell up, leave Heyes Landing at once, her reputation intact, and arrive in Washington as a grieving widow. Why not? No one would know; others had done such a thing—why not she?

At the very end, immediately before her condition became plain, God had relented. Link's fortnight had long gone; she must accept that, as Mrs Potts had said, he would not return, and she dared wait no longer. She must leave to make a new life. He had said forever and a day, and only the day part had been true. She would sell up and go, at once.

Which she did. Mr Potts bought the store—for less than its worth, but no matter; she ached to be gone. And if Mrs Potts suspected her condition she said nothing. And she told them nothing. Not where she was going. Only back East, she said, smiling, to a little inherited estate, and with Link gone there was nothing to keep her in Arizona Territory.

The wild land which she had once loved she now hated. She would forget it. Heyes Landing and. . . Link . . .had never existed. It reminded her too much of him, and of his falsity. Love her, indeed!

On that last day, she rode out on the stage without a backward glance; the only thing she took from the Territory beside a few clothes was her father's library, which filled the trunks which the Nelsons had brought with them. Nothing was left in Arizona of Charlie Nelson except the memory of her in the minds of those who had known her for a few short years.

And the wild girl she had been was gone forever. Look where that had got her! In future she would be cold, composed Mary Charlotte Nelson McAllister—never Charlie—the widow of poor, dead James, who had never made any dreadful jokes, frolicked in the sun, teased, and mocked and loved. Not he.

She grew her hair, wore skirts, inherited Miss Nessie and the little house, bore Sally-Anne, and the steadiness at first assumed came true.

Until. . . Until Jared appeared in her life, she had been cool, respectable Mary McAllister, wild Charlie forgotten. But Charlie was still there, hiding, and had reappeared again when she had seen something of lost Link in Jared.

And it was no wonder that she had found difficulty in identifying him as her lost love. His renewed image as a wild desperado fresh before her, she compared them— the slim boy and the strong, well-built man; the Texas drawl and the clipped Eastern speech; the bearded, pony-tailed rapscallion, and the harsh, clean-shaven face of the mature Jared; the wandering, no-account gun-slinger and the millionaire man of power, from a family with its roots deep in the American past.

A Tunstall had fought with Washington, and there had always been one among the nation's rulers. And Jared Tunstall was the friend and associate of the most powerful men in Europe, the lover of princesses, suave, sophisticated, not at all like the carefree boy with whom she had played in the water and made love with on a blanket in the Arizona desert. Small wonder that she had found difficulty in believing Jared was Link, as he had found it difficult to believe that she, who had changed so

much, was his boyish, tempestuous Charlie, so grave
and reserved as she now was.

Slowly, still in the clothes which she had worn when
Jared had come to her, to revive the past, she lay down
on the bed and slept. And, in her dreams, she was a girl
again, not with him, but alone, frantic, riding in the
desert, searching, searching for the lover who had left
her. . .and had not come again. . .

And Jared—what was he remembering, after their
delayed reunion? Only that beyond the sweetness of their
summer's loving there was the bitter memory of his own
return. . . He had been late, so late, riding back to
Heyes Landing, but he had had no doubts, no doubts at
all, that he was returning to her.

In his eagerness to see her again he had bypassed
Garrity's Ranch, tired and saddle-sore though he was,
for he had driven himself hard to try to make up for the
lost time. . .and the boy Link had gone straight to the
store.

Even now, the memory of it overcame him. He had
entered, to find Mrs Potts behind the counter, her face
an emblem of surprise at the sight of him. He had
thought nothing of her presence, thought that she was
keeping the store for Charlie for some reason.

'Charlie!' he had said. 'I have come for Charlie. Tell
her I'm here.' And, in his joy at his safe, if delayed
return, said impulsively, 'I've come to marry her.'

Mrs Potts paled. 'Land alive,' she said slowly. 'She's
gone, Link. Gone these three weeks or more. Sold the
store to Potts, and gone back East.'

There was a roaring in his ears, and he had put his
hands on the counter to steady himself.

'No, not gone,' he said. 'She can't have gone. Where?
Where did she go?'

All Mrs Potts's doubts about the sincerity of Link
Travis's feelings for Charlie Nelson disappeared in a
wave of pity.

'I can't tell you, Link. She didn't say. Only that she had a letter come telling her that she'd inherited a little estate back East, and she was happy to leave here to make a new life among her own kind. Packed up and went in a coupla days.'

'A message,' he said numbly. 'She must have left a letter or a message for me, shorely.'

'No. You wuz gone so long she thought that you'd deserted her. We all thought it, Link. I'm sorry to tell you this.'

Sorry? What did her sorry mean? Link Travis had meant nothing to Charlie Nelson but a summer's play. A letter from back East—and where was that?—and she had forgotten him and gone. Forever and a day had been a day for Charlie.

However could he have been so deceived? Women! They were all the same. He should have known better. He would know better. He would never give his heart away again, never.

He had made one last effort to find out where she had gone, but, true to the West, Mrs Potts had not asked, and the Nelsons had never said where they had come from.

He had visited Boot Hill once with Charlie, and her father's memorial was a simple stone with his name and dates on it, nothing else.

'Father didn't believe in what he called funerary nonsense,' she had told him. '"We are truly like the flowers which come up and are cut down, and we should not pretend that we are more," he always said.'

His flower had gone beyond recall, and only now, with Sally-Anne's existence, did he understand the true reason why Charlie Nelson had fled, single and pregnant, after one afternoon's loving. She had fled from ruin, shame and disgrace when it had seemed that her lover had used her and deserted her.

And all these years he had taken women for his playthings, despised them, because his common sense had not told him why she had gone. He burned at the thought.

And now he must win her again, and even more than before she was worth the winning. The raw boy had chosen better than he knew—the girl he had loved in the Arizona desert was á pearl of such great price that to win her again would take all the strength and resolution of the hard man he had become.

CHAPTER ELEVEN

WASHINGTON gossip, led by Sarah Lee Chase, was almost shrill with excitement. Two subjects titillated every soirée, ball, reception and dinner table. The first was that Boyce Hamilton had been given his *congé* by the widow McAllister and was behaving like a man demented, and that Jared Tunstall, the celebrated Don Juan of American society, was nearly as passionate in his pursuit of the said widow— had been caught at last, and by the Ice Princess, no less.

To add to the fun, the second scandal broke at the same time. Senator Warren Hulse, another noted womaniser, with a shrinking, down-trodden wife, whom he had betrayed on so many occasions that the wits said that even that celebrated Revolutionary War traitor Benedict Arnold might have been ashamed to have done it so often, had gone home unexpectedly one afternoon, to find her in bed with his secretary.

What was sauce for the goose was definitely not sauce for the gander, and both wife and secretary had been turned out of the house in the hour—the wife to seek refuge with her family, the secretary to embrace ruin! No one apparently saw anything odd in Senator Hulse's self-righteous fury—other than a few mad feminists, of course.

Both stories did the rounds, and it was difficult to tell which society found the more entertaining. The most maddening thing about the first scandal was the fact that both the widow and Tunstall showed not the slightest sign of being aware how much gossip they were causing.

Mary had told Jared that he might court her, but she could hardly have been prepared for the assault he mounted. It was almost as though Link were back again.

175

'Land sakes,' shrieked Miss Nessie, one balmy summer's evening. 'Whatever next?'

Mary and Sally-Anne had run to the window to discover that a small group of musicians had arrived in a little wagon, Jared Tunstall driving, set up their stools and instruments, and had begun to play Mozart's *Eine Kleine Nacht Musik*, for the benefit of the widow McAllister—and the rest of the street.

Mary emerged when the first movement was over to accost Jared, who was sitting on his stool, beautifully turned out, white gloves and all, ready to applaud the musicians.

'Oh, this is too bad of you,' she said to him, half angry, half laughing. An interested crowd had gathered. 'What do you think you're doing?'

Jared put his head on one side, saw Sally-Anne run to the gate, eyes wide, and said, 'I would have brung my geetaw, and sung you "Clementine" again, but I thought that the widow McAllister's taste had matured, and that Mozart would answer better. Don't you like the music I've chosen for you, Mary?'

'Of course I like it,' she wailed, memories of a night in Heyes Landing strong in her. 'That is not the point. Imagine the sensation when this runs round Washington tomorrow.'

The leader of the musicians looked at Jared. 'A moment,' Jared said gravely, then turned to Mary. 'You would not disappoint the players, would you? I told them I knew that you loved Mozart, and that you would be flattered by the honour they are doing you. And as for the gossips of Washington, how fortunate they will be to get their teeth into something real at last. Sarah Lee will have a syncope from excitement.'

'Oh, Mr Jared,' called Sally-Anne, 'this is nearly as good as if you had brought the horseless carriage with you. When are you going to take me riding in it?'

Before he could answer, Mary said repressively, 'Go in, at *once*, Sally-Anne; you are not to encourage him. I

swear he is no older and no more sensible than you are.'
She swung on Jared. 'This is no way to win me over.'

'It was last time,' he said with incontrovertible truth.

'That was then, this is now. What will people think?'

'That I wish to marry you, which I do.'

'This is no way to gain my consent. Yes, let the
musicians play, and then take them away. Why should
you think that making me the talk of Washington will
please me? You are demeaning me by doing this.'

His face changed at that. He said, suddenly grave
again, 'Yes, indeed, I forgot. We are not nineteen any
more and living in the Territory. But let them finish,
and then we will go away.'

'Quietly,' said Mary, through her teeth. 'And behave
yourself in future. I meant it when I said that you and
Sally-Anne are a good pair.'

After that, his pursuit was more decorous. He sent her
flowers, great boxes of chocolates, expensive perfume
from France, a giant ermine muff; paid visits, where he
sat and made love to her with his eyes and his voice,
never touching her. And still she was obdurate.

'You do not know me,' she said one day, when he had
eaten cake, and drunk tea, and had teased her lovingly.
'I am not that girl. I want your respect, as well as your
love. Are you giving me your respect? If not, you are no
better than Senator Hulse, with his double standard.
Don't you understand that while society admires you for
your brazen pursuit of me, and if you gain what you
want without marriage, you, like him, will be almost
admired, while I, if Washington knew the truth about
me, might as well wear the red A for Adulteress, because
my reputation and my position in life would be gone
forever? How can you be so thoughtless of me?'

What she said to him, and the manner of her speech,
struck home. He rose, and said quietly to her, 'I did not
mean to hurt you. I have associated too much with those
who have lost all moral sense. Yes, I do respect you, and
will try to show it.'

'If you don't,' she said, fierce, 'I shall turn you away,

and for good. I told you and I meant it—I will not be your plaything.'

His voice was stern too. He said, 'I will be good. I don't want to lose you, truly, or Sally-Anne either.'

'Then don't treat me as your whore. If I marry you, it will be as your partner, not your ornament. I will not be Mamie Hulse. You understand me?'

He did, and knew, wryly, that if he won her she would indeed be the pearl of price that he, and Washington, thought her.

Two could play at Jared's games with life. Boyce Hamilton, watching them, was consumed with rage and hate. He, too, had hired an agent to find out what he could to the discredit of Jared Tunstall, to use against him in a bid to win Mary back.

'There must be something disreputable in his past,' he had told the man. 'Something which he needs to hide. Such a pirate cannot have been so innocent that all of his life will bear inspection. Spend what you will, leave no stone unturned.'

Thus instructed, the man had been sent on his way the day after Mary had refused him, and now, like Jared before him, Boyce waited for his report. The man had wired him, saying that he had been successful, even beyond Boyce's wildest hopes, and would be in Washington by the weekend.

The Hulse scandal, and the ruin of poor Mamie Hulse, inspired Mary when she wrote her latest column for the *Gazette*. She knew only too well that, like Mamie Hulse, she would be destroyed if the truth about Sally-Anne were known, but that Jared, like Warren Hulse, would not only have survived, but would be admired for doing what, for the woman, was social suicide.

Now she stood in Garrison Firth's office. He had been reading her latest column, which she had brought to him that day, rather than post it. She saw him come to the end. She had risen from her chair and walked to the

window, to stare down Pennsylvania Avenue, full of the
afternoon's traffic, cabs, buggies and traps, all being
driven at speed in a light summer's drizzle, which was
breaking up the day's humidity and making the pave-
ments greasy.

The editor was silent when he reached the end. He
put down her script on his desk and said, 'I thought that
you told me that you had no wish to write of such
scandals.'

Mary turned from the window towards him.

'I was not writing scandal. I wrote of a principle. I am
not concerned with the unpleasant and scurrilous details
of the Hulse affair, only of its implications for all women.
You can surely see that.'

'I can. Of course I can. Others might not. Many will
call it muck-raking. They prefer to sneer at women's
rights, not to know of women's wrongs. They will call
an attempt like this to expose wrongs indecent.'

'So they may. I was pleased to show how little
Congress cared for working women when they refused
to regulate their working hours and their pay. This is of
the same order.'

'Again, I agree with you. But I am bound to advise
you that there are dangers in publishing this—for both
you and the *Gazette*. As to the paper, I am prepared to
risk that, and I think that the owners will agree with me.
Your column will, in future, be instantly turned to—as
you know, it is already a talking-point.'

He paused again. 'I am also bound to tell you that I
can see circumstances arising from this in which I could
not protect your anonymity—a lawsuit instigated by
Senator Hulse, for example. I would be sorry for you to
change your mind and not allow this to be published,
but, in fairness, I must warn you of the consequences.
They might be unpleasant.'

Mary stood silent for a moment, clasping her hands
together. I have been a hypocrite long enough, she
thought, and what I have written needs to be said, and,
thinking so, said, before she could change her mind,

'That is a risk I will take, Mr Firth. Print it. Print the truth.'

'Even if you perish in the flames of controversy?'

'Even so,' she said.

'As an editor I am pleased to hear you say that. As a man and—dare I say?—a friend, I admire your courage, but I doubt your judgement. I would not say this to many, mind, but you are a lady, Mrs McAllister, and a good woman——Are you as strong as you think you are?'

'I am not strong at all,' said Mary, 'But I must do my duty to my sex as I see it.' Her hands were trembling, and she put them behind her back.

'So be it,' he said gently. 'But be prepared for the storm.'

Mary, Sally-Anne and Miss Nessie had just enjoyed a late afternoon tea in the back parlour, the front parlour being in a state of what Miss Nessie called 'turned out'. All the furniture was in shrouds, the curtains were down from the windows, the carpets up, the paintwork and floorboards newly scrubbed, the many ornaments washed, cushions and runners laundered and ironed, waiting for tomorrow when everything would be put back and restored.

Sally-Anne hated the back parlour. 'Nothing to see out there,' she grumbled, nose snubbed up against the window-pane.

'All the late spring flowers are out, and the summer ones are arriving,' said Mary gently. 'Hardly nothing.'

'Flowers are not people,' said Sally-Anne unanswerably. 'I prefer people, and horses and dogs. Things happening. Flowers *are*. They don't happen.'

This was unanswerable and shrewd as well. Miss Nessie often sighed that Sally-Anne was frequently too clever for her own good.

'You could fetch your knitting, miss,' she said.

Sally-Anne sighed. 'Oh, that,' she said.

'Yes, that,' said Miss Nessie firmly.

'Or you could read,' said her mama.

'I spent the day reading,' answered her daughter restlessly. 'I want to *do* something.' She began to jump up and down on the spot.

Her mother's reproof was smothered by a knock on the front door. Livvie was heard to answer it, and a deep male voice began counterpointing her light one.

Livvie came in, self-important. 'Gemmun here to pay his respecks to Miz Sally-Anne.'

'Oh, surely not,' said Miss Nessie impatiently. 'Do you never get things right, Livvie? You mean Miz Mary.'

'That's what he said, mam. Miz Sally-Anne. Mos' pertickler 'bout it, he wuz.'

Mary suddenly knew who Sally-Anne's caller was. She did not know whether she was glad or sorry. She only knew that Jared, having tried in so many ways to win her back, was now, increasingly, beginning to attempt to reach her through their daughter. More, it was apparent from the first moment they had met, on the Mall, that they were twin souls. She was his true child, and, in all conscience, she could not refuse him access to her, and the emotions which tore at her were complicated by that knowledge.

For she wanted to accept him, to become his wife, to give Sally-Anne a father, but. . .but. . . She was suddenly as maidenly in her hesitations as she should have been so long ago. Having given him what he wanted so easily then, now she was hesitant, fearful still of herself, and of him.

Love must not blind her this time. She must know, truly know, that when she said yes it would not be to the glamour he carried around with him, but to the knowledge that his commitment to her was as deep as hers to him. That there would be no other woman, or women, to lure him again, when he had tired of her, back to the life he had lived for the past eight years. Did Jared Tunstall truly love her. . .? Or, perhaps more importantly, had Link Travis truly loved her? She had to know.

'Send him in, Livvie,' she said at last. 'Your first

gentleman caller, Sally-Anne. Mind your manners, my
love.'

'It's him,' said Sally-Anne suddenly. 'I know it is.'
And when the door opened she had half a mind to throw
herself at Jared as he entered behind Livvie, who was
saying importantly,

'Mr Jared Tunstall to see Miz Sally-Anne.'

He was dressed in what the three women all thought
were quite the strangest clothes which they had ever
seen: heavy brownish-gold tweeds, a funny hat, with a
small peak both at the back and at the front, thick
beautifully polished brown boots, long woollen socks
showing above them, and leather gloves with large
gauntlets.

He was carrying a small spray of carnations confined
in a lacy paper doily, which he gravely handed to Sally-
Anne, after he had bowed formally to her.

'My compliments, Miss McAllister. I wondered if you
would care for a jaunt in my horseless carriage as well as
this spray?'

Sally-Anne, who had begun to curtsy to him when she
received the flowers, paused, broke off on hearing this
invitation, and clapped her hands together, only saving
the flowers from destruction at the very last moment.

'Oh, yes, yes. Say that I may, Mama.' Her eyes were
shining, her face rosy as she lifted the spray to her lips.
'Oh, how absolutely swell. Thank you, thank you, thank
you. Do say yes, Mama.'

'In fact. . .' said Jared, his own eyes alight, and now
bowing to Mary and Miss Nessie. 'Your servant, ladies.
I must ask your mama to come with us to act as your
chaperon. It would not be at all proper for me to drive
alone with such a very young lady as yourself.'

For once Sally-Anne was deprived of speech. Mary,
who had risen to her feet, said gravely, 'Most improper
indeed, Mr Tunstall. I think that you should go with
Miss Nessie, Sally-Anne. Put on your best paletot coat
and your new spring bonnet. Miss Nessie will pin the
spray which Mr Jared has brought you to your coat.'

Sally-Anne was in ecstasies. 'My first caller! Just wait till the girls at school hear of this. Even Nancy Thayer has never had a gentleman caller, and she's years older than I am.' She took Miss Nessie's hand, obedient for once, and was led away to be dressed for her adventure, leaving Mary and Jared alone together.

'I, too, will have to make myself ready,' she said.

'I hope that you don't object to my doing this,' said Jared. 'But it is such a beautiful day, and Sally-Anne spoke so feelingly of horseless carriages that it occurred to me that she might value a ride in my Daimler.'

'Of course I cannot object to such a kindness,' said Mary, 'So long as you don't spoil her too much. Goodness knows, she is lively enough already. . .'

'And, of course,' said Jared, still grave, although his eyes were laughing at her, 'it is difficult in a case like this to know who is chaperoning whom. The world can hardly gossip with Miss Sally-Anne firmly ensconced between us. We may not picnic today, but I thought that a drive to the small park near here would be a good substitute. Propriety must reign supreme.'

'Indeed,' said Mary, who had begun to smile back at him, such charming impudence having its own effect on her, and reminding her strongly of how he had been at Heyes Landing. 'And if you will keep to that, Jared, then we shall be happy to accompany you; and now you really must excuse me. Like Sally-Anne, I have to dress suitably for such a grand occasion. I'm sure that she will entertain you while you wait for me.'

Sally-Anne was like to burst, as she said later to Nancy Thayer, particularly when they all three walked out to the carriage, and Jared solemnly described its best points to her as if it were a horse, so that Mary half expected it to raise a wheel for her, as though it were a hoof.

And then Sally-Anne was lifted by Mr Jared on to the long bench, which was all there was by way of a seat, reclined grandly back on its rail, her two most favourite people in the whole world on each side of her. She had

privately decided that such a perceptive man as Mr Jared
appeared to be would make her a most suitable papa.

'Are you wearing the correct clothes for a horseless
carriage, Mr Jared?' she asked. He had begged her to
use his Christian name, rather than the more formal Mr
Tunstall.

'Not exactly,' he said. 'These are the clothes English
country gentlemen wear to engage in sporting activities.
This funny hat with two peaks is called a deerstalker,
and this caped coat is worn with it to protect one from
the cold.'

'It is not cold today,' observed Sally-Anne.

'No, indeed. But to drive a horseless carriage is such a
splendid thing, particularly when one is with such a
pretty young lady, that I thought that I ought to dress
for it grandly.'

His manner with Sally-Anne was perfect, Mary
thought. He neither patronised her, nor appeared to
indulge her, but spoke to her as though she were a
sensible person like himself.

'The English,' she said reflectively. 'Miss Nessie said
that you were a friend of the Prince of Wales. Is that
true?'

'Yes,' he said, 'and of his wife, Alexandra.'

'Miss Nessie says that she is beautiful. Is the Prince
handsome? Like princes in fairy-tales?'

'Not at all. He is middle-aged and rather fat—but he
is very kind.'

'And are the English ladies beautiful? Miss Nessie says
that they are.'

He considered her, his expression quite serious, then
looked at Mary over the top of her head. 'Very beautiful.
But not so beautiful as an American lady I know—or her
daughter, either.'

Sally-Anne gave a little crow of delight, looked up at
him, and caught his arm.

'Oh! You mean Mama and me! Oh, my first compliment from a gentleman.'

Mary, watching them, felt her heart give a great lurch.

Jared was looking down at his daughter, laughing conspiratorially with her. And the two dark heads together, the expressions on the face of the man and the child, were so strangely similar, displaying the same sense of fun and joy of living, that it was as though she were seeing the two sides of the same coin—male on the obverse, female on the reverse.

They had reached a small park, tame among the scrub and trees which surrounded Washington.

Jared dismounted, helped down his two women and they walked to a bench near to the park's gate. Sally-Anne's hoop and cane were handed down to her, and she made the most of her freedom, flying off, her hoop bowling before her, Mary and Jared left alone.

'Yes,' he said, as though the recent conversation in the carriage had not stopped. 'you are more beautiful than the English ladies.'

'But you enjoyed knowing them, I am sure.' she smiled, teasing him a little.

'Ah, but I had not met you then.'

This line of talk was dangerous. Mary opened her parasol; the sun of late June was growing hot, and she walked a little way away from him, to say, over her shoulder, as he followed her, 'You must not spoil Sally-Anne.'

'You would prefer that I spoil her mother?'

'Neither of us. You must behave yourself.'

'I am behaving myself. See, I am not even touching you.'

How to say, It is not even necessary for you to touch me. Simply to know that you are near me is enough—and more than enough—for me?

'Be serious,' she said at last, an unwilling smile on her lips. 'I am sure that the man who plays Wall Street for his profit—and his amusement—must have a serious side to him.'

'Indeed. But you must also know that men and women are all of a piece. If I did not enjoy what I do in Wall Street, I would not do it.'

This sounded like something Sally-Anne might say—
when she was older, perhaps. He obviously liked what
he was doing now. A passing group pointed and grinned
at his absurd clothes. That amused him, too.

'I wonder why I cause such excitement,' he said,
laughing at her. 'Can it possibly be what I am wearing?'

'It is hardly usual for Washington,' said Mary a little
firmly, 'even though it might be eminently suitable for
the Highlands of Scotland. I believe that is where
deerstalkers are usually worn. People are amused by
what seems strange to them.'

'Yes, ridiculous, is it not? These garments are no more
absurd than Orrin's Western get-up. No one stares at
him. It must be me. Put your hand on my arm, dear
Widow McAllister. Confer respectability on me.'

Mary did so, laughing out loud, despite herself, the
glamour of him strong on her. 'Oh, yes, you are right. It
is you. You are absurd.'

He looked down at her. 'Suppose I proposed to you
now. What would you say to me? Could you be cruel
enough to refuse me, to deny me Sally-Anne? You see
how well we go together. She is very much my child;
that is plain to see.'

Mary pulled her arm from his, and turned away. 'Now
you are blackmailing me,' she said in a stifled voice,
'when I still don't know whether I can trust you. Can I
trust you, Jared, when you are unscrupulous enough to
use Sally-Anne against me?'

'But it is in a good cause,' he said, trying to take her
hand. 'Say yes, and you will make three people happy.'

'And that,' she answered him, retrieving her hand, 'is
how you won me at Heyes Landing. You see why I resist
you.'

For a moment he was almost angry. He caught her by
the shoulders and turned her towards him, regardless of
spectators. 'I loved you then, as I love you now, to
distraction, to death itself. If you hold against me the life
I lived until I met you again, think this—that losing you
destroyed me. I thought you faithless—as you thought

me. But, knowing that you were not, as you must accept that I was not, that which moved me for eight years is gone, over. You are my morning star, and I want no other.'

'If I could believe you. . .' she began.

'Believe me,' he said, 'and believe this. I will do anything to win you, and, enchanting though my daughter is, it is her mother I want the most, and I will lay siege to you until you surrender.'

He released her, stepped back, and held out his open hands to her. He saw the anguish on her face; reason and love struggled there, and neither was the winner. He felt a sudden pity for her torment—as well as his own.

'Come,' he said. 'Let us pretend that we have just met, that we are strolling together, idly conversing on matters of public, not private import. Orrin says that the silver issue is almost settled, and that when it is the great issue to which he has dedicated his political life will be achieved. He wishes to retire to the ranch. He wants me to take over the senatorship when I reach thirty.'

'And do you want to be a senator?' she asked.

'Ah.' And his smile at her was mocking. 'You do not think me sufficiently statesmanlike? But you must remember that I have made myself a fortune before I am thirty, and that needed some solid thought, I can tell you!'

There was no answering him, and before she could, Sally-Anne, who had been passing and repassing before them, ran up, panting a little.

'You look very serious, Mama, and Mr Jared, too.'

'That is because we have been talking about politics,' said Mary.

'Then talk about something else. I prefer you to look happy.'

'Most sensible of you, Miss Sally-Anne.' He bent suddenly, caught her under the arms, lifted her into the air. Squealing with delight, she looked down at him.

'Oh, now you are smiling,' she cried, and he sat her on his left shoulder for a moment, saying,

'Can you see the river through the trees, Miss Sally-Anne?'

'No,' she said. 'But I know it is there. Will you drive me to the Potomac one day?'

'One day,' he said, 'if Mama promises to come too, and you are a good girl.'

'Yes,' she said, adding severly, 'and you must be a good boy.'

'And Mama,' he answered her solemnly, putting her down again.

'Oh, Mama is always good.'

Both he and Mary began to laugh. 'I know,' he said, still holding the little girl's hand. 'That is our problem, yours and mine. We being so wicked and Mama so good. I shall try to persuade her to be less perfect.'

'And what a relief that will be,' said Sally-Anne frankly. 'Because, you know, I like being naughty. It's more fun.'

This open confession of wickedness amused both her hearers, and their journey home was even lighter-hearted than the outward one had been, after Jared had confessed to her that he, too, found naughtiness more exhilarating than behaving himself.

'But it doesn't answer in the long run,' Mary interjected quietly. 'We have to pay for everything we do, particularly our naughtinesses.'

'Oh, that is always later,' Sally-Anne replied, 'and we have had our fun first. Besides, later might not come.'

'An infant Machiavelli,' her father said, handing her into the carriage. 'And, seeing that Mama is so good, I think that we ought to reward her, don't you? How about taking over the monster's controls for a short time, my dear Widow McAllister?' And he looked at her over Sally-Anne's head, and there was something about his smile, his sheer delight in teasing her, and wanting her to play so innocently with him, that tugged at Mary's heart, and brought back memories of another time, and how he had taught her before, and always with such charming gaiety.

She began to say, 'No——' but Sally-Anne's squeal of delight interrupted her.

'Oh, do, Mama, do!'

'Now,' said Jared, 'you really must respond to such a cry from the heart.'

And, without waiting for her reply, he stopped the Daimler, and rearranged them on the front seat, so that Mary sat before the wheel, and he next to her, his arms about her helping her to control it, and Sally-Anne wriggling with delight on his other side. Mary had no alternative but to give way after such united pressure.

What with one thing and another, between her own amusement—yes, she was amused—and her interest in controlling the monster, and Sally-Anne's even greater delight that Mama was doing such a daring thing, and Jared's opportunity to hold and subtly caress her quite legitimately, their progress through Washington was by way of being as interesting to the many entranced spectators as any presidential procession.

But, listening to Sally-Anne and Jared, Mary did not care. Perhaps Sally-Anne was right: later might not come! But it had come for her once, and might do so again—and she was thinking of this when they reached home, and Jared helped them both down again.

'And I may call on you soon, for another spin?' he said.

Sally-Anne jumped up and down, crying, 'Yes, say yes, Mama. Tell him he may come to tea, and thank you—oh, thank you for the treat,' before running in to tell Miss Nessie and Livvie all about the wonders of a drive in the contraption, and the excitement which their progress had created.

'Like Sally-Anne, I prefer it when you smile,' he said softly, before he left. 'I think that the fortress is beginning to fall, dear Widow McAllister. I shall say *au revoir*, and soon, I hope, even *au revoir* will not be needed.'

Before she could stop him, he kissed her, there on the pavement, and then he was in the Daimler again, in one smooth movement, and the monster went clanking down the street.

CHAPTER TWELVE

WASHINGTON society responded to 'A Lady's' latest column with a mixture of amusement, excitement and disgust. Taken with the scandal which had provoked it, it provided material for every drawing-room and dining table for days.

If talk about the Ice Princess fighting off the Wall Street pirate flagged, then 'A Lady' and Mamie Hulse was sure to take its place. No one guessed that the Ice Princess was the mysterious 'Lady' who looked at Washington.

'Oh, the Lord preserve us,' shrieked Sarah Lee Chase at her husband that morning. 'Just read what "A Lady" has said now, will you? Will Senator Hulse sue the *Gazette*, do you think? And shall we find out who "A Lady" is?' She passed the paper across the breakfast table, and Senator Chase read it while he ate his bacon and beans.

A Lady Looks At Washington—
The Dual Standard.

I take up my pen this week to write only of sombre matters, not the light elegancies which have occupied me so far, but even 'A Lady' must occasionally look at matters which sadden, rather than gladden, the heart.

Some sixty years ago Lord Macaulay wrote of English society that, in one of its periodic fits of morality, it drove from its precincts the great poet Lord Byron for behaving no more and no less immorally than virtually all his fellow peers. We Yankees are inclined to sneer at Britishers for their hypocrisy in such matters, but A Lady must testify that we have no right to do this. We are as unregenerate as they.

For have we not seen, in the past few weeks, in the heart of our great capital city, a household where the master, arriving home to find his wife pleasing herself in exactly the same manner as he had seen fit to do these many years, drove her from the premises, and into complete social and moral exile, while he, the greater sinner, remains inside society's pale, still honoured as one of the Nation's legislators, and, indeed, even a little admired, for the same conduct which in his wife—or any other woman—is seen as a fit reason for her banishment and destruction?

A Lady would like to know how this conduct can be justified; how the poor girl who creeps shamed away with the fruit of her sin, shunned by all, can look up to see her seducer still brazenly laughing among his fellows, admired for the same conduct which has branded her with the equivalent of the red A which our forefathers inflicted on the woman who fell from grace.

A Lady has to admit that the banner of the double standard flies over Washington, and asks how long it will be before it is pulled down, and replaced by a flag to which *all* in our society may pay homage, whatever their sex or station?

Sarah Lee's husband, having read this, tossed the paper back, laughing grimly. 'Well, if Warren Hulse sues over that, he will be a fool as well as a cuckold. But he is not noted for his common sense. What next will "A Lady" say? Are any of us safe? She had a nice old fling at the Labour laws last week. At this rate, prostitution will be next on her list of subjects! One supposes that she is not married, or that her husband cannot keep her in order.'

'She may say what she pleases, so long as she leaves me alone,' said Sarah Lee gaily. 'I swear that I have not had so much entertainment in years since "A Lady" began putting men in their places. No doubt about it, that column was written from the heart!' She rose to fetch her best summer straw boater with the daisies, to

begin a round of visit to her friends to find out their
reactions to 'A Lady'—and smilingly retail them where
Senator Warren Hulse could hear every bitter word.

Boyce Hamilton's reaction was a different one. He was
reading 'A Lady', an expression of disgust on his face as
he did so. He was expecting his detective to report to
him that morning. He sprang up when the man arrived,
throwing the *Gazette* on the floor.

'You have something for me?'

'Oh, indeed. More, I believe, than you could have
hoped.' Satisfaction rode on the man's face. 'I think that
I can offer you a weapon to destroy Tunstall—if that is
what you want.'

'Never mind what I want. Tell me what you have
found.'

'Briefly, I will not trouble you with the details of my
search. I soon found that there was a year missing in
Tunstall's life after his family were killed in the so-called
Tunstall-Hughes feud. By working backwards—and for-
wards—from that, I have discovered what he did in the
missing year. . .something which I firmly believe even
his brother Orrin does not know of.' He paused dramati-
cally, savouring his prowess.

'Go on, man. Go on. Why do you stop?'

'He disguised himself, took another name; Lincoln—
Link—Travis, even spoke differently, by all accounts,
went hunting for the Hughes brothers in the south-west,
posing as an outlaw, a desperado, became one in actual-
ity, and ended up with Liam Garrity at his ranch in
Arizona.'

He paused again, but, aware of his employer's
impatience, rapidly continued, 'From there he seems to
have tracked down the Hugheses, who by then had
changed their names. The two middle brothers were
killed in a shoot-out at Ogallala; only the eldest, Rafer,
and the youngest, Barrett, whom the Tunstalls had
always claimed killed the old senator, were left. Tunstall
murdered Barrett Hughes—shot him, without warning,

or so Rafer claims—and then badly wounded Rafer. It was Rafer I found. Tunstall—Travis—left him for dead.

'He is willing to swear on oath to all this, and that Tunstall was undoubtedly Travis, although the local papers merely named him as Travis in reporting the incident, one more scuffle among banditti to them. Tunstall was wounded himself, went off, and was not heard from again in the West—was thought to have died. He saw Tunstall recently, by chance, when he visited Gary, Montana, and recognised him, even though he was greatly changed, as the man who killed his brother, and tried to kill him. The eye of hate sees true.'

'And Rafer Hughes will swear that Tunstall was posing as Travis, and murdered his brother—but who will believe his word against Tunstall's, especially if Tunstall denies everything?' said Boyce angrily. 'Are there no wanted posters for Travis, no tintypes of him?'

'Oh, he covered his trail well. Went warily,' said the detective. 'He meant no one to know of what he had done. As I said, I believe that even his brother Orrin knows nothing of his Western adventures. . .and wanted posters—yes, there is one, done after he and the Garrity gang robbed the railroad near Tucson and the bank at Bisbee. Only drawback is, it might be anyone. Looks nothing like Tunstall.'

'Tintypes?' queried Boyce.

'There is one tintype of Garrity's gang with him on it. Garrity was like Jesse James: vain, loved having his picture taken with his pals. But that won't help you either.'

'And why not?'

The detective laughed. 'Just shows a thin boy, bearded, wearing a pony-tail, a big grin on him. No use as identification—nothing like Tunstall; his own ma wouldn't have recognised him.'

'And that's it?' said Boyce. 'Just Rafer Hughes who saw him after eight years? That's a slim chance to nail him.'

The detective hesitated, looked keenly at Boyce. 'You

sure do want him bad,' he observed drily, then added, 'No, there's more. Something which might do for him— but you'll not care for this, perhaps; it's not like the other stuff, but it could be the clincher in court.'

'Go on,' said Boyce, frowning, 'Why do you stop?'

'It concerns Mrs McAllister. Are you sure that you want to hear?'

'Now I do,' said Boyce, 'Even more than before.'

'Mrs Mary Charlotte Nelson McAllister. Only she ain't McAllister, and she sure ain't Mrs. She lived for a piece about eight years ago in Heyes Landing near where Garrity had his so-called ranch, and where Link Travis lived for a coupla months or so. Charlie Nelson she was known as then, a regular tomboy, cut her hair short, wore a man's pants, and a Colt revolver.' He hesitated again.

'Go on,' said Boyce, his throat dry, stricken at this vision of a Mary such as he could never have imagined.

'Seems she and Travis were sweethearts—real close, joke of the town—folk still laughed about it after all these years. Only, he deserted her, sudden-like. Never came back for months, until after she had left, sudden-like again, telling no one where she was going. Guess where she turned up—only, you know, don't you? She arrived in Washington to inherit her ma's cousin's money, calling herself Mrs James McAllister. Only there wor'nt no James McAllister, and no marriage neether. Nine months after Travis deserted her she gave birth to her daughter. Like to bet who's the father?'

He thought that Boyce might faint on the spot. 'You're sure of this?' he said. 'Wouldn't do to be wrong.'

His voice was a distraught whisper. Mary, his pure and innocent love, the woman whom he had wished to marry, was Travis's whore, Jared Tunstall's deserted mistress, her daughter illegitimate, her stainless life a lie. He could not bear it. He did not know whom he wished to hurt more—Mary, or that hard swine, her lover.

'Sure as I can be. Seein' as how you told me to dig up everything discreditable I could find out about him, I

followed this through. No doubt at all: she left Heyes
Landing as Charlie Nelson, turns up here a week later as
Mrs Mary Charlotte McAllister. Who else could be the
father? Folk at Heyes Landing most partickler that she
only had one beau, and that was Travis—or Tunstall, as
we now know he was. My bet is that when he turned up
here she didn't even recognise him at first, but, from my
observation, she knows that he was Travis now.'

He paused. He saw that what he had said had hit
Boyce hard. Sweet on the woman by all accounts. Not
so sweet now, perhaps.

'There's your identification,' he said, a little sorry, for
all his cynicism. 'Put her on the stand, under oath, and
Tunstall's done for. She must identify him as Travis.
Your honest, if unwilling, witness.'

Boyce made an ugly face. 'Our honest witness? She's
besotted on the man. What's the odds she will lie herself
blue, will deny knowing him? And, with her known
character here, he'll be home free.'

'Not at all,' said the agent. 'Think, man, think. If she
lies to save him, then out it comes—that she was his
mistress, bore his child; who would believe a word she
said? Besides, there's more to damn her.'

'More?' said Boyce, at whom grief and rage tore with
iron claws. 'How can there be more?'

'Oh, I've had her followed in Washington, and her
life's virtuous enough now, except that my man discovered that she is the woman who writes the *Gazette*'s
scandalous column "A Lady Looks at Washington"—
imagine the furore when that comes out in court! No,
she's our ace in the hole; no word of her before the
Grand Jury, or even when his trial opens, and then,
when he—and she—thinks he's saved, his word against
that of a scallywag like Rafer Hughes, and wham! We
subpoena the good lady, and if she starts her tricks her
character's gone, and his with it. Couldn't be better.
Either she tells the truth and he stands to swing, or she
lies, and we use her relationship with Travis-Tunstall
against her, and still he swings. Pretty, ain't it? Like a

forking mate on a chessboard, he's damned either way, and she with him.'

What a revenge! To gain it on the pair of them at one stroke!

'Put her on the stand,' said the agent exultantly, 'and Tunstall's done for.' But you'll have to tear the mask of virtue from her face to do it.'

'Added to Rafer Hughes's testimony it should do for him,' ground out Boyce. 'And Hughes would be pre-pared to testify to this before the District Attorney—and then the Grand Jury?'

'I thought that you would ask that,' said the agent smugly. 'I have brought him here to Washington and have him holed up in a lodging house, ready to swear an affidavit out against Tunstall. His affidavit, and this——' And he waved at Boyce the file of documents which he had brought with him from Heyes Landing.

'And that should be enough for the Grand Jury to be summoned to swear out a True Bill for murder against Jared Tunstall, and have him deported to Arizona Territory to stand trial—if that is what you want.'

Indeed Boyce wanted it. All his love for Mary had turned to hate since learning the truth about her, Tunstall and Sally-Anne. He panted for revenge on the woman who had refused him but had been willing to lie with an outlaw and murderer, bearing his bastard, while pretending to a virtue which she did not possess.

'Do it,' he said commandingly. 'See that Hughes knows that he has financial support to enable him to remain in Washington, pass the evidence to the DA. As a lawyer I can tell you that, without doubt, on the Hughes affidavit alone, we have a prima facie case against him. With Mrs McAllister as a subpoenaed surprise witness, he is done for.'

That should wipe the smile from Tunstall's face, teach him not to drive around Washington, waiting to inherit his brother's seat in Congress, spending his ill-gotten millions as the friend and lapdog of European aristocrats.

His friendship with the great, and the women he had

enjoyed—none of it would save him if Rafer Hughes could make his accusations stick, and Mary McAllister be brought to her knees in the witness box!

Jared was another who read 'A Lady'. . .and when he reached the part about the woman branded with the scarlet A, and remembered his conversation with Mary, he knew who 'A Lady' was without a doubt. She possessed both the intellect and the courage to write such a thing. . .but could she conceivably be aware of the consequences if Washington discovered who 'A Lady' really was?

He must see her, speak to her, warn her, protect her. All his chivalrous instincts were up in arms. He ran out to his buggy to pay her a visit. He already needed to see her, to ask her to accompany himself, with Orrin as chaperon, to the theatre, and what better time than now to invite her, and to warn her?

Mary was leaving her home—it was one of the days when she worked for Senator Graves—when she saw Jared come dashing up, and wondered why he was driving to see her with such urgency.

She was wearing a prim dove-grey dress, with black and white trimmings, suitable for office work; only her hat was frivolous, a wide-brimmed straw with black and white ribbons, tied in enormous bows, with the ends left dangling.

'Mary! I must speak to you. It is not of us that I wish to talk, but of you. To warn you.'

'What is it, Jared? You look so strange. Are you ill?'

Worry for her was moving in his usually cool, impassive face. He held the *Gazette* out to her. 'This, Mary. It is this. The column. . . I fear for you.'

Heart thumping, she affected surprise. 'The *Gazette*, Jared? What is there in the *Gazette* which can concern me?'

'Oh, you should play poker! You should. But you cannot deceive me, Mary. I know you. You are playing a dangerous game by writing as "A Lady"—oh, yes, I am sure that you have written this; do not deny it. You spoke to me in almost these identical terms that day with Sally-Anne. If Warren Hulse sues the *Gazette* for printing this, what will become of "A Lady's" anonymity then?'

'True,' she said, her face preserving its lovely calm. 'But why speak to me of it?'

'Because I love you, and because, I repeat, I know beyond a doubt that you are "A Lady". It is your voice, your own sad condition of which you write so movingly, as well as Mamie Hulse's. Oh, what will they do to you in court, if Hulse should sue? They will rip your reputation to pieces. They are wolves, wolves, and will destroy you.'

He wanted to hold her in his arms, fight the world for her, take Sally-Anne and her to some sanctuary where he could protect them from harm, from the world's inevitable sneers.

They were face to face again. Anyone passing could see the strength of the passion between them. Mary's will was as strong as Jared had feared it would be when she said firmly, 'Even suppose I were "A Lady", and, mind, I am not admitting that I am, what concern is it of yours?'

'Only that what I felt for you by the lake that long-ago day is still with me, and in me—the desire to protect you, as all male animals wish to protect their mate, or the woman whom they wish to make their mate. Marry me, and you will no longer need to write such things to earn a living.'

It was the worst thing he could have said. Her face changed. 'To earn a living? Is that what you think? Not that what I write is as much a duty to me as anything else? Are you to censor what I do before we even marry? If so, what will you do afterwards?' She thought of Mamie Hulse's pain, of her own, of the pain of all betrayed women. 'Cannot you see why I hesitate to tie myself to you in marriage—however much I love you?'

'Oh, you wrong me,' he said passionately. 'I only wish to protect you.'

'I know that,' she answered him, head high. 'But you are a free spirit, and so do I wish to be.'

'But it is different for a woman,' was his reply to that. 'You need our. . .my protection.'

'Again, I must remind you, that I said that when we married—if we married—I would not wish to be your toy. Think; you must not deny me the right to be myself, to make my own mistakes, my own decisions. If. . .if. . . I decide to marry you, it will be as your partner, not your slave. You understand me?'

Oh, yes. He did, he did. He understood the raw courage of her, and loved her the more for it. He respected her right to be her own woman, and hoped she would go on being so should she marry him—though that might be hard for a man used to having his own way.

And to lose her now would be to lose more than the girl by the lake; it would be to lose also the strong woman she had become.

'Firth should not have allowed you to do it. . .' he began, only for his eyes to fall before her steady ones. 'No, I should not have said that,' he achieved. 'You are your own mistress. The decision was yours, not his.'

He took her gloved hand, and kissed the palm. He could feel her, warm, through the fabric—at least she could not deny him such a distant kiss as that.

For the first time they faced one another on equal terms, both now experienced, mature. Paradoxically again it was at this juncture, when Mary had asserted her right to freedom, and he had assented to it, if implicitly, that they understood that they now had the possibility of a life together.

'One more thing,' he said. 'I had intended to visit you even if I had not read your column. There is to be a gala night at Ford's Theatre, a special performance of *Hamlet* with Maurice Barrymore. Will you allow me to escort you there? Orrin will come with us to stifle scandal.'

Mary looked hard at him. It would be, in a sense, to make a public statement of her feelings for him. They had avoided being together at such occasions since the shock of their discovery.

She knew by his expression that he was as aware as she of what the world would think when it saw them together, even with Orrin there.

'Yes,' she said slowly. 'If you grant my right to be myself, then I will come with you. You do grant me that right, Jared, do you not? Now and forever?'

'Yes,' he said, 'It will be hard for the man I am; you must know that. But I do grant you that. . . Forever. . .and a day. You see, I have not forgotten.'

Their eyes met. They were both back on a hillside in Arizona.

'A renewed pledge,' she said. 'Oh, Jared, I think that there may be hope for us yet.'

It was as much as he could do not to take her in his arms and begin to make love to her immediately, but he knew what an error that would be. Instead, he took her hand, kissed it, and then stood back to let her go, the hope that there might be few more farewells strong in both of them this time.

Boyce immediately handed the papers relating to Link Travis, and Rafer Hughes's affidavit identifying him as Jared Tunstall, to the Justice Department, and started in motion the events which would lead to the District Attorney's serving a Bill of Indictment on Jared Tunstall to appear before the Grand Jury to determine whether he should be indicted for the wilful murder of Barrett Hughes, and the unlawful wounding of his brother Rafer.

Ignorant of the storm which was about to burst, Mary had reached her decision. After due thought, she was willing to accept again what she had accepted eight years ago—that, wild and unregenerate though Link Travis might have been, and to a great extent Jared Tunstall still was beneath his civilised mask, she was prepared to give herself to him once more, this time for good.

The love between them was as strong, if not stronger, than ever, and she had at last come to terms with her past. She had exorcised the sense of betrayal with which she had lived for nearly eight years, and thought, too, that he was ready to accept her, not as his mere partner in bodily pleasure, but as a person in her own right. Oh, yes, she would share the delights of love with him again, but she would also, she hoped, be his mate in more than that—would share his real life with him, not exist on its periphery.

She had no doubt that he would find it hard—he had had merely himself to please for so long—but then, she also had been her own woman, and giving that up would demand a real sacrifice from her, too.

Preparing herself for the theatre, she had decided that afterwards, when he drove her home, she would give him the answer which he wanted, and they would, at last, make 'Forever and a day' come true. . .

Once she had made the decision, Mary wondered why it had taken her so long, and laughed a little to herself at the contrariness of human beings. They had lost so much time together, she and Jared, and now they could take up their life again where they had left it off, and with Sally-Anne, who would at last have a father.

'Oh,' said Jared softly, when he arrived to collect her for the gala night, 'you look astonishing. You will kill every other woman stone dead.'

He looked at Orrin for confirmation, who smiled and said in his best Western drawl, 'Couldn't have said it better myself, Miz Mary. An honour to escort yuh. Playin' gooseberry takes on a new meaning when I look at yuh.'

She laughed up at them. Evening dress, the dramatic black and white of it, enhanced both the brothers' looks. Jared wore a cravat of flaming-red silk, while Orrin

sported one of royal blue. His Western boots were
particularly fine and shiny.

All Washington society was present, and walking into
the box, opening her fan and sitting down between the
two tall and massive men, Mary was only too aware that
every eye was upon her, and every busy brain was
drawing conclusions about her presence there with the
brothers.

She had dressed to impress, and knew by the
expression of those who watched her that she had
succeeded. She was wearing an evening gown of white
silk, ornamented with crystals, great crystal drops in her
ears, a starburst in her hair; her large fan was white,
with tiny crystals, and a single white carnation flowered
in her corsage.

At the first interval, the classier part of the audience
streamed into the upstairs foyer, to see, and to be seen.
It was a roster of great Congressional and business names
which collected there.

Mary was escorted by both brothers, bowing to all
those who wished to speak to them, for even on their
own the Tunstall brothers were among the great stars of
the day, and her presence with them sealed not only her
success in Washington but theirs as well, and the buzz
was that the Ice Princess was falling to Jared Tunstall—
but only at the price of marriage; Orrin's accompanying
them testified to that.

Surrounded as she was, Mary did not at first hear the
babel, the harsh voices, the gasps of surprise, the surge
in the crowd. A small group of uniformed men finally
reached the three of them, pushing her roughly to one
side to get at the Tunstall brothers, or, more particularly,
Jared, for Orrin was suddenly shouldered aside, too.

The District Attorney, Decimus Parker, desperate to
make a name for himself, to make a real killing, to show
that even though he was a Republican the law knew no
favours, would show none even to such pillars of the
party as the Tunstalls, had determined to arrest Jared

Tunstall in as public and sensational a manner as possible.

To pull down Jared Tunstall, perhaps lay Orrin low with him, would not only bring him great publicity, but would serve to further his own political career. Thus an arrest in such circumstances, before all the power and might of Washington society, would be a coup long talked about.

The leader of the group of policemen, the only one in plain clothes as befitted an officer of the court, thrust the Bill of Indictment into Jared's hand, his fellow put his hand on Jared's shoulder, while the court's officer recited the nub of the suit against Jared.

The tumult in the crowded confines of the foyer rose to a roar. Mary, watching, aghast, was pushed further back by the crowd which swirled and eddied around her. Orrin was loudly protesting at such a public affront, and the only unaffected person appeared to be Jared himself.

He stared at the Bill, held it out to the tipstaff, and said in his iciest voice, the voice of the man who dominated Wall Street dealings, 'Not for me, surely?'

The tipstaff stared back. . .began to recite the indictment again, and this time Jared tossed the Bill to the floor. 'And that is what I think of that,' he said, but hardly had he finished speaking than the leading policeman who had seen that he had taken the Bill in his hand grasped him by the arm, and attempted to lead him away.

It was Orrin, still shaken, who picked up the paper from the floor and said, 'What nonsense is this?' and, reading it, saw the words 'Arizona, 1881'. He turned to Jared, a question on his face, only to find Jared staring stonily at him, shaking his head.

'A mistake,' said Jared. 'Such an accusation will not stand up in any court of law. I deny the charge absolutely, now and in the future.'

Mary, as stunned as the rest, tried to push towards him. She had no notion of what Jared was accused, only saw that he had been arrested, and then, through the noise of the crowd, she heard something which stopped her where she stood.

'What is it? What is it?' people called. Others, nearer to the arresting officers, who had heard the indictment read, repeated the words, 'Tunstall, Jared Tunstall. Murder,' they said. 'Arizona,' and, 'Barrett Hughes, murder,' and, 'Arizona,' again, the words becoming a Greek chorus which accompanied Jared while he was being pushed through the crowd by the police, Orrin following, Mary herself forgotten.

Murder! Arizona! Mary was on fire. Charlie surfaced, as she was wont to do in moment of stress. She shoved, clawed and kicked her way towards him, her own momentum and the crowd's random motion suddenly bringing her before him, so that for a brief moment they were face to face.

Jared saw her. The control which he had so far shown did not falter for a moment, was not affected by his inward surprise that what he had done in Arizona eight years ago should rise from its grave and come to haunt him now.

How and why he had been discovered and pursued, the connection between Lincoln Travis and Jared Lawrence Tunstall Junior finally made, he could not imagine. But one thing he did know. He would lie and lie again about the killing of Barrett Hughes and the shooting of Rafer.

It was not that he was ashamed of what he had done—he was proud of it. For he had pursued the Hugheses, killed and wounded them in fair fight, because the law had refused to touch them for the murders of his father, his half-brothers and of Orrin's dear wife Clara.

But he had no intention of risking execution or even loss of reputation himself for remedying the law's defects. He had never forfeited a moment's sleep over what he had done, and neither would he do so over his determination to look the DA and the court in the eye, and use the poker face and the cunning with which he had made himself a power in Wall Street to cheat the gallows.

'Don't worry,' he said gently to her. 'It is nothing. They can have no true evidence against me; of that I am sure. I shall tell Orrin to see you safely home.'

Mary could not say to him, Arizona, they said Arizona. What were you doing there of which you could not speak to me, living under a name which was not yours? A thousand speculations whirled through her brain. She remembered what Orrin had told her of the Tunstall-Hughes feud, and suddenly thought, Is *that* why he was in Arizona? Is *that* why he was late back?

Face to face, there, when he was under attack, she said instead, the words flying from her, knowing at last that she would do anything, anything, to protect him, 'Oh, Jared, the answer you wanted from me is yes, always yes. Forever. . .and a day.'

His face lit up, and then he was gone. They had pulled him roughly away. She saw him speak to Orrin, who turned, and came towards her.

'Miz Mary.' Even in his evident distress and bewilderment over what had happened Orrin was still his courteous self. 'Jared has asked me to see you safely home, and then I must go to him, try to find out what mischance has brought about such a monstrous accusation. So far as I know he was never in Arizona in his whole life. I shall bail him out, and stop this nonsense once and for all.'

Mary nodded, almost mechanically. She felt rather than saw the many curious and mocking eyes on her. She allowed Orrin to take her by the arm and lead her from the theatre, many others leaving with them, the actors whom they had deserted wondering what had happened to reduce their audience, unaware of the wider drama taking place inside their miniature world.

In a dream, she allowed Orrin to drive her home, certain only of one thing. He had told Orrin nothing of his Arizona adventure, and she was suddenly sure that the only person in Washington who could testify that

Jared Tunstall had, for a short time been in Arizona, passing under a false name, was herself. And she would say or do nothing to hurt him, would remain as quiet as the grave. Not even to his brother would she betray her knowledge.

And, if she had ever doubted that she loved him, that doubt was gone. They had pledged their love beneath Arizona's burning sun, above the lake, and that pledge would hold good after eight years and over nearly two thousand weary miles, and despite any accusation.

'How amusing,' Sarah Lee drawled to her cronies in the Ladies' League, who met the next morning to plan the entertainment for the summer. 'The Senator assures me that both Mary McAllister's beaux are involved in this latest and delicious scandal. It appears that dear Boyce sent the papers which resulted in Jared Tunstall's arrest to the DA, and, of course, her latest victim being Tunstall himself, she has the satisfaction of seeing to what lengths adoration of her will carry a man.'

'Shush,' said the woman to whom she was speaking. 'Mary McAllister has just come in.'

Sarah Lee's brows rose alarmingly. 'Well, she does have courage, that I do grant her. Who else would brave the gossips this morning of all mornings?' And then, 'Oh, here you are, Mary. What excitements last night. One did not imagine that Jared Tunstall knew that Arizona existed, let alone that he chose to murder a man there.'

Mary stripped off her gloves, her hands, she was pleased to note, quite steady.

'No, indeed,' she said, inclining her head a little in Sarah Lee's direction. 'I suppose a fashionable location might prove more acceptable to you. Should he have confined his activities to the East Coast he might have been forgiven, do you think?'

'Oh, murder is murder wherever,' said Sarah Lee carelessly.

'Except, of course,' said Mary, advancing to the table,

and taking her seat among the other committee members, 'that he has not been proven guilty yet—not even had a True Bill found against him. The Grand Jury does not even meet until this afternoon—so that we do not yet know its decision. Unless, Sarah Lee, you are privy to some information to which the less informed among us do not have access? Do tell.'

Sarah Lee metaphorically ground her teeth. She had long since ceased to grind her real teeth where Mary was concerned, or they would have been worn down to the gums, since somehow she was unable to put her down, however hard she tried.

None of the women around Mary, who sat there, as composed as ever, offering suggestions for topics and speakers for the book meetings, and helping to plan a garden party in aid of poor orphans, could possibly have guessed at the emotions which swirled around inside her head.

She thought of Jared's arrest and the new knowledge that Boyce, of all people, had helped to bring it about, the dreadful chance that Jared might be convicted of murder—for while the rest of Washington, including Sarah Lee, found it difficult to think of Jared being in Arizona tracking down and killing his family's murderers, Mary, who remembered the wild, pony-tailed boy he had been, had no difficulty at all in believing that he had done it.

She never knew how she managed to get through the morning, facing down Sarah Lee, when that lady said sweetly to her of their next meeting a week hence, 'You will be able to come, Mary? You are sure you will be available then?'

'No reason why not,' she said coolly, pushing back her chair. 'I shall have no engagements to detain me, Sarah Lee.' She was aware that every avid eye was on her, but was determined to betray nothing of the misery and fear which tore at her. To wait, helpless, while the law dealt with him, unable to see, or even commiserate with him, was an agony in itself.

Somehow, she must see him, send a message; but
how? She walked steadily out of the room, a model of
etiquette, as she always was, the envy of every woman
there for her calm control of herself and her life.

And how long would that last, in the face of what was
happening to Jared?

'Now, little brother,' said Orrin to Jared, his manner
coldly serious, befitting an officer of the court which
would shortly try Jared for murder if a True Bill were
found, 'exactly what is all this about? Yuh bein' in
Arizona an' all, and killing Hugheses?'

They were in a room in the Police HQ the next
morning. A judge in Chambers had earlier refused to
free Jared on bail, listening to the DA's argument.
'Powerful friends in Britain,' he had said, in counter to
Orrin, who was acting as Jared's lawyer until the man he
had wired for—the famous, if not to say notorious,
Harry Hampden—had arrived from New York. 'He
might try absconding there if we set him free.'

Orrin had offered to put up as much as a million
dollars, but the DA had grinned infuriatingly. 'Chicken
feed to the Tunstalls,' he had said. 'Try forty instead.
And if a True Bill is found against him this afternoon a
king's ransom would not free him to you.'

Orrin had given up rather than be taunted by the man
opposite. He would try again, after the Grand Jury had
met, if a True Bill were found.

'Yuh've no real evidence. Only the unsupported word
of a scoundrel, Rafer Hughes,' he had said, for that news
had also travelled around Washington.

'Oh, let the jury decide this afternoon,' the DA had
said. 'Meantime, he can kick his heels in gaol.'

'Oh, come,' said Jared to Orrin. 'I wonder at the DA
for pursuing this, I really do. Are the Grand Jury going
to listen to the unsupported word of a thief and robber?
I shall deny the whole thing absolutely, here, and in the
Territory, if this nonsense is persisted with.'

'I shouldn't be too sure of yoreself,' said Orrin,

watching Jared closely. 'Remember there will be those on the jury only too happy to pull such a thruster as yoreself down. Envy and jealousy follow success about, yuh know.'

'Oh, but you know I was never in Arizona,' said Jared carelessly. He was aware of his brother's eye on him, knew that if he told him the truth he might even advise him to confess, and plead justifiable homicide. But the risk was too great, and Jared had no mind to swing for killing vermin. He had brazenly outfaced more than one enemy, sworn that lies were truth, and truth was lies— and hoped to do so again.

And faced with an outlaw and desperado such as Rafer Hughes, and the man of affairs and good family Jared Tunstall was, he thought that he knew who would win— and it would not be Hughes.

Orrin was inclined to agree with him. But something troubled him, and that was the year after their family had been murdered. Jared should have gone back to Harvard to continue his education. He had been accepted for a Master's degree, had a bright future as a scholar, but he had thrown it all up, and left the ranch saying that he would go north, travel and see life a little before he decided what to do with himself.

And, at the end of the year, he had reappeared at the ranch, said that he had no mind to be a scholar, but would try his hand in the great world outside, and started the headlong career which had brought him fame and fortune.

What was more, Orrin remembered, he had changed, greatly. There was a wildness about him, controlled, it was true, but vividly present, which he had not possessed before. The boy had become a man—very much a man— and Orrin had been able to understand why a scholar's life did not attract him any more.

What if his brother had gone south-west, not north, and tracked down the remnants of the family which had butchered those whom he held dear? Could he condemn him for avenging Pa, the boys, and his lost Clara? He

also knew that the man his brother had become had an
implacable will, and if he thought fit would not involve
his last surviving relative in what he had done for fear of
damaging him, too.

Orrin wanted to say, Tell true, Jared; did you kill
Barrett Hughes and injure Rafer? but he would not.
Jared was his own man, must make his own decisions,
and he would not push him into a corner.

Instead, he put out his hand, took Jared's and shook
it. 'Yours to decide, little brother. And I honour yuh for
what yuh did, whatever yuh did.' Which was as far as he
dared go. Jared might make of that what he would.

Jared looked at his brother steadily, and said, 'And
you will look after Mary for me. I would not have her
deserted at this juncture, and I can do nothing for her.
With luck, I shall be free this afternoon, and we can
forget this, but if not I trust you with her, Orrin, as I
would with my life.'

The big man said, 'Yes,' as he thought of his dead
wife as he had not thought of her for years, and flung his
arms around the younger brother, met late in life, whom
he had come to love and trust. 'Oh, Jared, I had hoped
that we might share a double wedding soon—yuh with
yore Mary, and me with Nella, my dear widow. God
grant that it may be so.'

CHAPTER THIRTEEN

BY THAT evening the news flew around Washington. The Grand Jury had found a True Bill against Jared Tunstall for the murder of Barrett Hughes and the unlawful wounding of Rafer Hughes.

Harry Hampden, the notorious trial lawyer, came to tell Orrin the news. Harry was famed for his successful defence of many a hopeless case, but he was not allowed to defend Jared before the Grand Jury, the accused having to rely on his own wits before the legal might of the DA, who was the prosecuting counsel.

'They allowed me to see him afterwards,' he said. 'The judge ruled, after the True Bill was found, that the affidavits, including those of Rafer Hughes, were enough to make out a prima facie case that Jared was the Link Travis who shot down Barrett Hughes. He ruled that Jared's denial was not in itself enough—that the court must decide which of the two of them was speaking the truth.'

'Well,' said Orrin vigorously, 'That's as may be, but no jury in Arizona would find against Jared, whether they thought him innocent or guilty, once they had heard of the truth of the Tunstall-Hughes feud and what was done to Pa, Clara and the boys.'

'And there's the rub,' said Hampden wryly. 'The judge allowed a plea from the District Attorney that he should be tried here in Washington, seeing that no fair trial could be held in Arizona Territory after the Moreno Case and others in the West had always found for the defendant. He claimed that, as all the material witnesses are here in Washington, for him to be tried here might ensure a fairer verdict. I hasten to add that there are precedents for this. I shall protest before the trial begins, of course, but I have no real hope of success.'

Orrin was despondent. He knew the truth of what had been argued, but seized on something else which Hampden had told him. 'Witnesses! I thought Rafer Hughes was the only witness they had.'

'Witnesses was what Mr Jared Tunstall told me. He queried the DA's statement, as was his right. The DA said that it was a slip of the tongue.'

Orrin sighed. He thought of Mary hearing the bad news that Jared's chances had been so diminished by the judge's ruling.

Mary was only grateful that the law moved swiftly in 1889. Jared's trial was scheduled to take place ten days after the jury had found its True Bill.

She had one brief interview with Orrin during that time. He had told her that Jared had retained the finest defence lawyer in these United States, had every hope of acquittal, that he constantly thought of her, and handed her a letter from him.

He had written only a few words, ending, 'I shall always love you——Forever. . .and a day. . .'

She had given Orrin a message for him, as short and as pointed as his.

'I meant what I said at the theatre. . . Nothing can change what I said to you before. . .and will say again. . . I love you ——Forever. . .and a day.'

Jared and Orrin had agreed that it would be best if she did not visit him in gaol—the DA had won his point about bail—and she had reluctantly assented. At the back of her mind was the knowledge that she knew of his presence in Arizona, using a false name, and she would do nothing which might betray that knowledge. . .and betray him.

She attended the Ladies' League, preserving her calm, provoking Sarah Lee into heights of silliness not yet reached, in an attempt to dent Mary McAllister's poise. She would attend Jared's trial: not to do so would cause more gossip, she thought, than going.

More people than the Tunstalls and Mary McAllister were touched by the trial. Senator Hamilton, on the day that the Grand Jury indicted Jared, called his son into his study.

'A word with you, Boyce.' His face was so stern that Boyce, although he was on his way to an urgent meeting, followed his father without hesitation.

'Yes, what is it?' he said impatiently—he was always impatient with his father these days.

'Tell me, Boyce. Is what I learned this morning true? That you handed the papers which enabled the Grand Jury to indict Jared Tunstall for murder to the DA, and that you are financing and representing Rafer Hughes?'

'Yes,' said Boyce glacially. 'Why do you ask?'

'Come,' said the senator. 'You know better than that. I am ashamed to hear your answer. I know, beyond a doubt, that you have done this in order to hurt Mary McAllister, and damage the man she preferred over you. This is not worthy, Boyce. I ask that you reconsider your actions. Give up this sorry feud.'

Boyce stared at his father. 'No business of yours,' he said.

'Oh, but you are wrong,' said his father sadly. 'You are attempting to hurt a good woman who has done you no harm. It is the action of a half-man.'

'A good woman?' said Boyce, sneering. 'You would not think so if you knew of her what I know.'

'There is nothing which you could tell me,' said the senator firmly, 'which could alter my opinion of her. Had you proposed to her before she met Jared Tunstall, I am sure that she would have accepted you, and made a man of you at last.'

'That is enough,' said Boyce, raising his voice. 'And, since you thought so highly of her, I wonder that you did not offer for her yourself. No fool like a deceived old fool, as you would have been had she accepted you.'

'No,' said the senator, his voice ice. 'I was a double fool, but not for the reasons you give: a fool not to offer for her, because I thought myself too old, not man enough for a young woman, and a fool not to realise that I was more a man than you will ever be. Sorry I am to say it, but I must ask you to leave this house for good, sir. You are not welcome here. And if, through you, any mortal hurt comes to Jared Tunstall, or to her, I shall offer her my name and my protection.' He turned on his heel, leaving Boyce standing there, his hate of Mary and Jared redoubled, because through them he had lost his father.

Jared's trial was one of society's most exciting events of the year. For once, the audience for a criminal case was as fashionable as that for a White House reception—men and women of power flocked to see one of their own kind on the rack.

Jared Tunstall was admired—and hated—by many. They came to gloat or to wonder at this belated epilogue to the Tunstall-Hughes feud, long thought to be over.

Mary sat at the back of the section reserved for spectators. Jared, pale but composed, beautifully dressed as usual, sat at the defendant's table, flanked by Orrin and his defence counsel Harry Hampden. Orrin's presence there was greeted with surprise, until some remembered that he had been trained as a lawyer, was there to fight for, as well as to support, his half-brother.

Old Glory, the United States flag, draped beside him, the judge, His Honour Mr Clarence Gilbert, sat, grave in his black robes, occasionally using his gavel to hammer for silence. His distinguished audience was as unruly as any other because of its interest in, and knowledge of, the defendant, and the scandal which lay behind the case—Boyce Hamilton's revenge on Tunstall for winning Mary McAllister away from him.

Jared smiled faintly once, his eyes raking the room. Mary pretended that the smile was for her. He had undoubtedly seen her, but his glance passed over her face, apparently unseeing; he would not embarrass her by his recognition.

Thinking of him, remembering the past, she missed

the tedious business of the *venire*, the challenging and
swearing in of a jury.

The indictment was then read, stating that on the
twenty-fourth of August, 1881, in the town of Broken
Rock, Arizona Territory, the defendant, Jared Lawrence
Tunstall Junior, did unlawfully kill Barrett Hughes by
shooting him down without warning, and did unlawfully
wound his brother Rafer Hughes.

The reading of the indictment caused such a stir of
gossip in court that a great deal more gavel-hammering
ensued, and a warning from the judge that the court
would be cleared of spectators if a decent silence was not
maintained.

Jared then rose, and formally pleaded, 'Not Guilty',
in a cool, firm voice. He even managed to look a little
bored by the whole proceedings, and turned and made
an amused comment to his defence counsel when he sat
down again. His counsel then rose to give the court the
first hint of his mettle.

'Your Honour,' he said, 'I should be failing in my
duty to my client if I did not place before you my, and
his, sincere objection to this trial's being held at all. The
Grand Jury were presented with only the evidence of a
known scoundrel who has already served time for criminal acts, and this against a man whose name and
reputation are unstained, relating to a supposed crime
committed eight years ago when my client was little
more than a boy, in a part of the world which he is
prepared to swear on oath that he has never visited.
Furthermore, it is understood from evidence already
presented to the Grand Jury that the man who killed
Barrett Hughes was one Lincoln Travis, and my client is
adamant that he is not that man. In all these circumstances I submit to you that the Grand Jury were
mistaken in ordering that my client should come to trial,
and I expect you to so rule, and order his immediate
release.' His confident smile encompassed judge, jury,
and spectators. He sat down with a flourish.

'Mr District Attorney,' said the judge, 'I think that it

is for you to answer Mr Hampden's plea. I consider that it has some merit.'

'Oh, Your Honour,' said the DA, equally confident, 'firstly, it is for the Grand Jury to decide the competency of the indictment, not, with respect, yourself. Secondly, I am certain that when you, and the jury, hear the whole case against Mr Jared Tunstall there, rather than the abbreviated version which is all that the Grand Jury had to consider, there will remain no doubt in their minds and in yours as to his guilt. For you to throw out the case before any further evidence is heard would be, again with due respect, an act beyond your power, and highly inadvisable.'

The judge steepled his hands beneath his chin, and considered the two lawyers whom he had called before the bench.

'I am bound,' he finally announced, 'to follow the advice of the District Attorney. If, Mr Hampden, your client is innocent, as he claims, then a trial cannot hurt him, and he ought to prefer, in fact, that the whole matter is publicly aired, so that his innocence is proved beyond a doubt. Such a consideration moves me to allow the trial to continue.'

Harry Hampden bowed his leonine head. His whole appearance, his manner, and the air of suppressed power which he carried around with him, were beginning to make an impression on spectators and jurors alike, Mary noted. She breathed a little more easily, knowing that Jared had such a master by his side to fight for him.

'I bow to Your Honour's decision,' he said. 'As I must. I must now, again in fairness to my client, urge that you should properly order that this case be tried not here in Washington, but in the Arizona Territory, where the alleged crimes took place.'

The DA's reply to this, and the judge's verdict, were again in favour of the prosecution. 'For,' finished the judge, 'all the evidence and the witnesses are here present, and in the current state of justice in the Territory the trial may be more fairly conducted here, and I so rule.'

Neither Jared nor his counsel had expected either decision to go their way, but the point had been made that Jared would be most strenuously defended, and Mary was not the only spectator to think that, with Hampden on his side, Jared Tunstall was in an almost unassailable position, given that the DA had so little going for him, with one tainted witness.

Finally, early in the afternoon, the District Attorney, Decimus Parker, rose, a powerful figure of a man, determined that this case would make his name.

'In the case of the people against Jared Lawrence Tunstall Junior, also known as Lincoln Travis,' he said, 'the people will seek to prove that Jared Tunstall, posing as an outlaw, under the name of Lincoln Travis, in the summer of 1881, hunted down and murdered Barrett Hughes by shooting him without warning, under the mistaken belief that he and his brothers had murdered Senator Tunstall, his father, three of his brothers, and his brother Orrin's wife Clara—a brutal crime of which Barrett Hughes's surviving brother Rafer will give evidence that he was entirely guiltless. He will also state that, on the contrary, the Tunstall family repeatedly endeavoured to destroy the Hughes family, and that Jared Lawrence Tunstall's act was merely the final one in——'

At this point Orrin, who had grown increasingly more agitated as the DA spoke, lost the almost Roman calm which distinguished him in public life, and, with Jared and Hampden vainly trying to pull him down, rose to his feet, shouting, 'Lies! All lies! The whole world knows that the Hughes family murdered my father, my brothers, and my dear wife Clara. . .'

All was tumult. The judge hammered vainly to still the uproar, the DA was protesting, demanding Orrin's expulsion, Hampden was on his feet apologising for his colleague, and Jared had an arm around Orrin, whose head was in his hands.

Finally, 'The jury will disregard the prosecuting counsel's statement,' ruled the judge, and then, 'Senator Orrin Tunstall will approach the bench.'

'Senator Tunstall' he said to an Orrin now quite white, but mastering himself, 'I understand your distress, but I am bound to warn you that you are an officer of the court, and as such know its rules. Mr Hampden was entitled to object to the District Attorney's statement, should he so wish—you had no such right. One more interruption and I will have you removed. You understand me, sir? Only your previous good name and your sufferings have prevented me from ordering your removal immediately.'

Mary suffered with Orrin, and if the DA had hoped to score a point he had lost. The sympathy, visibly, was with Orrin. The DA, a young man, had underestimated the detestation of what had been done to the Tunstalls, and to Clara. Few doubted the Hugheses' guilt.

After that, all might have been anticlimax, except for the unlikely tale the DA unfolded in his opening address.

'The people will prove, gentlemen of the jury, that, after the deaths of his family, Jared Lawrence Tunstall Junior, taking the name of Lincoln—Link—Travis, pursued the Hughes brothers into Arizona, under the mistaken belief that they were responsible for the Tunstall massacre. He disguised himself as an outlaw, and, indeed, became one—in fact, finally joining the infamous Liam Garrity on his ranch in Arizona Territory, near Heyes Landing, where he helped to plan and to successfully carry out several raids on banks and trains. Garrity and his gang were later killed to the last man in an ambush in the Bedford County War in Texas.

'But, before that, Jared Tunstall had already left to track down and then murder Barrett and wound Rafer Hughes at Broken Rock, in the Arizona Territory, being himself wounded in the action.'

On hearing this story, every eye in court wandered from the DA to Jared, sitting there, smooth, cool and sophisticated, the friend of princes, as unlikely an outlaw

as a man could be; and Mary, listening to this recital of
what Jared had done, after he had left her, knew, at last,
why he was in Arizona, where he had gone, and why he
was so late in returning to Heyes Landing. And—oh,
she feared for him, for she knew that the DA was telling
part of the truth.

She could not believe that Jared had wantonly murdered Barrett Hughes, but she could, remembering the
Link Travis he had been, believe that he had challenged
and killed him in fair fight.

'The people will bring witnesses to prove that Jared
Tunstall is indeed Lincoln Travis, who, it is uncon-
tested, shot down the Hughes brothers. Evidence as to
this is also available, and will be produced for the court,'
the DA ended. 'Evidence which is so strong that you
will be compelled to find Jared Lawrence Tunstall guilty
of murder, of a crime so heinous that the only punishment which the people will demand will be that of the
death penalty, death by hanging. Do not allow his social
standing, his name, and his wealth to affect your justified
revulsion for the crime which he committed.' The DA,
too, sat down with a flourish.

Witnesses! The DA had said it again. Jared looked at
his lawyer, who shrugged. The prosecution, like the
defence, was under no obligation to reveal its case, or its
witnesses to the opposition—might, indeed, and often
did, spring a surprise at any time. Many had begun to
argue that this was wrong, and should be changed, but
tradition was against them.

Mary, sitting there among the spectators, felt another
shiver of fear. He had said witnesses. In her brief
interview with Orrin, he had told her that before the
Grand Jury the DA had said witnesses, and had then
retracted. They, whoever they were, had traced Jared
back to Heyes Landing, that was plain—but had they
also traced her?

After all, Jared had traced her, had he not? And if
Boyce Hamilton, who sat in the spectators, too, eyes
unblinking, first on Jared and then on herself, had by

the same means as Jared traced Jared back to the Link
Travis he had undoubtedly been, might he not have also
found Charlie Nelson, Link's sweetheart, who had lived
in Heyes Landing—and who was Charlie Nelson but
Mary McAllister? Could it possibly be that they might
try to use Charlie Nelson to hang Jared, for she, and she
alone, could say with truth, Yes, I knew Link Travis
and, yes, he was—is—Jared Tunstall?

She tried to push the ugly thought away, but could
not. God could not be so cruel that He could arrange it
so that it was by her testimony that Jared could be
condemned to a dreadful death. She consoled herself
with what happened next, when Rafer Hughes was called
to give evidence of his brother's death at the hands of
Lincoln Travis, claiming that Travis had shot him down
without warning.

Rafer made a bad witness. Even cleaned up, wearing
a respectable suit, his hair sleeked down, and after heavy
coaching by the DA, he still looked and sounded the
desperado he had been. The contrast with Jared Tunstall
was even more vivid. Disbelieving eyes moved from his
battered face to Jared's smooth and civilised one. The
harsh Western accent, the total lack of *savoir-faire* which
accompanied him from the first moment he stepped on
to the stand, all told against him.

Harry Hampden was up and down like a jack-in-a-box
when Rafer gave his evidence.

'Objection,' he roared, not once, but several times, as
hearsay and vilification of the Tunstalls poured from
Rafer.

Red-faced, Rafer growled his fury, then the judge
turned to the DA. 'You must control your witness, Mr
District Attorney. Warn him that if he repeats his
accusations against Senator Tunstall again he will be in
contempt of court.' For Rafer had begun to abuse Orrin,
to accuse him of inciting Jared to murder, after previously helping his dead father to damage the Hugheses.

The DA, who had begun to see his case slipping away
from him, warned Rafer to be careful of what he said, to

answer questions and not to volunteer unwanted and damaging accusations. It was plain to Mary, and to the rest of the courtroom, that Harry Hampden was itching to get at Rafer, to discredit him, show him up for what he was, to use his hatred of the Tunstalls against him, by demonstrating that the case against Jared was founded on an act of unjustified spite.

Finally the DA was done, and, with a sigh, Rafer made to leave the stand. He had produced, during his evidence, a stained and grubby 'Wanted' poster, and several yellowed newspaper clippings, accounts of the incident in which Barrett had died and he and Travis had been wounded. These had been admitted as evidence, given numbers, and handed to Harry Hampden, Orrin and Jared for examination.

Hampden held the 'Wanted' poster in his hand when he approached the stand to cross-examine Rafer, who, by now, had already left it. Harry Hampden looked at the judge, eyebrows raised, and the judge said immediately, 'The witness will remain for further questioning.'

Rafer's expression was so sullen that Harry Hampden said poisonously, 'Come, come, *Mr* Hughes,' treading on the Mr, for the DA had been punctilious in so addressing Rafer. 'You have taken part in trials before, have you not? You are not so stupid as to be unaware that when your own counsel has finished with you, you are there for the opposing counsel to test your truth and to expose your lies. You are lying, are you not, *Mr* Hughes?'

Rafer glowered at him, but said nothing. Hampden smiled at him, and said, still sweetly poisonous, 'Come, come again Mr Hughes; you were not so quiet a moment ago. Are you lying? I am anxious to know—and so is the judge, the jury, and Mr Jared Tunstall, the victim of your inventions.'

'No inventions,' said Rafer sturdily. 'He is Link Travis, and you will not shake me, or stop me from so testifying.'

'So testifying,' drawled Hampden mockingly. 'You

are used to testifying, are you not? Tell me, how many
prison terms have you served, *Mr* Hughes?'

'Objection,' said the DA, 'on the grounds of being
irrelevant and immaterial.'

'I merely wish to establish Mr Hughes's credentials as
a worthwhile and trustworthy witness,' said Hampden.

'Overruled,' said the judge.

'Please answer me,' said Hampden. 'How many?'

'Two,' mumbled Rafe. 'But I wuz framed.'

'Oh, I'm sure,' smiled Hampden. 'Twice. For robbery
once and unlawful wounding, I believe.'

Rafer nodded.

'And now, before I begin to question you about what
happened in Arizona Territory on the twenty-fourth of
August, 1881, let us examine to what you are *testifying* as
to Jared Tunstall's being Lincoln Travis. The DA asked
you if you could see Lincoln Travis in court, and you
turned around and identified Mr Jared Tunstall as him.'
He turned to Jared. 'Would you have the goodness to
stand up again, Mr Tunstall? I wish to question *Mr*
Hughes further. Look again at him, *Mr* Hughes. You
are willing to swear that that man is Lincoln Travis?'

'I've said so, haven't I?' almost howled a goaded Rafer.

Hampden swung towards the judge. 'Please instruct
the witness, Your Honour, to answer my questions
correctly.'

The judge sighed, and so instructed Rafer. 'Well?'
said Hampden.

'Yes, that man is Lincoln Travis,' ground out Rafer.

Hampden held up the 'Wanted' poster. 'And this is a
drawing of Lincoln Travis? You swear to that?'

'I've already. . .' began Rafer, to change his mind and
say, still sullen, 'Yes.'

'Yes,' said Hampden, 'so you did. Now, I'm going to
hand this poster to the jury and ask them to look at it,
and at Mr Tunstall. And while they are doing so I shall
question you further. What does the poster show, *Mr*
Hughes?'

'It shows Link Travis.'

'A desperado with a beard, and his hair in a pony-tail. . . Let the Jury look at the poster and ask themselves whether it resembles Jared Tunstall in any way. I think that they will find it does not. And the text below—it gives the colour of his hair and eyes. Hair black, it says, and Jared Tunstall's is certainly black—like that of half the men in this court—but we aren't going to accuse *them* of being Lincoln Travis, are we. . .?'

'Objection,' roared the DA.

'I take it that this line of questioning has a further point, Mr Hampden,' said the judge, 'and that you are not merely embroidering?'

'Oh, indeed, Your Honour,' said Harry Hampden, face mocking. 'After the hair, it says eyes grey, does it not? Now, *Mr* Hughes, you see Mr Jared Tunstall there, standing so patiently; tell me, what colour are his eyes?'

'I can't see from here,' growled Rafer.

'No?' said Hampden. 'Then I will tell you, and we may ask his Honour to check what I say. Mr Tunstall's eyes are blue-black, quite remarkably so, not grey—and his height, it says, five foot eleven inches, and I dare swear that Mr Jared Tunstall, like his brother, is well over six feet tall—six feet two inches, at least, *Mr* Hughes——Now what do you say to that?'

'Oh, everyone knows "Wanted" posters are unreliable——' began Rafer angrily, to be stopped by Hampden.

'Do they indeed? And yet you have cheerfully put this one forward to try to hang Mr Jared Tunstall with it. I think that you may sit down, Mr Tunstall. The whole world, let alone this courtroom, can testify to your eye colour and height, and that they show Mr Rafer Hughes's "incontrovertible evidence", I believe the DA called it, to be a lie.'

'He's still Link Travis, sitting or standing,' called Rafer.

The judge's gavel was in action again. 'The witness will not speak until spoken to. Continue, Mr Hampden.'

'Yes, you continue to assert that Link Travis and

Jared Tunstall are one and the same. Tell me, *Mr*
Hughes, when did you first know that? When your
brother was shot? Five minutes later? A week later? Or
was it eight years later, when a private detective was
offering a reward for information damaging to Jared
Tunstall?'

It was the DA's turn to bellow, 'Objection. Counsel is
not questioning the witness; he is making a speech.'

'Let me rephrase that,' said Hampden, before the
judge could rule, 'since the DA does not like hearing the
truth. When did you first identify Jared Tunstall as Link
Travis?'

Mary leaned forward. She was fascinated by the
defence counsel, and by Jared's hard demeanour—the
more so since she knew that Jared was lying through his
teeth, and that Hughes, however much he might be lying
about Jared's wantonly murdering his brother, was right
to identify him as Travis.

'I didn't know that he was Jared Tunstall until eighteen months ago. I'd never met him when we lived near
the Tunstalls in Wyoming; he lived away, they said, in
the north. I saw him, accidently, when he came to
Montana about some mining business, and I knew him—
not when I first saw him, but later. Something about
him—and then, when I was told that he was Tunstall, I
recognised him, the way he held himself. Travis had that
same damnable sureness, the way he mocked at you
almost. He was in Broken Rock a week before he found
an excuse to kill Barrett, and his. . .impudence. . .was
the talk of the saloons.'

Mary shivered again. She remembered Link, the way
he had approached her, how sure he was of himself—
yes, it was almost arrogance. It was that same sureness,
his self-control, which had told her, more than anything
else, that Jared was Link. . .and she knew that Rafer
Hughes had seen it, too.

'You identified him,' said Hampden, smiling. 'He
didn't wear a beard then, in Broken Rock? He was clean-
shaven?'

'No. He wore a beard. But I knew him.'

'He wore a beard, and you knew him, clean-shaven? And his pony-tail? Did he wear a pony-tail in Montana like the one on the "Wanted" poster? Does Mr Jared Tunstall wear a pony-tail? Is he, was he, ever likely to have worn one?'

'Yes, Travis wore a pony-tail and. . .'

'And, yes, you knew him without one,' finished Hampden. 'Come, come. This evidence is meaningless. I would not hang a dog on it, Your Honour,' he said, appealing to the judge. And then to Rafer, 'I suppose Link Travis spoke with an East Coast accent, too, and wore a European tailored coat and suit?'

The spectators, fascinated by what had passed, broke into loud laughter at this. The DA roared objections.

'Oh, Your Honour,' said Hampden. 'Here we have the evidence of a witness who, after nearly eight years, sees a man of six feet two, not five feet eleven, without a beard, or a pony-tail, who has blue-black eyes, not grey, who speaks with an Eastern accent, and I dare swear Mr Link Travis spoke with a Western accent. Did he, *Mr* Hughes, speak with a Western accent? No need to answer; I see by your face that he did, and you identify them as one and the same. The mind boggles. I submit again, Your Honour, that this case should never have come to trial. Mr Hughes invented this in order to get a grubstake, to live high on the hog in Washington, batten on the Tunstall-Hughes feud, try to destroy another Tunstall.

'Now, Mr Hughes, what do you say if I tell you that we shall prove that Mr Jared Tunstall, at the time of which you speak, was in the north, completing his education? That he did so while dressed as a desperado, speaking in a thick Texan accent? Was in two places at once?'

Again, there was uproar, so loud that the DA's protestations could not be heard. Jared Tunstall's trial was providing even more entertainment than its 'swank audience'—for so the *Gazette* called it—had bargained for.

'Objection,' howled the DA. 'Mr Hampden is speechifying again.'

'Sustained,' said the judge wearily, 'But I am bound to advise you, Mr DA, that I, too, am not happy with what has passed so far. Have you further evidence? For, without any, I shall be compelled to call a mistrial, and stop proceedings.'

Mary, heart thundering, prayed that the DA had finished. She could tell by the expression on the faces of the jurors, the spectators, and even the judge, that on what had been heard Jared was almost free. Rafer Hughes was discredited. Whatever he said from now on would be suspect.

But the DA held his ground. 'Your Honour, I do have further evidence, which, seeing the lateness of the hour, I have arranged to call tomorrow. Since it will strongly reinforce the People's claim that Mr Jared Tunstall, however unlikely it seems, was Lincoln Travis in Arizona Territory in 1881, I must ask for Your Honour's patience, and that you allow me to call it.'

The judge considered, then said, at last, 'It is not like you, Mr Parker, to bring a case on insufficient evidence. But I must inform you that if what you produce tomorrow is as dubious as what has been heard today I shall stop the trial immediately, and reprimand you for wasting the court's time.'

The District Attorney bowed. 'I am grateful to Your Honour. I assure you that what will be presented to you tomorrow will be of a different order from today's evidence. I am also bound to submit that I consider Mr Rafer Hughes to be speaking the truth—only his manner is unfortunate when confronted with a skilled advocate.'

'That is as may be,' said the judge. 'But remember my warning.'

'I ask Your Honour to reconsider, and dismiss the case,' intervened Hampden. 'So far my client has been the subject of ill-informed and damaging innuendo. He should be released from further torment at once.'

'I will say what I said before.' And the judge was firm. 'If he is innocent, he has nothing to fear. We will recess for the day.'

First the newsmen and then the spectators streamed from the courtroom; the trial of Jared Tunstall had been even more sensational than anyone could have hoped. First the astonishing accusations, and after that. . . Seldom had a prosecution witness been so completely demolished.

And there was more to come; there was no doubt of that. Those who knew the DA well said knowledgeably that he would never have brought the case to court on such poor evidence as had already been produced. Who knew what might happen tomorrow?

Oh, if only it were over, Mary thought, going home alone. Orrin had disappeared with Harry Hampden and Jared after the judge had gone, and she could only imagine what he had thought as the evidence had unfolded. She had hoped at the end that the judge would throw the case out, ending Jared's ordeal. The thought of him being found guilty was almost too much to bear.

And what was worse was her terrible suspicion that somehow the prosecution might have found out who Mary McAllister really was, and that they might use her to press home their case against Jared!

CHAPTER FOURTEEN

EIGHT o'clock in the morning was not the best time for facing a crisis, Mary found. She was standing before her dressing-table, fixing her hair, tempted for once to use rouge and *papier poudré* to conceal the marks of sleeplessness on her face, when she heard a violent battering on the front door.

She had spent a distressful night worrying about Jared, and wishing that she could see him, to comfort him, to reassure him that she loved him. He had been so cool and controlled in court on the previous day that she could almost have thought that she had imagined he was Link Travis, and that he and she had lived and loved in that long-ago summer.

Standing there yesterday, wordlessly defying Rafer Hughes, the faintest of smiles on his face, he was the Wall Street pirate in action—or the boy, Link, who always knew what he wanted, and went for it. Had he been like that before the dreadful deaths of his family? Or had those deaths, as Orrin had hinted at the Sheldon house, changed him?

Harry Hampden had said yesterday that Jared had been in the north, thinking of returning to Harvard, where a scholastic career had awaited him. She had difficulty in thinking of him as a likely scholar, until she remembered the knife-like intellect, which he had devoted to money-making, the speed with which he spoke and thought and acted.

Downstairs, Miss Nessie was busy feeding a recalcitrant Sally-Anne. 'Why is the toast burned this morning? I don't like it all burned,' she was complaining.

Miss Nessie answered the door, shouting crossly, 'No need to break the door down; I'm coming, I'm coming,' only to be pushed backwards by a portly court official, followed by several policemen.

The official tried to thrust a piece of paper into Miss Nessie's hand, saying, 'This subpoena to attend court as a witness in the case of the people versus Jared Lawrence Tunstall, Junior, alias Lincoln Travis, is being served on you, Mrs Mary McAllister.'

'Lands sakes,' said Miss Nessie, angrily pushing his hand away. 'No wonder so many criminals go unpunished if the tipstaffs can't do their work properly. I'm not Miz McAllister.' And the subpoena fell to the floor between them.

Sally-Anne, drawn by the noise, stood in the doorway to the kitchen, face a little frightened. Mary, alerted by the commotion, came slowly down the stairs, a picture of cool dignity in a deep blue walking dress with cream silk bishop's sleeves merging from the shorter ones of the dress.

'What is it, Miss Nessie? Who are these people?' she asked, although, her heart sinking, she knew beyond a doubt who they were, and why they were calling on her. Her afternoon in the sun had created ripples in the pool of time so great that eight years later, two thousand miles away, officials and policemen were besieging her door.

'They say that they have a paper for you, Miz Mary.'

'Do they so?' said Mary steadily, advancing on the leader of the group. 'Then they had better give it to me, had they not?'

The official, having recovered his subpoena from the floor, recited his piece again, and pressed it into Mary's hand, adding, 'You are required to be present at the courthouse by nine of the clock, mam, without fail, or a warrant for your attendance will be sworn against you,' and then withdrew with his fellows.

Mary held the piece of paper in her hand, her face already so white that the subpoena's serving could not increase her pallor. An angry Miss Nessie shut the door on the intruders with a bang, then turned to see Mary sinking on to the bottom step of the stairs, head in her hands.

'What is it, Mary?' This was said woman to woman, all 'misses' gone, real concern on her kind old face. Sally-Anne, eyes wider than ever in a paper-white face, ran to her mother.

'Oh, Mama, who were those hateful men?' And, echoing Miss Nessie, 'What is it? Mr Jared, they said. What has happened to him?'

'Nothing, I hope,' said Mary, hugging her child to her. 'This paper simply means that I have to help him.'

'In court?' said Miss Nessie sceptically. 'But why come to you? What have you to do with what Jared Tunstall might have got up to in Arizona all those years ago?'

'A long story,' said Mary, who dared not tell Miss Nessie the truth for fear that it would somehow damage Jared; for she might yet outface them in court. She dared not even ask a lawyer for help in the little time remaining to her for the same reason. She trusted nobody, and what she feared had come to pass. They, and the they included Boyce, were going to use her to try to hang Jared. Never mind that. She would outface them all. The courage which had sustained her since she had first found herself pregnant was with her still.

She stood up. Her moment's weakness was over, and that weakness was all for Jared and not for herself. She thought how cool and steadfast he had been yesterday, and she would be the same. She wondered if he knew that they were calling her, but she somehow doubted it.

Sally-Anne, hearing yet another commotion outside, ran to the window, looked out, and said breathlessly, 'Oh, Mama, there are lots of men outside staring at the house!' While she watched, one of them walked boldly up to the front door, and hammered on it.

'Journalists,' said Mary numbly. The DA had informed the Press, and in the increasingly brash world of the 1880s the Press were becoming progressively more intrusive in their search for exciting stories to amuse their newly literate readers. She should know, thought Mary wryly, for was she not one of them herself? Although they were not aware of that.

'Go to the door, Miss Nessie,' she said. 'Don't open it, whatever you do. Shout to them through the letter-box. Tell them to go away.'

Sally-Anne ran to her mother again. 'Mama, I'm frightened. They won't hurt Mr Jared, will they?'

'Not if I can help it,' said Mary firmly. Miss Nessie's bellowed orders did not deter the reporter, however. Denied direct access, he trampled across Mary's flower-beds to look through the window—more of his colleagues and rivals joining him.

Miss Nessie shook her fist at them. She drew the curtains so that they might not see in.

'Vultures,' she stormed angrily.

Mary looked at the fob-watch pinned to the front of her neat dress.

'Miss Nessie, I will tell you everything later, I promise you, when I get back from court. In the meantime I must try to eat something. I shall have to leave soon, if I am due there at nine, and I must think how to reach the courthouse without having to run the gauntlet outside.'

Sally-Anne, her first fright gone, was beginning to find the whole thing quite exciting, especially as Mama seemed to think that there was no danger to Mr Jared.

'You can go through the back door,' she said, 'over the fence to the Brunts' garden, which backs on to ours. Jennie Brunt and I often visit each other that way. I'm sure that the Brunts will let you through if you explain about those horrid men.'

'So they will,' said Mary, having a picture of herself, the staid Widow McAllister, scaling the picket fence that divided the gardens. It would be like being Charlie Nelson again.

She kissed Sally-Anne, had breakfast, even managed to eat toast—burned, to drink coffee—cold, although both tasted of ashes. She must be ready and armed, for

she knew beyond a doubt that they were going to try to
break Jared through her.

'I see that Mary McAllister is not here today,' said Sarah
Lee Chase to her friend sitting beside her.

'Haven't you heard? The DA has subpoenaed her as a
witness to appear in court first thing this morning. We
were all speculating as to why on earth he would do such
a thing, when you arrived.'

Sarah Lee's pleasure that the stuck-up Widow
McAllister would be firmly in the eye of the court was a
little marred by the fact that she was so late in learning
such exciting news. She was usually the first to know,
and to patronise her clique because of it.

She might have guessed that something extraordinary
had happened by the buzz of excitement that ran around
the courtroom even before the leading characters arrived.

Jared had come in while she was talking to her cronies.
He sat between Orrin and Harry Hampden as he had
done the day before. Sarah Lee stared at him, wondered
if he knew that Mary McAllister was to appear, and
decided that he didn't, by his manner; but it was difficult
to tell, he was such an opaque creature, she thought
angrily, remembering how cool he had been the previous
afternoon.

Jared, completely unaware that Mary had received a
subpoena, had been more than happy with the way
things had gone the previous day. He had watched Harry
Hampden destroy Rafer with a wry amusement, and for
a delirious moment had hoped that the judge might
dismiss the prosecution's case forthwith and save him
the trouble of perjuring himself on the stand.

The only fly in the ointment was the DA's insistence
that he had more, and sounder, evidence than Rafer
might provide. And what could that be? The haunting
fear, which he shared with Mary—that if he had traced
her so could others—had made his sleep as disturbed as
hers. Perhaps he was wrong; for, after all, his agent had
been looking for her past, while Boyce's had been

pursuing him, and even if he had come across the name
of Charlie Nelson it would surely have meant nothing to
him.

He was not to know that Boyce's spite, based on
jealousy, the spite of a man who, disliking all women,
had finally persuaded himself that he did love one
woman, had driven him to pursue Mary's past as well,
and so the connection between Link Travis and Charlie
Nelson had been made.

'Jealousy is cruel as the grave,' said the Bible, and if
love conquered all, then jealousy had its victories as well,
and Boyce's jealousy encompassed a desire to destroy not
only Mary, but her lover, and to do so publicly would be
to add salt to his feast.

But, as yet, Jared knew nothing of this, and his fears
were not for himself—even though he had no wish to be
convicted—but for Mary. For if, by some mischance,
she was the prosecution's secret witness, then all that she
had striven for and built in the last eight years would be
destroyed, and she with it, in the revelation of their
consummated love-affair, and its consequence, Sally-
Anne, who would be destroyed too.

Nothing of this showed. He had joined in Harry
Hampden and Orrin's rejoicings of the previous evening,
although Hampden had nodded agreement when Orrin
had said, 'Remember, you're not home free yet, feller,
but the signs are good.'

Later, when Hampden had gone, Orrin had returned
to him for a moment, in the room set aside in the gaol
for accused persons to confer with their legal advisers,
guards standing at the door ready to take him to the cell
where he had been held for the past week.

'Something I have to say.' His brother stood tall in the
small room, dwarfing those who guarded him. He put
out a hand and took Jared's. 'Just this. You shouldn't
have done it, I know. But I thank you for it, and, God
willing, we shall see you free, and you may marry your
Mary, and leave all this behind.' He had wondered wryly

what Orrin would think if he knew, or ever discovered, the whole truth of what he had done in the Territory. . .

Like everyone else, he stood when the judge entered. The court reporter sat down, an air of expectancy filled the room—the only persons in it unaware that Mary had been called being the defence.

The DA finished his re-examination of Rafer Hughes. Hampden had indicated that he had done with him. Anything more from him might actually harm Jared's case.

The spectators sighed after some fifteen minutes of this—all apparently to little purpose. What the DA asked Hughes added nothing, was simply filler to take up time before he called Mary, and to lull the opposition into believing that, after all, he had no real further evidence to damn Tunstall with.

Hughes was stood down. The DA then rose, and said, 'The People call Mrs Mary Charlotte Nelson McAllister to the stand.'

Tumult again. Those who knew what was coming, and those few who did not, exchanged opinions. The judge gavelled for order again. Spectators noticed that Jared Tunstall's amused calm was, if not shattered, at least disturbed. He turned to his counsel and began to speak to him urgently.

Almost immediately Harry Hampden rose, and said to the judge in his lion's roar, 'Your Honour, I must protest this. We have had no warning that this witness was to be called. Her name has never been raised in connection with this case. I ask you to rule the district attorney out of order, and the witness refused.'

'Now, Mr Hampden,' said the judge, after gavelling furiously to subdue the noise. Mary, who was being led through the door into the court, was held back on Hampden's words to await the judge's ruling.

'I must have silence.' And now the judge was almost roaring. Spectators were standing, pointing at Mary, who stood calm, hands folded together before her.

'Mr Hampden, you know perfectly well that the

prosecution, like yourself, may call witnesses without prior warning. I have no alternative but to admit Mrs McAllister to the stand.'

Hampden, who had advanced until he stood before the bench itself, would not give way. 'Then, Your Honour, that being so, at least grant me a short recess so that I may speak with my client. Believe me when I say that this is the first I have heard of Mrs McAllister. I did not even know that such a person existed.'

The DA leaped up to protest this, but was silenced by the judge. 'Very well, Mr Hampden, I will grant you a short recess to confer with your client; but it will be short, mind. Be prepared to return when the officer of the court calls for you.'

'Now,' said Hampden, and he was almost angry, standing before the brothers, 'who the devil is Mrs Mary McAllister, and what has she to do with the case? What have you been keeping from me, sir, and you, Senator Tunstall?'

Both brothers began speaking together. Orrin: 'I have not the slightest idea; this is as big a surprise to me as to you.'

Jared: 'Mrs McAllister is the lady I hope to make my wife. She is a widow of good standing in Washington.'

He was in turmoil, but neither Orrin nor Hampden could have guessed it. He walked away from them, stood with his back to them both. He could almost feel Orrin's shock, and Hampden's anger.

'This is not good enough,' said Hampden. 'To have this sprung on me. You told me categorically that you had informed me of everything relevant to your life at the period when Travis killed Barrett Hughes. Now this woman appears. Is she the witness whose evidence will be damning to you, and if so, how?'

Jared swung back to them, a faint smile on his face. He knew one thing, and one thing only. He would tell Hampden nothing of Mary, of what had passed in Heyes Landing. He would wait to see what she was asked, what

she replied. And the moment anything occurred which
would damage her irretrievably he would stop the trial
by admitting that he had been Travis.

He would sooner swing by the neck than see her, or
Sally-Anne, hurt. The implacable will, which Orrin
knew he possessed, informed his every act.

'We shall have to wait to find out what she says,' he
said, 'and act accordingly. They may, for all I know, be
trawling—trying to upset us, make us do the wrong
thing. Nothing more.'

'And that's it?' said Hampden, almost disbelieving of
what he heard. 'Nothing more? I'm to make bricks
without straw?'

'Yes,' said Jared. His smile suddenly grew. 'After all,
it's only your reputation at stake. It's my life that's on
the line, and I choose what I do with my life, no one
else.'

Orrin, who had been staring from one to the other,
suddenly erupted. 'No!' he said, lunged forward, and
took his brother by the collar. 'Not good enough. Was
she there? How could she be there? What other games
did you get up to in Arizona Territory, little brother?'
He tightened his grip, stared, eye to eye, at his brother,
but Jared never faltered.

'None of your business,' he said. 'Any of it.'

'And Mary——'

Hampden broke in on them. 'What is this?' he said to
Orrin. 'You *knew* he was in the Territory then? How can
I defend. . .?'

Jared had pulled himself free and said, 'He knows no
such thing. And neither do you. Until Mary McAllister
goes on the stand, and even after. . .there is only one
decision which matters here. And that is mine. . .only
one reputation to be saved. . .and that is hers.'

'I've a mind to withdraw from this case,' began
Hampden. 'And I would do so, except that my
withdrawal——'

Again, he did not finish. 'The choice is yours,' said
Jared. He was almost indifferent. Payment is always

required of us, Mary had said. We cannot take what we want, as and when we want it. And now payment was on him. . .and perhaps Mary too.

Orrin, who had stood silent since Jared had broken away from him, said sadly to Hampden, 'I ask you to continue. I brought you here. He is my brother, and he has never told me that he went to Arizona Territory, nor that he killed Barrett Hughes. I have never consciously deceived you. And, as for Mary McAllister, that is as big a shock to me as to you.'

But he was no fool. He had made the connection, which had been there for him to see all along. Sally-Anne! She was his brother's child, wore Jared's mother's face, possessed his brother's will, his sense of fun. . .and his wildness, barely held in check. How could he have been so blind?

'Bricks without straw, then,' said Hampden, and then there was a rap on the door, and the usher told them to return. To what?

Mary entered the courtroom at last. She looked even more beautiful and composed than ever, Jared noted sadly, wondering how long her composure would last under the DA's hammering, how long before he rose to stop any real revelations about their past. . . Her face was almost luminous; the marks of tiredness added a lovely transparency to it.

Many who had heard of her but were seeing her for the first time, decided that her nickname was well earned. The Ice Princess was as coolly beautiful as her reputation, and her clothes enhanced her.

Mary stripped off her gloves before taking the oath, and placed them on the ledge in front of her. She sat down gracefully, a model of deportment, and looked straight at the DA, who was directly in her line of sight; Jared was a little to her right. She tried not to look at him, had been aware of movement at his table when she entered. She looked, instead, at the giant oil painting of the famed Chief Justice Marshall on the wall opposite to her.

To calm herself she pretended that she was alone in court with the DA and the judge; everyone else—jury, Jared and the spectators was non-existent. She was determined not to be ruffled, whatever was said to her. The cold reason which had ruled her life for eight years was ruling her now. Impulsive Charlie Nelson had never existed.

The DA rose, walked towards her, and saw that her eyes were unflinchingly on him, challenging him, almost. He decided that, above all, he would break her, and destroy that inhuman calm. Jared, watching, every nerve raw, was suddenly resolute. Whatever else, he would not allow her to be hurt. Never mind what might happen to him when he confessed his lie; she must not suffer through him.

The DA began to question her, and she answered him in a low voice, her diction so clear that in the sudden quiet of the courtroom everyone could hear every word she uttered.

'You are known as Mrs Mary Charlotte Nelson McAllister?'

The form of the question struck everyone, Jared and Mary in particular. War had been directly declared.

'That is my name. Yes.' Mary's hands, held quite loosely in her lap, were still. The DA watched them. He wanted to see them writhing.

'So you call yourself. Yes. What is your occupation, Mrs. . . McAllister? You do have an occupation, I believe.'

'I am Senator Barton Graves's political aide. I work for him for two mornings a week, and attend him in Congress and at the Executive Office when required.'

'And, Mrs. . . McAllister? And. . .?'

'And, sir?'

'And your other occupation, Mrs. . . McAllister. For I believe that you do have another. You are a journalist,

are you not? Pray tell the court of that occupation,
madam.'

Jared was whispering frantically to Harry Hampden.
Hampden rose, as Mary's face crimsoned a little,
although her hands remained still. There was another
excited buzz from the spectators when Hampden roared,
'Objection. The witness is being asked something which
is irrelevant and immaterial, Your Honour. What has
this to do with the matter before the court?'

'I, too, should like to know, Mr Parker,' asked the
judge of the DA. 'Pray explain to me why you deem this
line of questioning necessary.'

'Oh, Your Honour, I fear that although the prosecution has called Mrs McAllister as a witness we seek to
treat her as a hostile one. Moreover, it is likely that the
defence will claim her to be a witness of character. I am
bound to find out what kind of character this. . .lady
possesses.'

'I take your point, sir. Objection overruled, Mr
Hampden. You may procede, Mr Parker.'

'I ask you again, madam—and remember that you are
replying under oath. Is it not true that you are a
journalist, that you write for the *Washington Gazette*?
Please tell the court the name of your column.'

There was no help for it. She had told both Garrison
Firth and Jared that she would be brave. She was brave.
She could see Jared's eyes on her. She said coolly, her
voice and manner under perfect control, 'I write the
twice-weekly column for the *Washington Gazette* entitled
"A Lady Looks at Washington".'

Sensation!

The DA's reply to this was drowned in the noise from
the spectators. Several journalists dashed out of the
courtroom shouting, the *Gazette's* man as excited as any.

Sarah Lee's face when Mary replied was a picture.
'Whoever would have thought it? The Widow
McAllister, of all people. Wonders will never cease.
Well, no one will be able to call her the Ice Princess after
that!' she announced to all and sundry.

The judge's gavel came into operation. 'I will have quiet, or the court will be cleared of spectators. Ask your last question again, Mr Parker. No one heard it.'

The DA spoke into silence. 'That is a highly scandalous column for a lady to write, is it not, Mrs. . . McAllister?'

'No, sir. I cannot agree that it is scandalous.' She appeared the only unmoved person in the room. Jared closed his eyes, debated inwardly whether to intervene immediately.

'Come, Mrs. . . McAllister! Not scandalous? Do you not campaign for all society's moral rules to be broken? For there to be only one standard, and that women should be free to behave as men do?'

'Sir, I agree with you; I do campaign for one standard. But you are wrong when you say that I support immorality. I would prefer that men should behave as women do: virtuously and discreetly.'

A shout of laughter greeted this neat and witty response delivered in tones of the coolest impersonality. The DA thinned his lips. Jared winced. His gallant Mary might have won a battle—but she stood to lose the war.

'I see. Virtuously and discreetly. You have a ready wit, Mrs. . . McAllister, but that does not change the fact that, being ashamed of what you write, you shelter behind the cloak of anonymity.'

Jared's lawyer was on his feet again, bellowing objections.

'I am bound to ask you again,' said the judge, 'what is the point of these questions?.'

'Why, Your Honour, to show that this. . .lady is of such dubious moral standing when writing her column, and that she is so aware of her turpitude, that she shelters behind a pseudonym. Thus we gain an insight into her character and her reliability.'

'Not so,' replied Mary coolly, before the judge could make a ruling. 'The pseudonym was a mere journalistic ploy to create interest and to increase sales. As such, I believe that it succeeded.'

The DA was disgusted to see that her hands were still and easy in her lap as she spoke.

'The witness's answer,' ruled His Honour, 'makes it unnecessary for me to overrule you. Confine your questions to the substantive matters before the court, Mr Parker, if you would.'

Harry Hampden was on his feet again. 'The district attorney seeks to do this to disturb and unsettle the witness, Your Honour. I suggest that you reprimand him for such conduct not befitting the decent nature of this Court.'

'I am bound to say, Mr Hampden, that I have seldom seen a witness less disturbed by questioning. But yes, Mr Parker, do not seek to harass the witness.'

'I will obey Your Honour,' said the DA, casting a furious look at Mary, whose calm he appeared to be unable to break. 'Now, Mrs McAllister, I believe that you lived at Heyes Landing, Arizona Territory, between 1876 and 1881?'

This question caused another buzz of excitement among the spectators, although not sufficient this time to cause the judge to use his gavel again. Harry Hampden had already leaped to his feet, pushing down Jared, who was beginning to see the direction which the DA's questioning was taking, and did not like it.

'Objection, Your Honour,' he shouted, 'Counsel is leading the witness.'

'Yes, Mr Parker,' sighed the judge. 'I am bound to agree with the defence counsel again. Rephrase that last question, if you would.'

The DA bowed in the judge's direction. 'With pleasure, Your Honour.'

Mary, sitting there, controlling herself with increasing difficulty, knew exactly what the DA's tactics were. He was doing everything in his power to unsettle her. She refused to look at Jared, although she seemed to sense his internal distress, however cool he outwardly remained. She willed him to remain seated. They would learn nothing against him from her, come what may. She held to this one resolution as though it were a standard she was taking into battle.

The DA was questioning her again.

'Where did you reside between 1876 and 1881, Mrs. . . McAllister?'

'At Heyes Landing, Arizona Territory. My father, Robert Nelson, one-time Professor of Philosophy at Harvard, went to live there in an attempt to recover his health. He died in 1878, I remained there until 1881, running the general store which he had bought.'

'You were known at the time as Charlie Nelson, were you not?'

'Yes,' said Mary, 'that was my name then.'

These further revelations of Mary's past brought more excited and muttered comment from Sarah Lee. 'How exquisitely unlikely! A storekeeper! What next? One supposes that she did not ride with Garrity herself!'

'Cast your mind back to the early summer of 1881, Mrs. . . McAllister. Liam Garrity, the outlaw, owned a ranch, the Bar Y, just outside Heyes Landing, did he not? Who joined his gang during that period, Mrs McAllister?'

'Oh, sir,' said Mary, her voice as steady as she could make it. 'Pray tell me, which question do you wish me to answer? Or is it, perhaps, both?'

Jared was in agonies. His Mary was as quick and witty as a woman could be. She was running rings around the wretched Decimus Parker, but sooner or later he would ask the fatal question about herself and Link and Jared Tunstall, and what could save her then?

'I shall stop this,' he muttered to Hampden and Orrin, 'Whatever you say, if the questioning becomes dangerous, I shall end it.'

'You are a fool if you do,' growled Hampden, 'and she is destroying Parker, not he her.'

'But it cannot last,' answered Jared, to find the judge's eye on them all, his hammer going, as the DA turned to complain.

'Mr Hampden,' said the judge severely, 'I trust you to

keep your client in order while Counsel questions the witness. Continue, Mr Parker.'

'You are pleased to misunderstand me,' ground out the DA. 'Who joined the Garrity gang in the early summer of 1881?'

'Why, several persons, I believe, sir,' said Mary brightly, to laughter this time.

'Come, Mrs. . . McAllister, cease to toy with me. There was one particular person, was there not, with whom you became acquainted, and with whom this case is concerned? Tell me his name, and not that of any other.'

Every eye was on her. The news of her journalistic career had whetted the appetite of the spectators, together with the news of her life in Arizona and her name there, but a new buzz of excitement was beginning at the realisation that Mary McAllister had known Link Travis, as she was now compelled to admit.

'Lincoln Travis joined the Garrity gang then, I believe.'

'You believe, Mrs. . . McAllister? You met him yourself, shortly after, did you not? Became very friendly with him?'

'Objection, Your Honour,' said Hampden desperately, more to quieten his fractious client than to hinder Parker. 'The DA is leading the witness again.'

Jared's impassivity had finally cracked. It was suddenly obvious to the fascinated spectators that he was on the rack. He knew that, beyond a doubt, the worst had happened. Somehow, the truth about himself and Mary had been discovered, and the line of questioning was leading inexorably to it.

'What was your relationship with Lincoln Travis, Mrs McAllister? Virtuous and discreet, would you say?'

Even this innuendo could not move her. 'We were friends, sir.'

'Friends, sir,' he mimicked cruelly. 'Then, Mrs McAllister, seeing that you were a *friend* of Mr Lincoln Travis—virtuously and discreetly, of course—look at

Mr Jared Tunstall there. Is it not true that he was in 1881, and, to your certain knowledge, the desperado known as Link Travis?

'You may take your time in answering me, Mrs McAllister, but I would ask you to remember that you are on oath, and are required to answer me truthfully. Was that man, in the summer of 1881——' and he pointed at Jared '—Lincoln, known as Link Travis?'

The moment of truth was on her. No clever answer, no witticism could save her now. All that she had to do to save herself disgrace and obloquy was to tell the truth and identify Jared as Link. Her Calvary would be over—and his would begin.

If she denied he was Link, the DA would not let her out of the witness-stand, but, bit by bit, would drag out of her the events of that long-ago summer, and to cast doubt on her veracity would destroy her reputation completely, as he revealed the truth about Sally-Anne; he would also reveal that James McAllister had never existed—for she was sure now that the DA knew that, that somehow Boyce had found out, and told him.

He would prove that she, Mary McAllister, was a liar, a sham, whose word could not be trusted; that she had been Travis's whore, Sally-Anne illegitimate, and herself not fit for decent society.

But Mary had no doubt of what she was going to do. She had been a coward once, and run away, and been a hypocrite, afraid to tell the truth—for if she had outfaced the world and waited for him she and Jared would not have lost eight years, and she would have retained her integrity.

And, worse, once they had found one another again, she had had no more sense than to temporise with the man who loved her, had stupidly kept him dangling.

Before her was atonement. She raised her head proudly. Stared first at Jared, and then at the DA. She would lie, and lie again. She would not identify him as Link, would claim that there was no connection between the two men, that Rafer Hughes must be lying to damage yet another Tunstall. Her reputation must take its chance.

Jared saw her face change; he knew her well enough to know what she was going to do—perjure herself— and also knew full well what the consequences for her must be. He saw her lips beginning to frame the word no—and nothing, as he had told Hampden, could stop him.

Hampden was pulling at his arm, but he would not be stopped; he had left it too late, he should have stopped it the moment she went on the stand. He was on his feet, shouting, swinging an arm out towards the DA, towards the bench.

'Enough,' he said. 'That is enough. There is no need to badger or to question Mrs McAllister further. She has nothing to do with this. I admit it. I was Lincoln Travis, I killed Barrett Hughes and wounded Rafer Hughes in fair fight, and for just cause, and shall so now plead. Let her leave the witness-stand.'

Whatever uproar there had been before was as nothing to the noise that succeeded this announcement. Some were disappointed, half aware that there were going to be titillating revelations about what Mary McAllister and Jared Tunstall had got up to with one another in the past, but most were delighted by the heightening of a drama which hardly seemed to need further revelations to make it the most stunning event of the year.

Harry Hampden was silenced for once in his career. Orrin had his head in his hands, Boyce Hamilton, happy to see Jared Tunstall cornered, was sorry that Mary's ordeal had ended without her disgrace—that would have been the icing on his cake.

The judge, having gavelled for silence, said, 'Mr Tunstall, you and your counsel, and the DA, will approach the bench.'

'No,' said Jared firmly. 'Not my counsel. I owe Mr Hampden my thanks, but I no longer have need of him, and will not involve him further. I deceived him, as well as the court.'

'Approach yourself, then, Mr Tunstall. And you, Mrs McAllister, stay where you are, for the moment.' Mary, indeed, had made no move. Despite her inward turmoil she was the calmest person in the court, although full of a bitter regret at what Jared had done to save her pain.

'Now, Mr Tunstall,' said the judge. 'You are persisting in your declaration?'

'Yes, sir, I must. It is the truth.'

'The truth,' said the judge. He thought for a moment. He looked at the DA. 'You will agree with me, Mr Parker, that this changes the whole complexion of the trial.'

'I cannot disagree with Your Honour,' said the DA. 'If I may advise. . .'

'No, sir, you may not,' said the judge severely. 'You may both return to your seats for a moment while I decide what to do. Mrs McAllister, you may leave the stand.'

Mary rose, wondering whether her legs would support her. She picked up her gloves, and walked out into the main body of the court. The DA was already at his table, but Jared, on seeing Mary leave, hesitated, moved towards her, and for a moment they were side by side. Full of love and remorse, he put out his hand to her, saw her unreserved love for him plain upon her face.

The judge made to speak, whether to reprimand him or to make some comment to them both no one ever knew, for at that moment Rafer Hughes took a hand in the game.

He had been sitting quiet, to one side, but at the judge's last words rose slowly, his hand fumbling inside his greatcoat, and began to shout, 'That's all I wanted to know, fellers. No cause to trouble the law trying Tunstall. I'll save it time and money.' And before anyone could stop him, he pulled his hand from inside his coat to reveal his Colt .45, and, pointing it at Jared, fired.

In the screaming that started with his announcement, and before the fusillade of shots from the guards in the courtroom who shot him down rang out, Mary, seeing what he was about to do, flung herself in front of Jared, took the bullet meant for him, and fell, wounded and bleeding, to the ground. Her last sight before she sank into the dark was of Jared, as she pushed him away to save him.

CHAPTER FIFTEEN

FOR a moment there was a shocked and terrible silence, and then a noise which could be heard in the street outside as the realisation that Mary had been shot down struck home.

Spectators rose to their feet, some clamouring and shouting, some sobbing and turning away from the sight of two apparently dead bodies. Even Sarah Lee was reduced to speechlessness by the sight of hard-bitten Jared Tunstall bending over Mary McAllister's unconscious form, his face, for the first time in the trial, betraying the emotions which tore at him.

He had told Harry Hampden with all the confidence which had always ruled him that he, and no other, would choose what to do with his life. He had forgotten the dictum of the one philosopher whom he admired, Machiavelli, who had written that of all our acts only half were decided by ourselves—chance, and chance alone, ruled the rest. Worse still, for the three wrong things he had done—shooting down Barrett Hughes, seducing the young and innocent Charlie, lying to his counsel and the court —payment had been exacted not from him, but from the woman he loved.

Never mind that Barrett Hughes had deserved his fate, that he, Jared, had loved Charlie, and that he had lied to save himself from the punishment which the law had refrained from inflicting on the murderers of his family; he, in his pride, had taken on himself the right to play God, and God, or whoever, had reminded him sharply that he was no more than any other pawn in the game of life, and the piece which he had sacrificed was not himself, but Charlie, whom he loved, and was, in a sense, his victim.

Orrin had torn off his bandana and handed it to him

to staunch the blood which flowed from her wound and was soaking her clothing. He, too, knelt by Mary's body, unbuttoned her dress—to reveal to Jared's distraught gaze his battered ring on a blood-stained silk ribbon: Mary had recovered it from her workbox on the first day of his trial.

A doctor had been called for, but before one could reach her Boyce Hamilton, horrified at what he had provoked, pushed and shoved through the crowd to where she lay, dropping to his knees beside her.

'Say she is not dead,' he cried. 'She cannot be dead. Oh, God, I did not mean this, never this.'

Jared looked up at him, his face swollen with grief. 'If she dies,' he said, 'you may be sure that I will swing for killing you.' He was Link Travis again, coldly murderous. 'You caused this. You brought that homicidal madman here to do his worst.'

Orrin rose, pulled Boyce to his feet. 'Leave them,' he said, 'she is nothing to you,' and when Boyce would have struggled free held him forcibly away, adding, 'Behave yourself, or I shall do Jared's work for him now. I purely ache to kill you myself. She would never have been in this courtroom, on the stand, but for you.'

Agonised, Boyce watched them go, Jared carrying Mary, who was still unconscious. If Mary lived, which was doubtful, he had pushed her into the arms of his rival as surely as if he had made him a present of her.

Mary had been dreaming. She had been a girl again, on the hillside, with Link, under a brilliant sun, beneath a sky so blue that it was like the dream of a sky. She could not remember what they had said or done, only that they had been happy.

And then the hillside had gone, and Link, and she was alone and desolate, except that she had briefly awakened, and he, Link had been there, above her, his face altered, grown older, and sterner, full of sorrow. 'Link?' she had said, and he had replied,

'Oh, my darling, rest and live for me,' and he had vanished again, and the dark had claimed her.

The next time she was conscious she knew everything, and cried out, 'Jared?' and when the nurses came running asked, fearful, 'Does he live?' to be told,

'Yes, he is here,' before everything disappeared again.

Her hand was being held, and the dream was with her, for it was Link—or was it Jared?—who was holding it, and she turned her head towards him. 'Oh, you *are* safe,' she said, and her voice was a thread, 'And you are with me.' And the effort of speech was almost too much for her.

'Oh, my darling Charlie,' he whispered hoarsely. 'I am here, Link is here, and this time I shall never leave you.'

Her hand tightened a little on his. 'Now I can sleep, for you are safe.' She closed her eyes, secure in the knowledge that Link was with her—he had come back for her, after all—and, dreaming again that she was on the hillside with him, she fell into the pit of healing sleep which awaited her, Jared still holding her hand, and praying that the next time she awoke she would be with him again for good.

Jared saw that it was Charlie who lay on the pillow; Mary McAllister had gone with the long hair that they had shorn, but for the first time since she had been shot he felt that there was hope.

'And tomorrow. . .' Jared told Orrin, who had just informed his brother that all charges against him had been dropped since dead Rafer's last act had disqualified his own case. Furthermore, public opinion was firmly against any further persecution of the Tunstalls, particularly since Mary had so nearly shared Clara and the boys' dreadful fate—she had only just been pronounced out of danger. 'Tomorrow, I shall be allowed to take Sally-Anne and Miss Nessie to see her, and I can only hope that she, who nearly gave her own life to save my worthless self, will consent to marry me; for, after all, a man's sweetheart can hardly refuse him, when she has been responsible for saving him for his wedding day.'

'One more thing,' said Orrin quietly, before Jared left

him, to gain his first night's sleep since the shooting—
he had sat by Mary's bed until he knew that she was out
of danger. 'Boyce Hamilton hardly dares show his face
in public. They say that his father has forbidden him the
family home, seeing that his act in bringing Rafer here
precipitated the tragedy.'

Jared shrugged. 'Nothing matters,' he said, 'but that
she lives. Once, I would have gone after him, as I
promised him; but something good has come out of this
for me—that I must learn to control my own passions
lest they betray others, rather than myself.'

He was thinking of this when he collected an anxious
Sally-Anne, who could hardly believe that a wicked man
had hurt Mama so badly that she had nearly died. She
had rallied enough that morning to ask Miss Nessie if
Mr Jared would take them to the hospital in the horseless
carriage, but had been told by Miss Nessie that he did
not think it reliable enough, for he did not want to
disappoint Mama by being late.

'Perhaps,' he said, lifting Sally-Anne into the buggy,
'it will not be too long before you all come to live with
me in the Sheldon house—that is, if Mama is well
enough for me to ask her a certain question, and if the
answer is what I think it will be.'

'And what question is that, Mr Jared? That you might
be my new papa? Oh, I'm sure that she'll say yes. She
likes you so much, I can tell.'

And with that reassuring message ringing in his ears
he left Sally-Anne and Miss Nessie in the ante-room,
saying, 'I will not be long, I promise.'

Mary was, for the first time, well enough to be
impatient for him to come. And when Jared walked in,
a great bunch of carnations in his hand, she tried to
struggle up to greet him. There was a little colour in the
cheek he favoured with his kiss. 'Oh, you are better, my
darling Charlie,' he said softly. 'Well enough for me to
tell you how much I love you, and how much I hope that
you will consent to marry the faulty creature I am. For I
took the law into my own hands when I went after the

Hugheses, and again I showed you no consideration when I seduced you in Heyes Landing, knowing I would have to leave you—and it is no excuse to say that I went after the Hugheses because of what was done, unpunished, to Clara and my brothers. I was a heedless boy, who became a heedless man, and twice you were punished for my folly. After you were shot, I took a good look at myself, and did not like what I saw.'

'No,' said Mary gently, her eyes on his agonised face. 'You did what you thought was your duty by your family, and I can only honour your frankness now. Do not reproach yourself overmuch.'

She watched him put his hand into his pocket, and draw from it the blue ribbon, now black with her blood, on to which she had threaded the battered ring which he had given to her above the lake at Heyes Landing, long ago.

'They cut this from you when they brought you here, and I asked for it. You may guess why. This time I can tell you that the ring was my father's, taken from his body after death. Orrin gave it to me.

'Charlie, Mary—I hardly know which name to use—you are doubly precious to me now that you have taken the bullet meant for me. I want to renew my vows to you, if you can forget the past and what I did. Marry me, my darling, I beg of you.'

He took the ring from his palm and held it out to her.

'Yes,' she said softly, taking the ring from him. 'I did deny you in Arizona; I will not deny you now. I shall marry you as soon as possible. On the stand, in between that odious man's questions, I could only think what a fool I was to refuse you for so long, denying Sally-Anne a father. After all, I loved her so much because she was all that I had left of you.'

'Oh, my Charlie,' he said, giving her the most gentle of kisses, 'so wise you have grown, and now we must ask Sally-Anne in; she is longing to see you, and longing for me to be her papa, and we must tell her—and the world—the truth, whatever it costs us. You said once that we must not sanctify a lie, nor shall we. I told Orrin I could not possibly succeed him as a senator now, and he laughed and said, "Whoo, boy, it'll be a shoo-in, such family feelin' as you showed by killin' Barrett Hughes, and havin' a woman who loved you enough to take a bullet for you."' And, imitating Orrin, his voice was Link's again.

He went to the door and called them in.

Sally-Anne was clutching her doll to her for comfort, and her eyes were enormous, fixed on them both; Miss Nessie, for once, was nearly as overawed.

He took Sally-Anne on his knee. Her eyes were wider than ever as he asked her, 'What would you say if I told you that I was your papa?' He heard Miss Nessie's gasp as he spoke.

'Really and truly my papa, Mr Jared?'

'Yes,' he answered. 'Really and truly your papa, Sally-Anne.'

'Why,' she said, 'why, I would like that more than anything in the world. . .' And she hesitated, suddenly shy.

'Yes, Sally-Anne?' he said, her sudden smile, missing since her mama had been shot, shining at him again.

'And. . .if you are really truly my papa, I think that you ought to marry Mama *as soon as possible* so that I can have both of you all the time, and not just you for visits,' she finished.

'Oh, Sally-Anne,' he said, looking at a blushing Mary over his daughter's glossy blue-black curls, his face and hers male and female versions of the same vital image. 'I think that can be arranged for you—I really do.'

Look out next month for Sally-Anne's own story in
AN AMERICAN PRINCESS.
Further details in the following pages!

The other exciting

MASQUERADE
Historical

available this month is:

A DARLING AMAZON
Sylvia Andrew

In an effort to make her father's final days easier, Lady
Julia Marchant decided to take advantage of an
ambiguous newspaper article to pretend that she and
Hugo, 6th Marquis of Rostherne, were to be married. In
the privacy of her father's sick room, how could Julia
guess she was overheard? Or that the small white lie
would gather pace like a rolling stone, until she had no
alternative but to truly marry Hugo – the man over
whom she made such a fool of herself as a green girl!
How could fate be so unkind?

Look out for the two intriguing

MASQUERADE *Historical*

Romances coming next month

AN AMERICAN PRINCESS
Paula Marshall

Sally-Anne McAllister, driven by a traumatic experience into
espousing the women's movement, had decided to write
articles about the hard life of women in the East End of
London. But to do that, she felt she should experience such
work at first hand. By denying her background, and spinning
a long line of 'whoppers', she was employed by Dr Neil
Cochrane. He knew there was something odd going on –
those beautiful hands had never done a day's work in Sally-
Anne's life! – but at least she was safe in his household.
What he hadn't bargained for was how such a lovely and
vibrant young woman would so disrupt his peace!

THE ERRANT EARL
Marlene Suson

Alienated from his family, Stephen Kendall had fought for
Wellington, but now he had to return home, for he had
unexpectedly inherited his father's earldom. Tired, dispirited,
and upset to find the estate in poor heart, Stephen knew he
had yet another hurdle to face – his wife. Manoeuvred by the
earl into marriage with their neighbour's daughter, Laura
Milford, but in love with another woman, Stephen had badly
botched their wedding night, and for six years man and wife
had not communicated. What was in store for him. . . ?

Available in March

TWO HISTORICAL ROMANCES & TWO FREE GIFTS!

Masquerade historical romances bring the past alive with splendour, excitement and romance. We will send you a cuddly teddy bear and a special MYSTERY GIFT. Then, if you choose, you can go on to enjoy 4 more exciting Masquerades every two months, for just £2.25 each! Send the coupon below at once to – Reader Service, FREEPOST, PO Box 236, Croydon, Surrey CR9 9EL.

NO STAMP REQUIRED ------ ✂

Yes! Please rush me my 2 Free Masquerade Romances and 2 Free Gifts! Please also reserve me a Reader Service Subscription. If I decide to subscribe, I can look forward to receiving 4 Masquerade Romances every two months for just £9.00, delivered direct to my door. Post and packing is free, and there's a free Newsletter. If I choose not to subscribe I shall write to you within 10 days - I can keep the books and gifts whatever I decide. I can cancel or suspend my subscription at any time. I am over 18.

Mrs/Miss/Ms/Mr _____ EP29M

Address _____

_____ Postcode _____

Signature _____